KNOW HER LOVE HER

JACK & DAISY #1

Z.L. ARKADIE

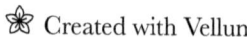 Created with Vellum

PART I
THERE HE GOES AGAIN

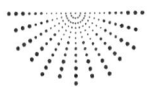

MR. ENTITLED

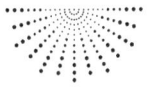

DAISY LORD

The cold mugs me as I step out of the hotel lobby and onto the sidewalk. It's the middle of May and forty-three degrees in downtown Chicago, a stark difference from the ninety degrees of dry heat I left in L.A. I shake off the chill and take long, fast strides up Pearson, across Michigan Avenue, up State to Grand and Clark, slowing only when halted by Don't Walk signs. I have a lunch meeting with Dexter Frampton, an independent television producer who's producing a show for Travel Station X, a new cable network. Everything that could go wrong this morning went wrong. I knocked over my bottle of mouthwash, and it spilled all over the floor. The dress shoes I packed don't match. Toothpaste squirted on my dress suit, and I had to put on the outfit I flew in wearing yesterday. I'd left my cell phone in the hotel restaurant last night, but I didn't realize it until fifteen minutes after our meeting was to start this morning. I had to rush down to the front desk to claim it.

I'm hot and sweaty when I rush into King's Corner Bistro.

"Welcome. How many?" the sprightly hostess sings before I reach her station.

"I'm here to meet Mr. Dexter Frampton," I say.

Her eyebrows crumple as though I just asked her a trick question. I wish I could offer more information, but he and I have never met.

I lift a finger. "One second." I step away to call him.

"That would be me."

I look up at a man with light brown skin, piercing blue eyes, and chiseled facial features. I'm momentarily caught off guard by how attractive he is.

"Daisy Lord?" he asks.

"Um, yes." I take my hand out of my purse and offer him a handshake. "I'm so sorry I'm late. My day got off to a rough start."

His smile enhances his classic good looks. "No worries. Our table is this way."

It's eleven thirty a.m., and the lunch crowd is arriving in droves. Our table is on the quieter side of the restaurant though. I order a seafood salad, and Dexter asks for the rib-eye steak.

"The network has ordered four episodes. They'll run one per week. If we get the ratings, then they'll order six more," Dexter says.

The waitress brings my coffee and his whiskey. He studies me as I sip my morning glory.

"You do know that I'm a travel writer, not a TV personality?" I clarify. "I won't be able to pull off the smiley, cheery TV host act."

"I want the person who wrote the book, and no one else."

"Oh, her…"

He frowns.

"It's just that I haven't written anything for over a year. I'm not sure…" I shake my head and look out the window. Rain beats down on the cluster of cars stopped at the red light. "If I'm still good at it."

A lot has changed since I married Belmont and gave birth to Joella. My daughter died. She went into cardiac arrest in the hospital, and they were unable to revive her. Belmont and I went from never arguing to saying mean things to each other almost every day. He's said that he's tired of competing with a dead man, referring to my brother, Daniel, who was struck by a car when we were kids. He's accused me of being unable to love anyone. I've said he's controlling and he smothers me. One day, Belmont said that he should leave, and I said fine. That was four months ago. We haven't seen each other since.

"Then why did you agree to see me?" Dexter asks.

"My agent wants me to give him permission to sell you the TV rights to my book. Initially I said no, but he convinced me to at least hear you out."

Dexter cocks his head and inspects me. "I don't think that's why you came here."

"Well, it is," I say cynically.

"I was adamant about you hosting the show. You're curious," he claims.

I shrug. "Of course I am, but I'm also sensible."

"If you don't mind, may I ask you a personal question?"

"Sure." My tone says I'm guarded.

"Are you still married to Jack Lord?"

"I am." A knot forms in my throat. "But we're separated."

Dexter doesn't look surprised. Probably everyone in the universe has read in the tabloids that billionaire Jack Lord separated from his wife.

"I'm sorry to hear that," he says.

"Me too."

The moment of silence is appropriate.

"I really want you to be our host. If anything, the audience will tune in just to look at you for an hour." He cracks a smile.

He doesn't sound or look as if he's flirting, but I think he is. "If that's what you're counting on to boost ratings, then you're in trouble." I only smoked for one year while I was in high school. I stopped after my health teacher showed us a film of what lung cancer looks like. I could sure use a cigarette right now.

Dexter laughs. "Come on, Daisy. I've heard that you're adventurous. You don't have to worry about a thing. I'll make this a pleasant experience for you."

"You've heard I was adventurous?"

"It's in every page of your book."

We grin at each other as the waitress puts our plates in front of us. My salad smells so good. I'm starving because I missed breakfast. Yet another thing that went wrong this morning.

"How long will it take to shoot the first four episodes?" I ask, digging into my food.

Dexter explains how they plan to feature domestic destinations like the Florida Keys, the states of Vermont and Rhode Island, and wrap in Chicago. The starting budget is small, but they'll go international if they're picked up for a full season. They want me to help write and produce the segments as well as host them.

"How about La Côte d'Azur?" I suggest.

"Ah, the French Riviera."

"Yes, but you can start in Barcelona, Spain, and end in Genoa, Italy. I could make it economical and interesting. I don't think many Americans know how easy and safe it is to vacation along the blue coast. The articles I wrote on that region weren't part of the taxicab series—"

"Because you took trains, busses, and rented cars," Dexter finishes my sentence as if I'd quizzed him.

I crack a smile. "You're trying to impress me?"

He tosses his head back and lets out a quiet laugh. "Is it working?"

I chuckle. "Maybe. But you never said how long it will take to shoot four episodes."

"About two months. If you can come up with a

proposal and shooting schedule that won't break our budget, then maybe we can do Europe in, say, three months?"

I gaze across the room to ponder. I don't expect to see anything interesting, but a familiar set of eyes meets mine. I blink to make sure I'm not hallucinating. Is Belmont sitting at a table with an attractive brunette? The neckline of her purple dress plunges down over her plump cleavage. Out of all the restaurants in the world, I can't believe he's in this one.

I panic and retrieve my purse from the back of my chair as I shoot to my feet. "I have to go."

Dexter stands. "You have to leave?" He's observing me as though I'm a crazy person.

"Did you arrange this meeting with him?" I nod toward Belmont, who's still watching us.

"Huh?" He turns to see who I'm referring to. His frown deepens. "Is that your husband?"

"Yes," I whisper.

"He has nothing to do with me asking you to be part of our show."

"Then why is he here?"

"Perhaps to eat lunch. This is a popular spot."

"Right." I'm distracted by the mystery woman reaching across the table to touch his hand. "Dexter, it was nice to meet you in person. I'll arrange the television rights with my agent."

I turn to leave, but he catches my shoulder. "Daisy, wait. What about hosting and producing?"

"I'm not a host or a producer," I say through my constricting throat.

Dexter smiles. "But you're an adventurist, and that's better than a pretty talking head."

I look at Belmont, who's now standing. "I don't know. Give me time to think about it."

"Twenty-four hours?"

"That soon?"

"We have to get started by next Monday if we're going to make this happen."

"I'll think about it," I say.

He removes his hand from my shoulder. "I'll be waiting. But, Daisy, this show won't work without you."

How many times have I heard Helena say that to whomever she was trying to persuade? "Right."

I rush out into the afternoon rainstorm. The first Walk sign I meet is flashing red. I dart across the street before the last twelve seconds expire just in case Belmont is chasing me. It's a shame that I'm running away from my own husband. People trot around me, all trying to make it to dry destinations.

I don't slow my pace as I turn down streets I didn't use to get here.

The rain stops, but my dress is soggy by the time I cross Michigan Avenue. I glance over both shoulders to see if Belmont has followed me. I'm slightly disappointed that he's nowhere in sight, but if he had caught up to me, I wouldn't know what to say to him. The doorman and I exchange greetings as I enter. He's gracious enough to ignore the fact that I look like a wet cat. After reaching my suite, I strip out of my clothes and draw myself a hot bath. The moment Belmont and I saw each other loops in my head.

I get in the tub, close my eyes, and pretend as if that lunch didn't happen. *But it did happen.* Since Belmont left me in our Malibu home, I haven't been happier, sadder, or more content. I've been stuck in a constant state of insouciance. My marriage has fallen apart, and feeling nothing is the only way I know how to cope. Four months, and I haven't received a phone call, email, or surprise visit from Belmont. When I saw him, it was as if I were looking at a handsome ghost. He accused me of not loving him, but that's not true. I'm just not sure he loves the real me, or even if he's able to love the real me.

I'm struggling to reach a state of complete relaxation when my cell phone rings. My heart flutters. Could it be him? I spring out of the tub, splashing water on the tile. My hopes are thwarted when I read the name on the screen.

I brace myself for the unexpected. "Hi, Angel."

"Daisy, are you in Chicago?"

"Yes, why?"

"Did you see Belmont today?"

I sigh and tiptoe back to the bathroom to wrap a towel around myself. "He told you?"

"He wanted to know if you're seeing the producer."

I stop rubbing the towel down my leg. "How does he know Dexter's a producer?"

"He said he asked him."

My mouth falls open. "He spoke to Dexter?"

"Well, you know Belmont. I didn't."

"You didn't what?"

"I was talking to Charlie. So how long are you two going to keep this up? It's just crazy that you've been apart this long."

"Well, he's the one who had a date, and they looked pretty cozy." I twist my hair up into a bun. Angelina's silence speaks louder than words, and I ask, "He's *with* her?"

"Well…"

"What's her name?" My heart wants to implode.

"I don't know what's going on between them but… She has to know," she says to Charlie.

I hate when she cuts away from our conversations to talk to Charlie.

"I have to know what?" The walls of the bathroom are closing in on me. Belmont's and my separation finally feels real.

"All I know is he brought her to Curtis's wedding, and I thought they were behaving like a couple."

"Don't tell her that," Charlie says from somewhere near her.

"Oh, that's right, Curtis got married in February."

Curtis Levin is Belmont, Maggie, and Charlie's cousin. Belmont and I were invited as a couple, but it seems he's already replaced me. Oh well—my heart is broken, but easy come, easy go.

"I was going to tell you, but Charlie talked me out of it. He said all you needed was a reason."

"A reason for what?"

"You know," she says.

"No, I don't know." I'm a little huffy. "He left me, remember?"

"But you didn't care."

"I care."

Angelina is silent. "Maybe you should talk to someone. Papa has a friend."

"He has lots of friends."

"This one's a psychotherapist, and he specializes in intense couple's counseling."

I blurt a sarcastic laugh. "You think I need a shrink? And one who's a friend of Jacques? Who, by the way, could stand some shrinking himself."

"He's won awards."

"Oh well, good for him."

Angelina sighs. "What are you afraid of?"

"Nothing!" That's not true. I'm afraid that Belmont might be right about me.

"Just consider it. He's one of the best in the world."

"Angel, please. I'm hungry."

I hear Charlie ask, "What did she say?" Apparently he thinks I need to see a psychotherapist too.

"Just think about it, okay? His name is Luc Calvet. I've already talked to him, and he's willing to make himself available whenever you're ready."

I can hardly believe what I'm hearing. The walls

have stopped closing in on me. Now they've expanded, leaving me naked and exposed. I study my image in the mirror. *Look sad, Daisy. Cry. Let yourself feel a powerful emotion.*

"Angel, good night. I love you," I say, studying my reflection. I do love her even though Belmont said I wasn't capable of loving anyone.

"I know, Daisy. I love you too. And hey, you never RSVP'd."

Finally, I feel tears welling up. "RSVP'd for what?"

"Our engagement party."

"Who is the 'our' you're referring to?"

"Charlie and me!"

I'm taken aback. "When did you and Charlie get engaged? I thought you were against ceremonies and crap like that."

"Well, Curtis's wedding convinced us that we were wrong. We got engaged a few months ago. I thought I told you."

"Apparently you hadn't."

"Well, we are. The party is on… June 12th in Iberville. You have to come. I mean it."

"I would never miss it. I'll even put up with Belmont and his girlfriend if I have to."

"She's not invited."

I smile. "My hero."

She chuckles.

"How awkward will it be when Belmont and I are divorced, and you and Charlie are living happily ever after?"

"Don't say that. You guys are going to fix this. Just wait and see," Angelina says.

I fall silent. I hope she's right. I remember our eye contact at the restaurant, and my heart skips a beat.

"I can't wait to see you," she says. "Maggie will be there."

We spend fifteen minutes talking about how Maggie has left her position at A&Rt Media Group to branch out on her own. It's a good move, and a brave one, except she's in business with her friend Monroe. Angelina insists that Monroe isn't that stable. After we hang up, I put on a pair of jeans, white tank top, leather jacket, and ankle boots and take the elevator down to the hotel restaurant for dinner.

A jazz ensemble is performing, and since I'm by myself, the host convinces me to sit in one of the cushy throne chairs in the lounge area. The décor is art deco, a modern take on the decadent Roaring Twenties. I take off my jacket. Before I can get comfortable and drink in the ambiance, Belmont sits in the chair across from me.

"Hey," I barely say. I'm shocked to see him.

Belmont regards me with the same cold expression he used before he up and left. "Congratulations on your new job." He stands to take off his black overcoat. He's wearing heather-gray slacks and a navy-blue V-neck sweater.

I can hardly concentrate. He's as scrumptious as he was this morning. We definitely have our issues, but attraction isn't one of them. "What new job?"

"Aren't you the host of *The Lone Traveler*?"

"So you *are* behind the whole thing," I snarl.

"I didn't have anything to do with it."

"Then we just happened to be in the same restaurant in Chicago at the same time?"

"What are the odds?"

I narrow one eye suspiciously. "Yes, what are the odds."

He sets his ankle on his knee and steeples his hands in front of him. "Of all the shit between us, you would be angry if I interfered with you getting a job?"

"I would be more upset than angry."

"Is there a difference?"

"I think so."

His expression is indiscernible. "You're so beautiful, Daisy."

I turn my gaze toward the stone fountain in the middle of the lobby. It's an obscure piece of work.

He leans forward. "We haven't spoken in four and a half months, and when you see me, you run away."

He's waiting for me to respond, but I don't know what he wants me to say. "Should I apologize?"

He sniffs disdainfully. "You have a lot of shit to apologize for, but fleeing a restaurant isn't one of them."

"You don't have to make me feel lousy. I already do."

"Do you?"

"Yes, I do."

"Why?"

I glare at him. To the world, it looks as if Belmont's the bad guy for leaving me. However, he and I know the truth. After Joella passed, he handled the cremation, the paperwork, and planning her memorial service, which I missed because I couldn't get out of bed. I only woke up when the nurse Belmont had hired changed the dressing over my incision, gave me a sponge bath, or tried to convince me to eat homemade soup. Belmont had never badgered me about doing my part. He'd consulted Heloise, my mother, and her advice was for him to wait until I got out of bed on my own, which I did a week and a half later.

Of course, things weren't the same. When we had sex, I asked Belmont to wear a condom. He was fine with that for the first couple of months, but then he wanted sex more frequently and spontaneously. I was always worried about being safe. Slowly, we stopped having sex so frequently. Belmont slept in another room. I didn't complain about that either. Then we started saying cruel things to each other. He would bring up how I missed Joella's memorial ceremony and question whether I ever cared about her or him. I refused to try to convince him of my love for our daughter. I told him that me being catatonic for a week and a half was right up his alley since he liked me being weak.

"You're not weak. You're void," he'd said.

I didn't recover from that comment until he moved out. I still don't think I'm over it.

The waitress steps between us to take our orders. I'm no longer hungry, so I just order a club soda.

"Did I ruin your appetite?" Belmont asks, scowling.

"No." Finally I feel my own anger. "Yes, actually. I don't know why you're behaving this way. You're the one who had a date, and I know you took her to Curtis's wedding. The invitation was for you and me, not you and her. I've seen the reports about you and other women. You've moved on. Maybe I should too."

Belmont puts his hands on my knees and leans in. "There are no other women."

"Um, should I come back?" the waitress asks.

I forgot she was standing there. I swallow. It has been too long since he touched me. The band starts.

Belmont stands and put on his coat. "We're leaving." He glares at me as if I should automatically follow.

But I came here to eat and listen to music. As soon as I sat down, all the men in the room paid attention to me. Not until this very moment have I considered finding myself a lover just as he did. I know exactly what Belmont wants, and every part of my body wants to comply. I rise to my feet. I'm disappointed with myself for being unable to resist him.

Belmont takes my hand—his palms are damp. He leads me to the elevator and slides his card through the reader, unlocking access to the 30th floor.

My jaw drops. "Are you serious? You have a room here?"

He chuckles. "I do."

"Is this coincidence, or are you following me?"

"Neither. I used our reward advantage."

"Ah, yes…" I did too.

As the elevator rises, he slams his lips against mine. His mouth tastes the same. The way he's so hard for me hasn't changed either. My chest, pelvis, and thighs rise to meet his. We whimper with frustration. We can't seem to sink into the other's skin.

"I do love you," I say breathlessly.

I tilt my head. His tongue slips up my neck to my chin, and his teeth pull my bottom lip into his warm mouth. Ravenous hands squeeze my ass and rub me against his unyielding erection. I'm soaked and ready for him. The elevator door slides open. Belmont leads me to my suite. Of course he knows which room I'm staying in.

He shoves me against the door and tugs at my jeans. "Why did you wear these?" His tongue circles mine.

"I didn't know I would have to accommodate you."

"You must've known I wouldn't let the night pass without having you." He grabs my pussy.

I gulp. I'm so sensitive to his touch.

"Give me your key," he commands.

My hands shiver, but I manage to get the key out of my pocket and give it to him. Belmont swipes it. He doesn't let go of my crotch as he backs me into the room. The desk lamp fills the room with dim light. Our mouths are incapable of pulling apart, but he releases my pussy to take off my jacket.

"Get on the bed." His voice is thickened by desire.

I sit on the edge, but Belmont sweeps me up and drops me in the middle of it. He snatches off his coat and spreads himself on top of me. We wrap ourselves around each other. My tank top goes over my head and separates our lips, but our mouths soon reconnect. He tugs the cups of my bra up over my breasts and sucks my erect nipples deep into his wet mouth. I whimper with every stir of his tongue and nibble of his teeth. Excitement makes me overly sensitive.

"Belmont?" I breathe heavily into his mouth.

He unsnaps my pants and pulls down the zipper. "What?"

"Do you have a condom?"

He sighs as he rolls onto his back and covers his eyes with his forearm.

My body and soul screech from his abandonment, but my face shows no signs of it. I stare at the ceiling and recall the last time we made love. It was the night before he walked out. I couldn't enjoy all the pleasurable things he did to me because I was too busy worrying about what could happen since we hadn't taken precautions.

Belmont sits up. "I think I want a divorce."

I close my eyes to bear the ache in my heart. It passes, but my stomach is still queasy. "Okay."

His glare stops my heart. "That's it?"

"You've already left me and started seeing someone else. Yes, that's it." Fueled by rage, I try to sit up.

All of a sudden, Belmont yanks off my shoes and throws them on the floor. He pulls me close to the foot of the bed and tugs off my pants. He grabs my ankles, spreads my legs, and admires my pussy. Without another word, he puts his face in it, swirling his tongue around my clit. The impact is immediate. I moan and claw at the sheets. He watches me squirm as his

23

fingers dig into the flesh of my ass, pinning my clit to his mouth. He makes me feel pleasure and pain. My knot swells against his tongue, and he squeezes harder.

I close my eyes tightly and, like our relationship, focus on what feels good. I whimper and try to wriggle my butt out of his grasp, but Belmont won't let go. His hands are like a trap, and my ass is the bear.

"Ouch," I whine. "You're hurting me."

He frees me, and I hear the clasp and zipper of his pants. Before I can lean up on my elbows, he lifts my thighs and pulls my hips up toward his erection. I gasp when he slams himself inside me. Belmont pounds me against his pole, hitting bottom. He groans as though screwing me is the best thing in the world.

I have no control over what he's doing. My tits bounce like paddleballs. He's shifting me so fast that he's a blur. Belmont is in this for himself. I should shout stop, but it feels so good being handled by him again, even if we're engaging in risky, condomless sex.

"Fuck!" He pulls out, pushes my bottom against the bed, and sprays my belly and tits with his juices.

"Did you come?" he asks, breathing heavily.

I frown. "What was that?"

"Did you come or not?"

"Of course not…"

By the way he's behaving, I expect him to say good, put his pants back on, and leave me unfulfilled. Belmont's gaze rolls up and down my nakedness.

"One second," he says and retrieves a towel out of the bathroom. He wipes my stomach then digs his fingers carefully into my pussy. "You're still wet." His thumb rolls around my clit, and his fingers thrust into me.

He watches my stomach muscles roll as sensations surge under the hood of my pubis. Belmont is an expert at this. I bite my bottom lip, arch my back, and let myself enjoy how good it feels. He bends over to suck my bottom lip into his mouth, then my top one.

Belmont breathes heavily. "Shit…"

He stimulates me faster. I run my fingers through his hair and grip his scalp as he bites and licks my nipples. I let him hear me when my walls pulsate around his fingers.

"Daisy, baby," he mutters and prods me faster to make my orgasm last.

I release the tension in my body when the sensation subsides.

Belmont takes his fingers out of me. "I didn't know you were in town."

I swallow the lump in my throat. "I believe you."

"I've been waiting for you to call." He stands and puts on his pants. "I don't like that guy— Dexter. If you want to work in TV, I'll talk to Vince."

I groan. It's the same old, same old. "Screw you, Belmont." I roll off the bed, go to the wardrobe, and put on a robe.

"Do you like him or something?"

"Don't insinuate things. We met for the first time today. But you don't get to walk out on me and then control me too."

He opens his mouth but studies me instead. He picks his coat up off the floor. "If I had known you would be at that restaurant, I would've chosen a different one. I didn't want to see you until you made the first move."

I roll my eyes. "That's ridiculous."

I think he's surprised by my brashness. "Come here?"

I recognize the way he's looking at me, so I

shake my head and plant my feet. He looks stunned. I hardly ever say no to him.

"You want to know why I haven't called you?" I ask. "It's because you're entitled."

"Entitled?"

"You're Hubbell Gardiner."

"Who the hell is Hubbell Gardiner?"

"He's a character in a movie, *The Way We Were*. And it's not your fault. You're good-looking and rich—a valuable commodity in our society. You walk out on me. You get a new girlfriend. You want to screw me, so I let you. Everything comes too easy for you."

Belmont flings his coat onto the sofa as he walks over to stand in front of me. "Stacy's not my mistress. We're friends, and she's working with me. I'm in Chicago because an investor here is selling off prime real estate to the highest bidder. But if money was all it took, I would've negotiated from the Vineyard. That's where I've been living for the past four months."

I'm not willing to let him off the hook so easily. "Then why did you take her to the wedding?"

He shrugs. "I didn't want to go alone."

"Have you ever had sex with her?"

Belmont's eyes shift.

27

"Don't lie to me," I warn him.

"Not since I met you." I try to walk away from him, but he grabs and embraces me. "It would be a hell of a lot easier to love her."

I try to pull away from him again, but he hugs me tighter. He's hard again.

"Daisy," he whispers, "don't deny me, please."

"Do I ever?" I sound disappointed in myself.

"You could if you want."

"I thought you were leaving?"

"Do you want me to go?"

I stare into his eyes. *Belmont is here in the flesh.* Four and a half months without him felt like a very long time spent in limbo. When I first met him, his eyes were mostly hazel. Tonight they're a combination of blue, green, and hazel. The flecks are never in the same arrangement.

I shake my head. Belmont takes my hand and leads me to the bed. He lays me down, parts my legs, and puts his mouth on my pussy. We've only just begun. I'll let him do whatever he wants. After all, he is entitled.

I moan...

2

A CHIPPED HEART

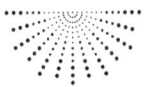

DAISY LORD

*M*y eyelids are heavy. The clock on the nightstand says it's 1:34 p.m. It's past my check-out time, and I've missed my flight back to L.A. It takes all my energy to sit up. My body feels as if I put it through a strenuous workout last night.

Belmont seizes my waist. "Where are you going?"

"To the bathroom."

His tongue and lips make out with the small of my back. I inhale. It's such an erotic sensation.

"Hurry up," he says and lets go.

I pee and study myself in the mirror. Belmont has left passion marks all over my neck and on my waist and hips too. My nipples are tender, and so is the entrance of my pussy. I have no idea where Belmont gets his stamina. He comes, and ten minutes later, he's back up. He says it's not him, it's me. He says he's never been so aroused by a woman, but I don't believe him. That would make little old me a powerful sexual stimulant, which is insanely ridiculous.

I wash my hands, rinse with mouthwash, and wipe the stickiness off of my belly. We did it six times throughout the night, and Belmont never came inside me. Instead, he came on me. I don't really like it, but I'm happy he's honoring my wishes.

As soon as I climb in bed, Belmont gathers me against him. His penis is erect. He parts my legs and plunges his fingers inside me.

"You're so hot," he whispers, pinning his cheek against mine. His fingers shift in and out, and he strokes my G-spot, which makes me gasp. "I need to go take a leak."

We kiss.

"Damn it," he complains and abandons me to empty his bladder.

I feel sexual again. Just to prove it, I fuck two of my fingers and roll my thumb around my clit.

Belmont's right—it's hot, wet, and very tight. In and out my fingers plunge.

"Oh shit," Belmont wheezes when he sees me.

In a matter of seconds, he pins my hands over my head and shoves his rock-hard erection inside me. I gasp.

"You've made me jealous of you," he says.

I chuckle. "I've never been this horny in my life."

He jabs me with his erection. I feel his girth and width. Belmont grabs my hips and angles his penis to rub my sensitive spot. I claw the pillow as he bounces me against his dick. He's in control, handling me as though I'm as light as a feather. I scream as my walls pulsate around his throbbing penis. Belmont moans, thrusting me deeper, faster, harder… He lets go inside me.

"No!" I shriek and try to squirm out of his grasp.

He holds me tighter. I don't move a muscle, and we don't say a word. Belmont kisses and nibbles my shoulder. He massages my breasts and pinches my nipples.

I force my body to not respond. "Why did you do that?"

"What are you afraid of?"

"You know what I don't want."

Belmont pulls out, and our juices pour out of me. I curl into a ball and listen to him zip his pants. I'm still horny, but I have to process what just happened.

"I just don't want us to make the same mistake twice." I wait for him to respond.

He's all dressed when he bends over to kiss my forehead. "I'll call you." He casually pulls open the door and leaves.

I let my gaze linger on the door for the longest time. The silence and stillness isn't as peaceful as it was when he first walked out on me. It feels as if he's gone for good this time. Tears roll freely from my eyes. Yes! I'm crying. I am part of the human race.

THE ROOM PHONE RINGS. I OPEN MY EYES. IT'S dark, and I check the time on the clock. It's six o'clock. Belmont's scent rises from the abandoned side of the bed. When he and I committed to spending the night together, we turned our cell phones off so that we wouldn't be disturbed. I stretch across the mattress to answer the call.

"Hello?" I sound hoarse.

"Daisy?" the man sounds surprised to hear my voice. "Hi."

"Dexter?" I ask, remembering that I gave his assistant my itinerary.

"We just took a chance and tried you at this number. You're still in Chicago?"

I flip onto my back and sigh. "I missed my flight." Belmont must've paid for the extra day because the front desk hasn't called, nor have the cleaners knocked on the door.

"Are you okay?"

"I'm fine. I guess I owe you an answer."

"Not if you're going to say no."

"Okay, I'll do it," I say, choosing to go against Belmont's wishes.

It's Wednesday. We decide I should be in the office on Monday. I power on my cell phone and set it on the desk while I take a quick shower. I dry off and check my messages. I delete all the ones from Dexter and his assistant. Maya called twice asking if I want to have lunch this week. She and I have rekindled our friendship. She and Adrian, my ex-boyfriend, actually tied the knot. There's one message from Maggie. She wants me to call her right away. I rebook my flight before ringing her back.

"Hi, Mags," I say after she answers. I zip my jeans.

"What's this about Vince conceptualizing a traveling show for you?"

"You talked to Belmont?"

"Vince wanted me to call and make sure it's what you really want."

I can picture the sour look on her face. "I was offered a job by Travel X Channel. They want me to produce and host a show. Belmont doesn't want me working with the executive producer."

"Dexter Frampton?" she asks.

"Do you know him?"

"I've heard of him. He does goddamn good work. Dais, I'm on your side in whatever's going on between you and Jack. If I were married to Jack, he would drive me bat-shit insane."

"Yeah," I say with a sigh.

"He said you called him entitled. You were dead-on. Vince is too."

"Speaking of Vince, how are things between you now that you've struck out on your own?" I say in an effort to change the subject.

"We jumped off the rails for a moment but now we're back on track. So you and Jack hung out last night?"

I clip my bra closed. "Sex has never been our issue."

"Communication is your issue!"

I slip on my tank top. Belmont's scent lingers on the fabric. "Maybe." We both know she's right. "He asked for a divorce. Well, he said he thinks he wants a divorce."

"Oh, he was just pouting. Jack wouldn't know what to do with himself without you. He's barely made it this far," she says nonchalantly.

Hearing her say that makes me feel better. "Oh, did you know that Charlie and Angel are engaged? They're throwing an engagement party."

"When?"

"On the twelfth of next month."

"Checking my calendar…"

I narrow one eye suspiciously while I wait.

"Oh, right. Yes. I'll be there. So will you, right?"

"I just don't understand why they're throwing a party. They were so anti-wedding."

"People change, Dais."

I shrug. "I guess so."

"I just never thought Charlie would get a woman to say yes to marrying *him*, especially one of Angelina's caliber," Maggie says.

I chuckle as I check the room to make sure I'm

not leaving anything. Maggie congratulates me on my new gig and assures me that taking the job is the right thing to do.

I finish getting all of my things into my luggage, call a cab to take me to the airport, and go downstairs to check-out. I was right. Belmont took care of my bill and asked that I not be disturbed. He's always looking out for me.

AFTER GOING THROUGH THE SHENANIGANS OF getting a new flight, a boarding pass, clearing TSA, waiting around to board, and enduring the four-hour flight to L.A., I'm finally in Malibu. I'm back in Belmont's and my house. I go to the kitchen and take a tuna steak out of the freezer so it can thaw before I head upstairs to change into a tank dress. Then I walk down the hallway to my office to work on travel plans. I start in Nice and Marseille.

I email some of my contacts in those areas to see if any local festivities are going on in the next two months. It's amazing how fast they reply. Of course they all ask the standard, "How are you?" I lie and say fine. I accept my old friend Javar Les's offer to be my companion since he speaks six different languages. I also email Maya to arrange lunch. She replies immediately and asks me to meet her tomorrow in front of Abbot's Habit on Abbot Kinney.

Time flies. It's pretty late, but I'm starving. I sauté the thawed tuna steak with onions and spinach and put it on a whole-grain bun. Being alone in the house was easier before my trip to Chicago. To keep my mind occupied, I work as I eat. Two hours later, I take a quick shower and crawl into bed. I take deep breaths and force myself to think of nothing. Eventually it works, and I fall asleep.

THE WORST PART OF LIVING IN L.A. IS THE TRAFFIC. The best part of living in L.A. is being a native, which means I know how to navigate my way around the tough spots. One p.m. approaches, and freeway traffic is atrocious. After creeping south on Pacific Coast Highway, I exit onto Lincoln, which is fairly light considering the time of day. Other than a few speeding idiots, my drive is stress free. I park on Electric Avenue and meet Maya on the corner of Abbot Kinney and California Street.

I see her sitting outside the coffee shop under the green awning, tapping out a message on her cell phone. I haven't seen Maya since after we loss Joella. Belmont believes she's one person I should leave in my past. But Maya is the only person in the world who gets me.

When we saw each other last, she pleaded her case. "You didn't love Adrian, Dais," she said. "You never did. He's the one for me. I'm the one for him." She was as dramatic as an aspiring actress would be.

However, I had been forced to admit that she was right. It was a relief to share my true feelings with someone.

"I knew you couldn't carry on forever for Jack," Maya said. "He's one of those guys who has specific tastes, and you're it. And that includes your goddamn issues. I bet you were miserable while you were pregnant."

I sighed. Only Maya could comprehend the depths of my despair. I poured out a lot of what I had been keeping inside over my Humble Indian curry bowl at Café Gratitude on Larchmont. Before parting ways that night, we'd made a promise to work harder to maintain our friendship, no matter what crazy things Maya did to fracture it.

Maya looks up when I make it to the corner. She sets her cell phone on the table, pulls her long, dusty blond locks over one shoulder, and waves. I wave back. The light turns green, and she stands as I cross the street. I've never seen Maya in something so loose-fitting, but she's seven month's pregnant with her and Adrian's first child.

"I know…" she says as we hug. "I look like a walrus, but you look hot as usual."

"I don't know about that. You look beautiful."

"I try." She links arms with me. "Let's go somewhere not so Venicey."

"But it's all Venicey." I chuckle.

"True."

We head north past the small dress shops and art galleries. I tell her about my new job and my trip to Chicago.

"You're going to be gone for a while?" she asks.

"Yes, but at least I'll be on La Côte d'Azur for the majority of the time. It'll give me the chance to put my life in perspective."

"Your life is already in perspective. Here…" She opens the door to a restaurant.

A huge bar is situated in the middle of the restaurant with tables on the sides. The lunch hour is ending, so it's not so crowded. As usual, Maya knows almost everyone who works here. The hostess compliments Maya on how beautiful she looks, and suddenly I'm struck by illumination. Maya is the male version of Belmont. She seems to know everyone in L.A., and she's used to getting what she wants, even me as a best friend.

But she never questions whether or not I love her. She steals my boyfriend and never questions it. She flirts with men who are interested in me to make herself feel worthy and never questions it. She outs my then-boyfriend, now-husband as a male escort, and still, she never questions my affection for her. I say "I do" to Belmont in front of God, friends, and family, and he questions my affection for him.

We're seated at a table where we can be seen but not heard. It's the best seat in the house. The waitress pours spring water into our glasses and sets the carafe on the table. We order our obligatory salads. Hers is avocado kale, and mine is spring greens with sliced cherry tomatoes and ginger cherries.

Maya rubs her belly. "They only buy fruits and vegetables from local growers who don't use pesticides. And the meats here are all organic, no antibiotics or hormones."

I smile. "Motherhood suits you."

"Who could've guessed? But I don't want to talk about me. What's going on with you and Jack?"

I sigh and slump my shoulders. "He said he wants a divorce."

"Is that what you want?"

"No. I don't know. If it's what he wants, then what can I do?"

"You can try fighting for him. I mean, he's Jack fucking Lord for goodness' sake!"

I roll my eyes. Sure, he's at the top of the food chain, but he's just a man. "I never believed love is something you should have to fight for."

There's a pinch of perplexity in her expression.

"Why are you looking at me that way?" I ask.

"You're all fucked up when it comes to love. You have this opinion that love's supposed to be easy, but that's so not the case. The sticky shit can be love too, and if you're stuck in shit, then you should try to fight your way out of it. Like, throw the shit out, not your love—just the shit."

I fall silent. I'm not sure how much of what she said is true. "Yeah…" I sigh. "I love Belmont even though he doesn't think so. I'm just tired of being agreeable. I hate living in that big house. You know me. I like the simpler things in life. The real things."

"I know. Well, then stop being agreeable. Just be you."

"I can't help it. I change when I'm around him. I don't even know how it happens. All I want to do is make him happy."

Maya nods. I can see the wheels turning in her head. "Does he make you happy?"

I smirk. "I'm the happiest when he's making love to me."

"I bet. I've heard Jack Lord can fuck a girl in a million and one ways."

My eyes expand, cautioning her to lower her voice. "Maya, come on. You're talking about my husband."

"Hey, that's what I heard."

"Well, it's true, but what we have is more profound than that. We have a connection, and it doesn't require us to be friends or even like each other to want to be together."

"No, I get it," she says.

I frown. "You do?"

"I do. He's in your pores."

I nod. She does get it. "But, hey, maybe I was meant to be alone."

She blurts a laugh. "You're too hot for that. You'd still be leading Adrian around by his stupid dick if I hadn't convinced him that there's more to a relationship than fucking you whenever you let him. You treated him like Pavlov treated those monkeys."

"You mean dogs."

"Monkeys, dogs, rats…"

I make a face. "I did not treat him like that. However, I will admit that I wasn't the best girl-friend. Do you attend his silly wrap parties?"

"Every single one of them." We share a laugh. "I also read his scripts and tell him everything he writes is brilliant."

I sniff cynically. "Is it though?"

"As long as we're married."

I sigh. "I think everything Belmont does is bril-liant. He landed on the Forbes list, and he's still unstained by his past."

"That's because Jack only fucked women who could lay golden eggs."

"Wow, that sounds… horrible."

"It was brilliant."

"Right now he's working with someone named Stacy."

Maya takes a moment to think. "Stacy Pruitt?"

"I don't know her last name."

"Hot? Dark hair? Desperate?"

"She's definitely beautiful and has dark hair, but what do you mean by desperate?"

"She's a bitch who doesn't respect boundaries."

"Kind of like you?"

"A hell of a lot like me. Actually, I heard she and Jack had a thing. Watch out for her."

I close my eyes to bear the ache that crushes my heart. "He told me that they used to be together but he hasn't made love to her since then."

"And you believe him?"

"I do."

"Okay, making love and fucking are two separate actions. Did he cover both of those? Because men, they're tricky."

I roll my eyes. "Oh my God…"

She shrugs. "All right, whatever. At least you can take solace in knowing that Jack isn't the sort of guy who can't control his dick. As you know, I've tried, and he didn't want any part of me."

"Don't remind me."

"Okay, I won't. But what next?'

I shake my head. "He's angry because he thinks I'm unburdened by Joella's death."

"Are you?"

I stare into Maya's eyes. "The answer isn't so simple. By the time I had her, I was ready to be a mother. I love her. I didn't even get a chance to hold her. I'll never get that chance, and I think that's what hurts the most."

"So you're ready to be a mother?"

"I didn't say that. I was ready to sacrifice all of my ambitions to be a good mother to Joella. I don't know how happy that would've made me, but I was ready to make her happy."

Maya takes a swig of her water. "Do you honestly think your daughter would've been happy if you weren't happy? Kids can see right through their parents' fucking masks. You know what I think?"

"What?"

"If it were just you and Joella against the world, then she would've been like an extension of you. But you have to think about Jack and what he'll *allow* you to do. He's like your fuckable daddy."

"That's disgusting," I say.

"It's true, and you know it. He's your problem, but he's a hot problem. You just have to figure out how to fix him. He's so fucking worth it."

"But shouldn't I want everything we have? It's the American dream right?"

"The American dream? There's no such thing. I thought you knew that."

I lean across the table and whisper, "I hate that my beautiful flower died, but…" I sigh. "I feel like I've been given a do-over. I don't choose to become what I almost became."

Our salads arrive, and the dense silence lingers. The waitress says she hopes we enjoy them and to let her know if we need anything else. She leaves us quickly because even she can feel the tension around our table.

"If I don't want what Belmont is offering, what does that make me?" I ask Maya.

"It makes you, you. And let me tell you, Dais, if I were a guy, I'd move heaven and earth to fuck you whenever my dick got hard. Not to mention you're just great company. Jack will change for you. All you have to do is mold him." She points her fork at my salad. "Now eat."

I snort a chuckle and pick up my fork. "I wish you could've seen my Joella. She was a beauty." I narrow an eye. "But she looked like Charlie."

She gasps. "The hot brother? Do you think he drugged you and fucked you and you had his kid instead?"

I laugh. "Only you would say something so preposterous."

We spend the rest of the afternoon gossiping

about mutual friends. Maya invites me to a clam-bake they're throwing on Sunday near my house. It would be the first time Adrian and I have seen each other since our altercation on Martha's Vineyard, so I tell her maybe. I'll call her if I decide to go.

I sleep easy alone in our big house. On Friday night, I have dinner with Heloise, my stepdad, Joseph, and Daphne, my half sister, who's home after graduating from Georgetown University this past weekend. She and I aren't close, but we are cordial. It's kind of sad that the last time I saw her was ten years ago. She used to be a brat, but now she's a sophisticated, thoughtful young lady. She's returning to Washington, DC, in a couple of weeks to pursue a career in government. The evening passes pleasantly.

Saturday goes by without any word from Belmont. On Sunday morning, I lay in bed with my phone in my hands. I'm ready to have that difficult conversation with him, but I'm not positive he's ready to hear it. I sigh, sink my head deeper into my pillow, and call him. I'm antsy. On the fifth ring, I'm about to end the call when…

"Hello?" a woman says in a sultry voice.

I hesitate. "Sorry, I must have the wrong…" But

I know this is the right number. "Is Belmont there?" I'm struggling to keep my breathing even.

"He's in the shower."

I end the call and tuck the phone under the other pillow as if hiding it will make what happened go away. I stare at the ceiling. Did some woman with a bedroom voice really just answer Belmont's phone? I close my eyes to restrain my tears. I've already cried too much.

A while later, I wake up to the muffled chime of my cell phone. I retrieve the device from under the pillow and check the name on the screen. "Hey, Maya."

"This is the third time I've called you. What the hell's going on?"

I tell her what happened before I fell asleep. "He never lets anyone answer that phone, not even me."

"Are you coming to the clambake?"

"No. I'm too tired."

Maya grunts. "When's your flight?"

"My flight... I don't know if I want to take the job anymore."

"Goddamn it, Daisy. I'm coming over."

"Don't..."

She's already ended the call.

3
UNDER A ROCK

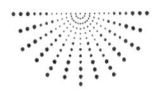

DAISY LORD

"*I* can force you to get out of that bed, or you can do it yourself," Maya says.

I struggle to sit against the headboard, rubbing my eyes. "How did you get in here?"

She's standing in the doorway of my bedroom, wearing a very short sundress that shows off her thin but toned legs. "Your maid let me in."

"Oh." I sigh. "Today's Sunday."

"Daisy, do *not* do this."

"Don't do what?"

"Fall the fuck apart! Like you did after I made that post on Facebook."

I grimace. "Don't remind me."

Maya sits on the edge of my bed. She and the baby in her stomach get comfortable as she faces me. "I'm going to remind you that you wouldn't have lost your shit if you'd taken at least one of my phone calls or answered the damn door. We could've talked it out."

I set my weary eyes on her. "No need to rehash the past."

"But I need to explain this because I never did."

I sigh wearily and motion for her to continue.

"When we came to Martha's Vineyard, Adrian was supposed to tell you the truth. He got derailed when he found out you were fucking Jack."

"Don't say '*fucking* Jack.' It sounds so belittling."

"Making love?"

I shrug. "That's better."

"You should know that I didn't post that picture of the ring until after Adrian assured me he had told you everything. He lied to me. That's what he was supposed to admit to you. I should've never believed him. He still lies to avoid dealing with difficult shit. Wimp."

She makes me chuckle even though I don't want to. "You sound like Heloise."

"Thank you. I want to be just like your mother when I grow up."

"Then congratulations, you've succeeded."

She laughs. "However, I should've never left it

up to Adrian to tell you about us. I should've invited you over for dinner, made your favorite meal, and told you myself. I just felt so ashamed."

I sigh deeply. "I know. It wasn't losing Adrian that hurt. Oh goodness, he got on my nerves."

She chuckles. "What hurt? That I betrayed you?"

I nod.

"Well… it was an unusual situation."

I bend over to cup her hand. "No, really, Maya. We don't have to rehash the past. I understand how complicated it was." I smile. "Plus you're having a whole human being."

"Fuck—whoever puts it that way?"

"Okay, you're having a baby."

She smiles. "I am."

"You are."

We stare into each other's eyes.

"I love you, Dais."

"I love you too."

"Don't ever stop being my friend again, okay?"

"Okay."

"Now…" She struggles to stand and stretches her back. "Get your ass out of bed and come to the clambake."

I groan and fall back onto my pillow.

"I'm not going to let you fall apart because life tossed an obstacle in your way. You deal with it by living, not crawling under a rock until you don't feel the pain anymore."

I'm taken aback. "Did you just say that to me?"

"Yes. I'm wiser now." She snatches the blanket from my legs. "So get your ass out of bed."

I PUT ON MY BLUE BIKINI AND A WHITE CROCHET cover-up, and we walk down the bluffs near my house. The gathering isn't far away. Out of the seventeen people in attendance, I haven't seen most of them in ages.

Keeping with the theme of the day—which is facing my issues—I answer all their questions regarding what I've been up to. Married. Yes, Belmont Lord, the billionaire. Lost a baby. Separated. New job that involves traveling. My job is what interests them the most. They want to know which network and who I'm working with. A few people in "the business" have heard of Dexter.

"He's not an asshole, good at what he does, and is easy on the eyes," Marla, a friend from our undergrad years at UCLA, says. "Don't sleep with him though. I heard if you fuck him, he loses interest."

"I'm not going to have sex with him," I say.

She raises her eyebrows as if she's doubtful.

Adrian avoids me like the ebola virus, although I feel him glaring in my direction from across the fire pit. The afternoon changes to evening, and everyone except Maya is liquored-up. I've even had a couple of glasses of wine. Instead of dancing, kicking up sand, and making fools out of ourselves, we sit around the fire and exchange memories of the wild, uninhibited Maya we used to know.

Trista raises her hand impatiently. "I remember when she talked me into posing as a stripper so we could give Guy Henley, the actor, a lap dance."

Justin Carp laughs. "We or she?"

"Sadly, *we*. She thought we'd get more out of him if we teamed up."

"Get what out of him?" Justin asks.

"Shush," Maya says, rubbing her belly. "Children are present—and so is my husband."

Adrian smiles when our gazes meet. I reciprocate the smile and raise my hand. "I have something to say."

Adrian looks worried.

"This morning, some woman answered my husband's phone."

There's a round of exaggerated gasps.

"She said he wasn't available because he was in the shower."

"Dick…"

"Stupid ass…"

"Man whore…"

"Dummy," Adrian says.

"Idiot," Maya says.

I giggle, accepting the support. "I wasn't going to get out of bed, but Maya came over, rubbed my feet, and said she wouldn't let me fall apart. She dragged me out of bed, made me put on a bathing suit, and that's why I'm sitting here now."

Adrian starts clapping, and the others join in. I have two more glasses of a fruity alcoholic beverage —the sort that sneaks up on you. The stereo has been turned on and everyone is dancing, but I'm sitting because ducks are swimming around my head.

"Let's get you home," Adrian says, offering me his hand.

I frown.

"It's okay. Maya sent me to your rescue," he says.

I search for her face around the fire pit. She shows me a thumbs-up, and I take Adrian's hand. It feels strange to be close to him. He still wears the same loud cologne that used to make me nauseated whenever I had one too many. His hand is still too soft. It could be the drinks, but I feel his fingers massaging my waist as he helps me up the wooden steps that lead away from the beach.

"I'm glad you and Maya made up," he says.

"Me too." I look to see if we're closer to my front door.

"I heard you're divorcing the gigolo."

"Belmont's not a gigolo, and you know it." My stomach is queasy.

"Once a gigolo, always a gigolo."

"That's just like saying once a cheater, always a cheater. And you cheated on me."

"A mistake I've had to live with."

"Let's not talk about this anymore." I feel as though this conversation is going in the wrong direction.

"I miss you though," he says.

To say that I miss him would be a lie. "I meant what I said. I'm happy you and Maya are together. Lord knows it wasn't going anywhere with us." I give an uncomfortable chuckle.

"Is that what you think?"

"That's what I know."

"I thought what we had was pretty good until I messed it up."

"Ha! You did?"

Now there's no doubt that he's feeling me up. His hand is clearly clutching my hip. I'm caught in a cloud of confusion. We make it to my house and stop at the foot of the steps to my door.

"Okay…" I sigh and take a giant step away from him. "Good night."

I turn my back, and he grabs me. I can feel his knot bump my butt.

"I didn't want to give you up," he whispers.

"You know what? It's all water under the bridge."

"How about I come inside so we can talk some more?" He breathes against my ear as his hand slides up my sternum.

"Adrian, take your hands off me," I say, enunciating every word.

"Just one more time."

I break out of his clutches and raise a hand. "Stay."

"Damn it," he mumbles and rubs his head anxiously. "Are you going to tell her?"

"No way." Once again, I enunciate. "Just don't ever touch me like that again."

I take a deep, steadying breath and walk up the steps. I take my key out of my fanny pack, open my door, and close it without giving him a second look. I engage all three locks, drag myself upstairs, and groan as I fall facedown onto the bed.

I WAKE WITH A STOP. DID ADRIAN TRY TO HAVE SEX with me last night? I sit up. My head is swimming, and it's chilly.

My cell phone chimes, and I swipe it off the nightstand. It's probably Maya. I meant what I said —I would never tell her what Adrian did. It doesn't matter because he's never experiencing any part of me. What a tool.

"Hello," I say without looking at the screen.

"Hey."

I go rigid. "Belmont?"

"Did you call me yesterday?"

I summon all my strength and hop into my big-girl panties. "She told you I called? I didn't think she would."

"Did someone answer my phone?"

"Yes. A woman." I trot out of the bedroom and down the hallway to turn on the heater.

"What did you want?" he asks.

"Forget it. I have a flight to catch."

"What did you want?" he persists.

"Nothing. I forgot."

He's silent.

"Belmont?"

"I'm here. What have you been up to?" he asks.

"Hanging out with family and friends, and doing a little work in the process."

"Is your flight to Chicago?"

"Yes."

"What time do you land?"

"I don't know. I'd have to check my ticket." I'm so pissed, I can feel the steam shooting out of my ears. He would never know by my tone though.

"Then check it."

"Why?"

"Because I want to see you."

I take a deep breath. "You're such a selfish prick."

"What?"

"She said you were in the shower. Were you?"

"I probably was," he says as if it's nothing serious.

"Are you having sex with other women?"

"Not other women."

"Are you having sex with Stacy Pruitt?"

He's silent again.

"Nice talking to you. Good-bye," I say.

"Daisy!"

"What?"

"I was probably in the shower. She shouldn't have answered my phone."

"Have you had sex with her recently?" I'm stern.

He takes a long pause.

"Belmont?" I ask.

"Daisy, I don't want to lie to you."

"Then you have?"

"I don't want to answer that over the telephone. Let's have dinner tonight."

I'm speechless. This is one of those moments where I can let the truth TKO me. I could miss my flight, go to my mom's house, wrap myself in a blanket, and sleep until my misery subsides.

"Oh well," I say with remarkable pose. "We'll figure out how to split amicably later. You never made me sign a prenup—"

"Daisy—"

"You should've."

"Babe—"

"But you're lucky, because I don't want half. I don't want anything from you. Just file for the divorce, and I'll sign."

"Daisy, let's have dinner."

"I don't want to have dinner," I whimper. I'm sobbing, and I can't make myself stop.

"Daisy, honey, don't cry…"

"I have to go… I can't have this conversation right now." I end the call.

4
GETTING DOWN TO BUSINESS

DAISY LORD

*J*ust because I know my husband and it's likely that he'll try to intercept me, I cancel the car for hire that he often uses and call a taxi. I also purchase a brand-new ticket for a flight on a different airline that leaves an hour and a half later than my original flight, and I fly coach like I did in the early days of my career. The major difference between first class and coach is the legroom.

Once I land at O'Hare, I take a taxi to my mom and stepdad's urban condo. The building, which is the shortest among giants, faces a park with lots of trees and flowerbeds. When the cab driver takes my bags to the door, I have a funny feeling that I'm being watched. I turn around to examine the area.

It's seven o'clock in the evening. People are jogging, walking their dogs, pushing strollers, playing soccer, or just lounging on the park benches. Not one soul is paying attention to me. I half expect to see Belmont somewhere out there.

On the table near the doorway, I find a note written on behalf of my mother. She had the refrigerator stocked with foods that I eat, but if she missed anything, then there's a grocery store down the street. The housecleaners are scheduled to come every Tuesday and Friday. They have their own key.

I sigh as I look around the living room. The space is large and full of furniture. This is the first time I've been here, so I leave my bags by the door and take a self-guided tour. There are four bedrooms, four bathrooms, a gigantic chef's kitchen, a great room, a den, two offices, and a dining room. There's also an elevator that stops at all three levels, plus the terrace. The condo is larger and more modern than I expected. Their house in Pacific Palisades isn't this big.

Gluttonous or not, I take the elevator to the third flood. The master bedroom has an infinity bathtub in the en suite bathroom, but I choose to sleep in one of the cozier guest rooms. My cell phone rings as I unpack my suitcase.

"Hi, Mom," I say after looking at the name on the screen.

"What's happening? Jack has been calling me all day. He wants the address to where you're staying."

"Did you give it to him?" I shimmy out of my dress. I forgot how sticky I get flying in the main cabin.

"No, but he was persistent. Did something else happen between you two?" she says in a trivializing tone.

"He's seeing someone else."

"Well, of course he is. Men are always the first to stick their dicks where they don't belong."

I sit on the foot of the bed and gaze out over the slit of Lake Michigan that's visible through the window. "I asked him for a divorce. Mom, this place is huge. I thought this was a flat."

"Then you're fine."

"Fine with what?"

"You've gone from telling me your husband is fucking another woman to complaining that our condo is huge."

"It's just not what I expected. I wanted something cozier. I'm tired of big houses. What happened to modesty?"

"Do you want me to give him the address or not?"

Apparently I'd hit a nerve. "Not." I don't sound certain.

"He's going to find you sooner or later."

"I know, but at least I'll have some time before he does."

"Time for what?"

"To get over him."

I can picture Heloise rolling her eyes. She thinks Jack and I are just trying to keep things exciting between us. When I first told her we'd split, she rolled her eyes. She thinks we should get a divorce but remain lovers.

"While you're getting over Jack, there's food in the refrigerator and freezer. It's what you like."

"I got the note," I say.

"One second, *ma fleur*. What do you want?" Her voice is muffled. "Daisy, I have to tend to this. Call me if you need me."

"Okay," I mutter, and we end our call.

I take a long, warm bath in the infinity tub and carry on practicing keeping Belmont out of my head. Instead, he becomes the faceless person in my memories.

I'm sitting at the table in a hotel bar. A man

shows up. The energy flowing from him makes my heart flutter. I don't picture his face, but must I? My back slips across the bed sheets, and the man on top of me makes me feel immense pleasure. Our tongues tango. They dance so well together. I touch myself. The water stirs around my hand as I stimulate myself. Only it's not me who's doing it. It's...

I rush out of the tub, splashing and dripping suds all over the floor. What in the world is wrong with me? I miss Belmont, that's what's wrong with me. But things between us have gotten worse. He has physically connected with a woman he used to be in love with. That's heartbreaking.

Tears glaze my eyes as I dry my skin, set the alarm on my phone, and crawl into bed. I curl up and stare at the flower pattern on the French chair. My cell phone chimes. I stretch my neck to see who's calling. Finally, it's Belmont. I want to answer, but I don't. The ringtone stops, and I anticipate the next time it goes off. Thirty minutes later, it does, then again an hour after that. The final chime, which occurs after midnight, is like the end of a lullaby. If he's calling me, then he's not making love to her. I'm content enough to close my eyes and fall asleep.

. . .

THE ALARM CHIMES. I ROLL OVER TO TURN IT OFF. It's seven thirty a.m., and I'm scheduled to meet with Dexter and our team at nine. I rise and shine, preparing myself for the day. After fixing my hair in a bun, I take one final look at myself in the mirror. I'm wearing a black pencil skirt, a sleeveless tank, and my orange suede Cole Haan ankle boots.

Finding my way around the kitchen is simple. I know my mother's habits. I make a cup of coffee in the K-cup machine and whip up a quick breakfast of one egg and a slice of turkey bacon folded into a slice of whole-grain toast. I eat it way too fast for it to keep me full for long. The hour and a half I gave myself has dwindled to nothing. I run upstairs to grab my leather briefcase.

"Shoot," I mumble when I realize that I forgot there's an elevator. I take it downstairs.

According to the weather woman, it's seventy-nine degrees with eighty-three percent humidity. I join the sprinkle of men and women filing out of nearby skyscrapers. I shuffle up the concrete steps at the end of the street to get to Columbus Avenue. The walk across the bridge reminds me why I wanted to leave Manhattan. I'm not a fan of tall cities—not living in them long-term anyway.

I prefer the countryside and antiquated fishing

villages. I really love Martha's Vineyard. I wanted to ask Belmont to build us a pretty little three-bedroom, three-bathroom cottage near a pond and make it our home. Why didn't I? Perhaps because I knew that Belmont loves to live larger than that. There's nothing wrong with it. He's earned it. He works hard. I'm just different.

I make it to the media building and take the elevator up to the Travel X suite on the fifteenth floor. The receptionist gives me a stony, wide-eyed glare.

It's clear she's not going to speak first, so I say, "Hi, my name's Daisy Lord."

She lifts her eyebrows pretentiously. I'm waiting for her to say something, but she doesn't.

"I'm here to see Dexter Frampton," I say.

"About what?"

I feel the tension in my forehead when I hear, "Daisy! You made it!"

I turn to see Dexter walking toward me. His smile is infectious.

"I did!"

We shake hands. I put whatever issues the receptionist may have behind me and follow Dexter to my office. It's small. The desk, chair, and one long wooden filing cabinet are against one wall, and a white board is tacked onto the other. I haven't worked in an office outside my house since college. I shared that space with three other interns who took a lot longer to become paid travel writers than I did. Jamie Rotherham, a friend of Heloise and editor at *Road Climb Magazine*, published my first three articles six months after I graduated.

"Have a seat," Dexter says.

I sit, clinging to my briefcase. I feel as though I'm ready to jump up and leave without notice.

Dexter studies me with a frown. "Are you comfortable, Daisy?"

I release the tension in my shoulders and sit back in the chair. "I am now."

He chuckles. "Good. I have something I want to read to you." He opens a folder I hadn't noticed and flashes me a quick smile. "'My parents inflicted me with the need to travel without even knowing it. My mom was a bitch before Alexis Carrington made it *en vogue*. Mom got away with it because she was a stunning French woman working in Hollywood. She used to say that the executives didn't know if they wanted her to blow them or if they wanted to slap her. It was because of that confusion, she went from fetching coffee to calling the shots in less than five years.

"'My father is famous. When you read his name, you'll think, "I've heard of him." You'll think of him in all of his perfection and genius. He is Jacques Blanchard, award-winning musician and composer. As long as I can remember, my father referred to himself as the music man. He trained my brother and me very early to respect that part of him. When Papa's practicing, he's not to be disturbed. When Papa's working in his studio, act as though he doesn't exist. When Papa's on the road, he doesn't exist.

"'That was fine with my brother, Daniel, and me, because we ran wild and far. We would tell our parents we were going to the neighborhood park, but instead we'd skateboard half the way and bus the rest of the way to Olvera Street in downtown L.A. My brother and I used our allowance to buy sweet rolls and *paletas*, and we ate them as we sat around the white stone fountain and listened to the rancheros in their hats and ponchos sing from their souls. Then we happened on Chinatown, north of the 101 Freeway, and the Chinese New Year parade. We ran the streets of L.A. like feral kittens!'" Dexter snickers. He's reading the introduction of my book.

Dexter's expression turns stern, changing with

the tone of the passage. "'It's a wonder that the most devastating event of my life occurred close to home. My brother and I had set up a plank in the middle of our driveway. We were jumping willies off it. As always, Daniel had let me go first, and then it was his turn. He promised to show me how to get more speed and height. He took one last jump, soaring high above the ground, faster than he'd ever gone. Our smiles were as wide as the Grand Canyon. That was the last time we celebrated perfection together.

"'Mr. Joe Haywood was returning from a long day of crunching numbers. He was an independent accountant, and his wife, Melissa, was a caterer. Mr. Haywood always made it a point to drive the speed limit and watch for the sprightly kids in the neighborhood, who were known to dash into the street out of nowhere. He couldn't have been more cautious when he collided with that Blanchard kid, going Lord knows how fast on his skateboard. Mr. Haywood's car was unscathed, but my brother was dead. Our traveling days, my traveling days were over…'"

Dexter's voice becomes distant as he continues reading about how my strained relationship with my parents made me reclaim my love for traveling.

The memory of Daniel lying in the street with his head busted open and dead eyes makes me want to weep. I constrain my tears though, because I'm not alone.

"'Life was peaceful on the road, and moments were perfect—like sitting on that stone fountain, licking a *paleta* with the sweltering sun directly overhead, mothers chasing their little ones, people in business suits rushing back to the offices. But it's summer, and we have no place to go, and just like then, Daniel is always beside me. He says, "This is cool, isn't it?" and I say, "Yep."'"

I smile, choked up.

"That's the voice of our narrator and the face of our host," Dexter says. "After reading your book, I realized you're not a traveler; you're an explorer."

"You convinced me." I clear my throat. "I have both feet in."

BELMONT LORD

Belmont ended the call before hearing the buzz. He'd already left four messages. Daisy was playing hardball, choosing to return his call when she saw fit. He hated waiting when it came to matters of the heart. She'd accused him of being entitled, and that had vexed him. Perhaps that's why, early that morning, he'd tried to give it another go with Stacy. Once again, he couldn't finish. Stacy was physically flawless, but Belmont didn't find pleasure in having sex with her. He only wanted Daisy. Always had, probably always would.

He and Stacy had just ended a three-hour meeting with the Voyager Group. They would've sold all of their Chicago holdings to him if he had included two of his properties along Miami's South Beach in the deal. Did they really think he would give up any part of Miami for Chicago? Voyager was the one with its head caught between the ropes, not him. In the last few days, Belmont had gotten them to drop the price significantly.

Initially, five investors had been interested in purchasing Voyager's riverfront properties. They were all equally matched when it came to holdings, so Belmont had had to dissuade the competition. That's where Stacy came in. She was one of the best investigators in his employment. She sniffed out their other projects, and Belmont used his contacts to sweeten those deals if they abandoned their interest in Voyager's holdings. Their new contracts would remain legitimate but pending until Voyager's properties were acquired by Lord & Lord Holdings.

There was one holdout: Reece Holdings. They were just as judicious as Belmont was. Although Belmont was impatient in love, meaning in matters concerning Daisy, he wasn't when it came to business. He worked on one major project at a time, and so did Reece Holdings. They were just as focused as he was.

Belmont grabbed lunch at the same restaurant where he'd run into Daisy. He hoped to run into her again, so he sat at a table near the window, waiting for Stacy. She was on a fact-finding mission to unearth anything she could on Matthew Silver, the CEO and son-in-law of Holden Reece, even if it was a jaywalking ticket from 1975. Belmont was about to put his cell phone in the breast pocket of his jacket when he remembered that Daisy had asked him not to do that any more. Angelina had convinced her that it might cause cancer. He sat it on top of the table instead.

Stacy waved as she passed by the window. She always looked appealing, but unlike Daisy, she worked at it. Her dresses were always tight, and her hair cascaded down her back like the women in magazines. She wore sweet perfume and dark eye makeup, which contrasted with her light eyes. Men liked looking at her. At one point, Belmont had too.

"No one's ever clean, are they?" she said as she sat across from him.

She gave him an envelope. He eyed her curiously before he opened it and read the contents.

"It's not a crime, but it's a crime in the public's eyes," she said.

"How in the hell did you get this?" Belmont asked.

They were certified bank statements made payable to a high-level politician. Basically, the man had been bought, and from the amount of money Matthew Silver had given to his campaign, strings were attached.

"Just thank your lucky stars that there's nothing you can do to get on my bad side." She winked at Belmont.

Belmont flexed his eyebrows and slapped the pages in his hand. "This, I can work with. I think our business here is finished."

"Is that your way of asking me to exit stage right?"

Belmont regarded her shrewdly.

Recognizing that look on his face, she shrugged. "I have to go to Tokyo for a little while anyway."

"Oh, what for?" he asked, pretending to be interested. He wanted Stacy gone because he was already working on his next big project—getting his wife back into his bed on a full-time basis.

"Would you want me to disclose that I've been working with you to any of my other clients?"

Belmont sniffed a chuckle. "Right. Then have a safe flight."

They let the silence that fell between them settle things.

"Hey, have you ever seen that movie…" Belmont snapped his fingers. "*The Way We Were?*"

"I have it loaded on my home theater. Why?"

"I've never seen it, but I want to."

"I can access it on my computer." She narrowed her sultry eyes. "How about a nightcap?"

Belmont was inclined to decline her invitation, but he wanted to see that movie. He was eager to know what Daisy really thought of him. So he said yes to the movie and maybe to the nightcap.

They walked to his hotel, which was the same one he'd been staying in since arriving in Chicago two weeks ago. It so happened to be the same hotel Daisy stayed in. Stacy asked what he planned to do with the lakeside property once he acquired it. The easy answer was make it better, but for a moment, he embraced the truth.

When he'd heard that the Voyager Group was selling off their Chicago assets, he thought getting into the bidding would be a good way to forget he had walked out on the only woman he could ever love. It had worked in conjunction with keeping company with Stacy, but then he saw Daisy in that restaurant. Since then, he had craved Daisy constantly, just like he had when he saw her in the Day Harbor Café on Martha's Vineyard. Fate had been on his side then. Belmont hoped *she* hadn't abandoned him.

He entered Stacy's room, which was one floor below his. He took off his jacket, loosened his collar, took off his shoes but kept his socks on, and sat against the headboard. Stacy excused herself into the bathroom to get comfortable. She came out in a silky slip dress. Belmont pretended not to notice how scantily clad she was. He wasn't in the mood for sex.

As she crawled to the foot of the bed to set up her computer, she made sure Belmont got an eyeful. "You never told me why you want to see this movie."

"I heard it was a classic," he replied.

"So is *Casablanca*. Have you seen that?"

"Here's looking at you, kid," he said in his best Humphrey Bogart voice.

"That's a yes. What about *The Maltese Falcon*?" She posed her body in a sexual way to look back at him.

"I haven't," he admitted. Suddenly he recalled Daisy inviting him to divorce her. He squeezed his eyes to stop his head from spinning. Hell, they'd been throwing that word around a lot lately. "*Vertigo*. Now that's a classic movie I've seen."

Stacy giggled. "And it's on." She crawled up the mattress to cuddle.

He put his arm around her because that was what she wanted. The movie started. Belmont studied every frame, trying not to miss a thing.

"He's chewing the hell out of that gum," he said. That bothered him. Right away he found Hubbell to be a cocky son of a bitch.

"What did he say?" Belmont later complained.

"He said he was a lot like the country he lived in," Stacy replied.

"Yes, that. If he thinks everything came easy to this country, then he's a stupid ass."

"It's just a movie."

Belmont gave Stacy a quick side-eye. It wasn't just a movie, not when his wife had compared him to that prick. He seethed but decided to keep his outbursts to himself.

Stacy was frisky, kissing him and massaging his dick until it turned firm. At one point, she tried to give him a blowjob, but he rejected it. He didn't want to miss a beat. Hubbell was a dick. A stupid dick who chose the boring chick because she fit the mold. Belmont wasn't that guy, and he was pissed that Daisy thought so. Hell, she really didn't know him at all. When the movie ended, he sat against the headboard staring at the credits.

"What the hell's wrong with you?" Stacy asked.

He threw up his hands. "'Your girl is lovely'? That's it? That's all she could say?"

"That line's a classic."

"But all she had to say was, 'Hubbell, I want you,' and he would've given up that other woman in a heartbeat. She just had to say something."

"Then maybe you should've written the script. I didn't know you were this sentimental about movies," she said.

Belmont shifted to sit on the side of the bed. "I'm not. But I don't get why that's considered a masterpiece?"

"Because it's Barbara Streisand and Robert Redford."

He bent over to put on his shoes.

"Are you leaving?" Stacy asked.

"I'm tired."

"What's going on between us, Jack? I'm ready to know."

He sighed despairingly. Finally, the time had come. "Let's not do this now."

"Then when? Tomorrow? Because you clearly want me to get the hell out of Dodge."

"You're the one who said you had to fly to Tokyo."

"I said that because you were being a jerk!"

Belmont studied her angry face. He wished Daisy would fight that hard for him. When he'd walked out on her, he hoped she would run after him. He wanted her to tell him to stay until she figured shit out. He knew Daisy had no idea what her problem was, but he knew. She was void. Daisy probably didn't know that he'd read her book multiple times. Each time, he came to the same conclusion. He shouldn't have to compete with the deceased, especially her brother.

Belmont grabbed his jacket. "Breakfast in the morning," he said and got the hell out of there.

It was late when he walked out of the hotel lobby and made a series of right turns until he ended up on Grand Avenue. He stepped over fresh vomit as he passed a half-empty parking lot. It was chilly, but his brisk pace helped him work up a sweat. The Chicago skyline boxed him in, changing constantly to give him different angles of the same skyscrapers. He crossed under a bridge and admired the concrete, steel beams, and multidirectional lanes of traffic. Mankind's inventions momentarily took his mind off of that lousy movie.

Maybe Daisy didn't know that nothing came easy to him, not even her. The first time he saw her inside the Day Harbor Café, it hadn't been easy to muster up the courage to say something to her. The day before on the docks, she had walked by him as though he didn't exist, which rarely happened to him. But when she passed him, everything about her felt right. So the next day, when she happened to show up at the café, Belmont figured he couldn't go wrong by inviting her to his birthday party. But hell, she left the card he gave her on the table! When he saw her again in the grocery store, he knew that he had nothing to do with them meeting. Fate did.

He made a right on Dearborn and continued

north. For some strange reason, the rustic brownstones made him think of Daisy. They were just the sorts of homes that turned her head. He made a left on Elm, hoping Fate would continue working her magic and make him collide into Daisy. When that didn't happen, he turned up Clark Street. A kid was barfing into a sidewalk garden while his friends stood around laughing.

Belmont had never been that stupid and young. He'd never equated being inebriated with having a good time. He was his own unique brand of stupid ass in his early twenties. He'd probably had a bit of Hubbell in him back then. He'd been good-looking all his life. Where he came from girls threw themselves at him, and guys respected him for it. He would give Daisy one point for that. He had benefitted from his good looks. He'd subconsciously despised it, so he jumped at the chance to be different.

Belmont was seventeen when he left home. He'd spent a year at Chicago University, but he believed his destiny was in Los Angeles, so he transferred to USC in L.A. He wanted to be free of his father's money, and he convinced himself he could be the next Brad Pitt. If looks were all it took, then he surely could've been the next major heartthrob.

Acquiring an agent had been easy. He had no headshots or previous acting experience, but he did have the gift of persuasion. His agent's name was Francis Lineman, and she was nothing like the women where he came from. Francis wasn't polite, and she distrusted charm, but Belmont knew how to make her feel less like a hard-ass. She didn't drop him from her client list even after she received warnings from male producers never to send him back to their auditions. Certain female producers requested him continuously. They came on to him, and he succumbed to their objectification. Not because he wanted the parts, but because he loved taking their hard shells and turning them into jelly.

Lorena Sheimann, a TV producer, had been the one to tell him to stop making a mockery out of acting and put his talents to better use. She knew he had just bought a couple of properties in the Holly-wood Hills and that he was interested in commercial real estate. Lorena told him the way into a man's wallet was through an ambitious woman who wanted to be pounded by someone like him while married to someone like her husband.

"You'll always have your daddy's money, but if you're going solo, then they'll get you there just as fast as you can get them off," Lorena said.

He'd moved to Vegas to start his corporation and to service those powerful women. They were interesting, so making love to them was easy. Their husbands never suspected a thing. They couldn't believe someone like him would have sex with their wives, especially when the husbands were chasing tail that was twenty to thirty years younger than them. Those women came through for him in many ways, and sometimes, they still did. But seven years later, after he'd acquired his first set of beachfront high-rises off South Beach, the sex without love had started to erode his soul, and he knew it was time to give it up.

Did he regret being their gigolo? No. Was any of it ever easy? Hell no.

He trudged up Wells Street and gazed at the vodka bottle on the billboard along the side of a building. Seeing it made him want a nice stiff glass of whisky, so he plopped down on a stool inside an Irish pub. Girls giggled. Guys laughed. He was out of place in his Armani suit, even if he had loosened his tie and unbuttoned his jacket.

"Shit," he muttered once he realized he'd put his cell phone into his breast pocket.

That was when Belmont saw that Daisy had returned his calls. She'd even left a message. He hadn't planned on tossing back his drink the way he did. It had been a long time since he'd had whisky, and it went straight to his head. It was too noisy inside to listen to the message, so he shot off the stool.

"Hi, I'm Lacey," a girl said, blocking his path to the door.

He frowned at the girl. She had that look that made leaving Chicago when he was seventeen easy. When she stepped out of her house and into the bar, she did it with the intention of enticing the opposite sex. Her goal was to attract, fuck abundantly, six months later pressure him for a ring, and the rest became the shit that used to give him nightmares.

"Nice to meet you, Lacey. You can have the stool. I'm leaving." Belmont walked around her and out into the night. He pulled up the message.

"Hi... Sorry I didn't call you back sooner. I guess you're busy." She took a long pause. "I don't know. Okay. Bye."

The sound of Daisy's voice made his chest tight and his dick hard. Belmont gritted his teeth and roared at the sky. He dialed her back. The call rang over and over. He didn't leave a message. If he didn't need his cell phone, he would've crushed it under his foot.

"Hey, are you okay?"

It was that girl, Lacey. Belmont glared at her.

"Yeah, I'm fine." He stomped down to Chicago Avenue toward his hotel.

MISSED MESSAGES

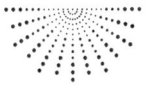

DAISY LORD

I huff and shove my phone into my purse, trying to make room for it. I could kick myself for leaving Belmont such a dumb voice message. I just didn't know what to say other than ask if he was with *her*. Since he didn't answer, I couldn't keep myself from assuming the worst.

I'd spent a long day in the conference room, determining where and how to shoot the first episodes of *The Lone Traveler*. There was a lot of back and forth regarding parts of New England as opposed to the Blue Coast. After being impressively guided in the right direction by Dexter—who made us realize that the show is not just a travelogue, it's about seeking and finding happiness—we decided on Provence, the South of France, and a trek from the Sonoma Valley to San Francisco. Tomorrow, I'm supposed to dial up my contacts to let them know I'm coming and bringing a camera crew with me.

Tonight, I've accompanied Dexter and the others to karaoke, which is something I've never done. After a girl skipped on stage and belted out a very bad rendition of "I Will Survive" by Gloria Gaynor, I excused myself from the table. I went outside to finally listen to the messages Belmont had left. In every single one, he simply asked me to call him so that we could talk. They all concluded with, "I miss you."

So I did as he asked, and he didn't answer. I wish I still smoked. I just want to grip the cigarette between my fingers and tremble as if I'm nervous. I get this funny feeling in the pit of my stomach as I gaze up Chicago Avenue. It feels like déjà vu. Foot traffic is heavy with lots of couples dressed up for a night on the town and people in their twenties hanging in packs. There's very little digression from these two sects of the population. I miss L.A. No, I miss Martha's Vineyard. My cigarette craving subsides, and I go back inside to rejoin the group.

The team is comprised of seven people, including Dexter and myself. Kristin, the beautifully pale Midwest type, is the other producer. She has been pleasant in an insincere manner. I can tell she wishes I would go back to wherever I came from. Damien, Emma, Braden, and Kate are associate producers. We're sitting in a horseshoe-shaped booth with a square table in the center.

"I told him he has two months to ask me to move in with him or else," Kristin yells over a horrible rendition of Beyonce's "Single Ladies."

"Or else what?" Kelly says.

"I don't know. I just hope it works!"

"It will." Kelly's tone sounds hopeful and rehearsed.

I half regret coming out. There's a lot of work to be done. The executives want the shooting schedule and script for the first two shows by next Friday, and I can't understand why these people want to waste precious hours listening to horrendous renditions of famous songs. We should all be working, especially since the sun is soon to rise in France. Dexter and the others are laughing and singing along. They have a high tolerance for the spirits. I try not to look bored.

Dexter smiles at me before he comes over and sits beside me. "Having fun?"

I want to say yes, but instead I say, "I'm sort of

worried about finishing that shooting schedule and script by the deadline. Aren't you?"

I'm confused about why he's chuckling, and it must show in my expression.

"All work, huh?" he asks.

I snort cynically. "Not lately."

"Is that so?" Now that he's gotten me to admit something personal, he's like a dog with a bone. "You said you're still married to the billionaire?"

I thought the girls weren't paying attention, but they seem to have heard that.

"Yes," I say and shrink into my seat.

Dexter nods. He looks as if he wants to know more.

"How long have you been married?" Emma asks.

I think she's Emma. I get her mixed up with Kate. They're both frail with fine light brown hair.

I really don't want to answer. "Almost two years."

"You were married to Belmont Lord, right?" Kristin asks.

I caught her phrasing—very tricky. "He's my husband."

"Oh," she says.

"Do you like 'Staying Alive'?" Dexter asks me.

"Sorry?"

"The song. 'Staying Alive.'" He takes my hand. "One song, and then I'll walk you home."

I shake my head. "I don't sing"—cheesy karaoke in cheesy bars.

The girls' eyes bob between Dexter and me. They're intrigued. He tugs me out of my seat, and now that I'm standing, I fear there's no backing out. *Great.* I get to sing my own bad rendition of a classic.

I feel as though I'm walking the line between reality and a bad dream. I've never done anything like this. I'm a voyeur, not a participant. Dexter helps me onto the stage before he shuffles over to tell the operator what song to play. I look out over the sea of curious gazes. I feel naked. I want to race out of here, and I'm on the verge of doing that when Dexter shuffles back. Standing behind me, he puts the microphone in front of my face.

The music starts. The words roll. Dexter is singing in my ear. I keep my eyes on the words, singing them with a severe lack of enthusiasm. Some people find this fun, but I don't. I'm eager for the words to stop and the music to end. Finally the place erupts with whistles, claps, and hoots. My skin runs hot.

"Another!" a drunk guy slurs.

My eyes expand in horror as a new song starts. I've heard the song before—it's by that Disney kid gone bad who always sticks out her tongue—but I've only heard it once or twice. Dexter wraps his arms around me and starts singing. I'm shocked by the liberty he's taken. Thank God his knob isn't stiff.

I stumble through the lyrics, skipping words and singing off-key. It's embarrassing, but people seem to be enjoying the show. Maybe because they're all smashed. Dexter sways my hips so we're moving in unison. Great, now I'm off-rhythm because the music is moving faster than I am.

Kristin runs up on stage to join us. The men hoot and holler again. Soon Kate and Emma join us. Dexter is still holding the microphone in front of my face. Kristin tries to take it from him, but in a subtle way, he refuses to let go. *I wish he would give it to her.* Finally the song concludes, and another starts immediately. I don't recognize the song, but my coworkers are singing it with gusto. Two guys and three girls climb on the platform with us.

I turn to Dexter. "I'm leaving." I break out of his grasp and step down.

Everyone seems to be watching me, wondering why I've decided to abandon the fun.

"You're over it?" Damien says once I make it back to the table.

"Pretty much." I collect my purse.

"Me too," Damien says. "By the way, I really dug your book."

"Oh, thanks." For some reason, I'm thinking twice about leaving.

"You want a drink?" he asks.

I shake my head. "No, I'm a lightweight. What I can go for is some coffee. I'm going to be up all night trying to map out a scheme for the South of France."

He snickers "You won't find much coffee in Chicago outside of Starbucks. This is a bar town."

"I noticed."

He scoots closer to me. "So you're going home to work?"

"Yep."

"We take a commuter flight from Paris to the Provence, unload all our shit, get situated, and then what?" he asks.

"We do what I did when I first visited the region."

"You climbed a slope to a hillside village in Provence."

I smile. "You read my book."

"I did. I don't normally read books like that, but it got me excited about working with you on this series."

"Wow, thanks."

"You know what I think? If we stick to the pages, then we can't go wrong."

"I agree." I turn my attention to Dexter, who's walking our way.

"Are you ready?" he asks.

I shoot straight to my feet. "Yep." I turn to Damien. "See you tomorrow."

He lifts his glass. Dexter says good-bye to him and escorts me out of the bar. Once I'm outside, I squeeze my eyes a few times. The sudden change in the noise level has clogged my ears.

"Getting acquainted with the team, I see," Dexter says as we start up Chicago Avenue.

"Oh, Damien? He seems excited about the project."

"So, Daisy, tell me more about yourself."

I glance at him. "Like what?"

"I don't know if I should tell you this, but your husband called yesterday."

I flinch, taken aback. "He called you personally?"

"On my cell phone."

"But how did he…? Forget it. Belmont can do anything he puts his mind to. What did he say?" My heart is beating so fast.

"He wanted your address. I told him I couldn't give it to him because that violates our policy."

My eyes expand. "What did he say?"

"He said he understood."

"Ha. He was charming you."

"Why do you say that?"

"Well, what did he say next?"

Dexter's eyebrows furrow. "Shit, you're right!"

"What?" I'm anxious to hear it. Belmont's ability to charm the socks off the Grinch is one of the things I love about him.

"He started talking about your book and how observant you are. He said you hardly have any fun and he's probably the reason for that. We just talked more about *you*."

"Then you gave him my address?" I can hardly breathe. Belmont could be waiting right outside my door. I want him so badly. We can make love tonight and resume fighting in the morning.

"Which leads me to the next course of business: you need to process in with HR tomorrow."

I grin. "You didn't have my address?"

"That would be a negative."

I'm disappointed that my address didn't miraculously find its way into Belmont's hands, but I laugh anyway.

Dexter chuckles a little. "So is that how he got you to marry him?"

"Like I said, he's very convincing."

"So you're the one who wants the divorce?"

I finally realize that we're stopped at a light. The bridge over the river is just up the street. "It's complicated."

"That means it's none of my business."

I snort a chuckle. "Kind of... But he's the one who left me."

"Get the fuck out of here!"

"Apparently I make a really bad wife."

"Why do you say that?" he asks.

We walk again.

"I was pregnant. Had a baby. Lost her. I didn't want to have another one."

"And he does?"

"I think so."

Dexter nods. "I was married, now divorced. I have two daughters."

"What's the divorce rate again?" I ask.

"High."

We chuckle.

"Well, I'm sure there are a host of women who want to pick up where your wife left off," I say.

"First of all—likewise. Secondly, I was twenty-four when we got married. I just turned thirty-seven. The next time I do it, there has to be fire-works and shit like that."

"It wasn't like that with your wife?" I'm getting too personal, but he started it.

He shakes his head. "No, it wasn't."

"Well, I experienced the fireworks."

"And yet you're separated?"

"Yep. And I still see them whenever he's near."

Dexter grunts thoughtfully. We walk past one of the many tall buildings in my neighborhood.

"So you stay over here?" he asks.

"Yep."

"Near a park?"

I tilt my head suspiciously. "Why, what's wrong with the park?"

"Have you ever been out in the neighborhood in the daytime or on the weekend?"

"No, why?"

"Nothing…"

"No, there's something."

He shrugs. "You let me know if there's something."

I grin. "Okay."

We gallop down a sloping road. Dexter walks me to my front door, which is right off the street, and says he'll see me in the morning. He adds that he'll try to avoid calls from Belmont now that he knows where I live. Five minutes with Belmont, and he'd spill the beans. We share a good chuckle before we say good-bye.

I go into the kitchen and cook the tuna steak I sliced in half before leaving this morning. I have to hand it Heloise—she knows me better than I thought. I find spinach and onions to sauté, and the Greek feta salad dressing is one-hundred percent organic with nothing on the label that's hard to pronounce. Unless I'm on the road, I'm a clean eater.

I make a tuna burger and a cup of mint tea, and go upstairs to work. However, I sit at the desk unable to lose my yearning for my husband. He's been screwing another woman, and my soul just knows he's done it more than once. Regardless, I want him to ravish me. I run my fingers through my hair, messing it up, as I try to stave off the anxiety. I get up and take long steps to my bedroom. I stand in front of my cell phone, which is sitting on top of the dresser. After a deep breath, I pick it up and dial him. It rings once.

"Hey," Belmont answers.

"Hey."

"How are you?"

"Fine."

It's silent.

"Where are you?" he asks.

"Where are you?"

"I'm just walking into the hotel. I was at a bar. I got your message."

I squeeze my eyes, regretting what I said in that message. "Oh, sorry about that. I totally jumbled it up."

"You're in Chicago, right?"

"Um-hum."

"You want some company?"

I release the breath I've been holding. "Um-hum."

"What's your address?"

I give it to him, wolf down the rest of my tuna burger, and brush my teeth before jumping in the shower. Belmont likes my honeysuckle-scented lotion, so I put it on. I don't want to look as though I'm in it for the sex tonight, so I put on an oversized T-shirt and leg warmers. Belmont knows the outfit as my work-in-the-home-office clothes, and this look usually drives him insane with lust. I fluff out my hair, the way he loves it. I smooth on a little matte dusty-rose lipstick.

The doorbell chimes. I jump. That was fast.

.

6

DIRE CONSEQUENCES

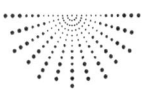

DAISY LORD

*B*elmont looks divine and smells delicious.

"Hey," he says as though he's out of breath.

"Hey."

I wonder if I'm staring into his eyes like he's staring into mine. He puts his hands on my waist and comes in for a kiss. It starts slowly, as if we're rediscovering each other. I forget where I am. The taste of his mouth is gratifying. The door slams. He lifts me off my feet, walks me inside, and our tongues and lips are entangled as my backside meets the sofa cushion.

"You know what this outfit does to me," Belmont says as he pulls down my panties.

Next thing I know, his face is between my legs,

and he's latched on to my clit. I whimper and moan. He's looking at me, but my eyes won't stay open long enough to meet his gaze. He moans as though I taste delicious. I run my fingers through his hair. His hands knead my stomach as my muscles tighten. My wriggling and moaning excites him even more. He whimpers louder, intensifying whatever he's doing with his tongue. The impact is immediate. I cry as pleasure streams through my pussy. He never fails to take me there—never.

We're kissing, and my taste is in his mouth. The tone of our kiss has changed. The warmth of life emanates from his body. His strong frame and the depth of our kiss are the conduits that flood my heart with love. Belmont forces his mouth off mine, and we squeeze each other tightly. My ear is against his chest, listening to how fast his heart is beating.

"I love you," I whisper.

He doesn't reply.

"You still don't believe me?" I ask.

"I believe you," he whispers.

"You don't sound as if you do."

"Do you want to go for a drive?"

I hesitate. That was out of the blue. "Now?"

"Let's go." He frees me from his embrace.

I'm inclined to resist. It's just another instance

of Belmont calling the shots. But I love his spontaneity. "I'll go put something on."

He caresses my wrist. "You're fine."

"I can't go out like this."

"The driver is out front."

I narrow one eye. "You arrived intending to take me somewhere?"

He smirks. "I arrived intending to do what I did. But I've been in town for a while without you. We have some catching up to do." He folds his fingers between mine and kisses my knuckles.

"I didn't think of Chicago as a romantic city."

"It can be what we make it." The look in his eyes is sexy.

"Well, I should at least get a coat. It's chilly outside."

Belmont holds out his jacket for me to slip into. He always has the answer.

"Okay," I say.

We hobble down the steps to where a black limousine awaits. I haven't ridden in one of those since prom.

"A limo?" I ask.

Belmont rubs my back. "I ordered one special for us."

"That fast? I just called you about an hour ago."

He winks. "Money talks, baby."

The driver is pretty young, about college aged. He opens the door to the back, which is decked out with white leather seats that look like sofas. Rose petals have been spread on top of a furry runner in the aisle. A bottle of champagne is chilling on a lit bar. We slide inside and get comfortable in each other's arms.

Belmont orders the driver to keep driving until he knocks on the window and not to turn down the same street twice. The driver seems to welcome the challenge. He glances at me before he closes the window separating us.

Belmont and I gaze into each other's eyes. We have so much to talk about, but I'm just happy to be with him. I don't want to ruin the mood by bringing *her* up. I always knew Jacques was involved with other women while he was married to Heloise, and I swore I would never marry a man who cheated on me. Belmont and I are separated, but we're still married. If they'd just shared a kiss, then I wouldn't care. But sex is the betrayal.

"Come here," he whispers.

Our lips touch. The kiss starts slow, tenderly. I squeeze him tighter, separate our mouths, and press my nose against his neck. Dear God, I love the way he smells. His cheek strokes mine, then the other. Each touch stirs an energy that makes me giddy. I'm intoxicated, floating on air. Our lips brush as our faces continue to pet each other. Every molecule of me desires him.

My hand comes down on his crotch. He's so hard that he just might burst. I unzip his pants and wrap my hand around his shaft. Belmont moans on contact. The head is already slippery. He pinches my nipples and tosses his head against the seat as I ride my hand up and down his rigid shaft.

I lock eyes with Belmont and run my tongue across my lips. His dick twitches, and his eyes shine with lust. I let my mouth water and lower it over his pole. I suck until his tip touches the back of my throat. Belmont whimpers and shivers. I restrain my teeth and keep up the suction as I bob my head. Then I do what he loves the most: I suck the tip and circle my tongue around it. The taste of his salty, sticky wetness fills my mouth.

"Fuck," he mumbles.

The next thing I know, he's lifting me onto his lap. His fingers test my wetness before he separates my legs. We gasp as he breaks through my inner sanctum.

"Oh, baby," he whispers. "You're so fucking tight and wet."

After three slow, indulgent thrusts, he pins my hips against his cock and mumbles something about my pussy. I know to keep still. He's overstimulated and doesn't want to come yet.

Belmont sighs deeply and presses his forehead against mine. "So how are you liking Chicago?"

We laugh. I look out the window, and he moves my hair to nibble on my neck.

"It's lovely." My voice trembles. That tickles.

My gaze falls on the brownstone row houses. I've always adored their bulging, oblong windows and the way the steps make you feel as though you're approaching a king's throne.

Belmont's gaze follows mine. "You like this neighborhood."

I recognize his tone. "You want to buy me a brownstone now?"

"Whatever you want, baby." He thrusts into me carefully.

"I know." My eyes let go of the way leaves dangle over the street like ruffled feathers. I slip my tongue into his mouth, and he prods me deeper, filling me to the rim.

He moans then halts. "Take that off." His eyes point at my oversized shirt.

I lift it over my head. I feel his hot, wet mouth on my lace bra before I can toss the T-shirt on top of the rose petals.

He tugs on my bra. "Free those."

I reach behind me and unclip it, exposing my breasts. His tongue and teeth work in unison to stimulate my nipples as he rapidly shifts my hips. I bite on my bottom lip to keep from screaming. His dick and mouth, they know what the hell they're doing. He's riding me to orgasm.

"I'm going to come, baby," Belmont grunts.

"So am I…" I grasp him tighter as he keeps doing what he's doing. I want to join him in muttering a string of profanities.

"You first…" he says.

I move a little to the right and concentrate on the sensation that wants to explode and send waves through my pussy. I'm making sounds that haven't come out of me in a long time.

"That's it, baby…" Belmont says.

I toss my head back and shriek when my orgasm detonates. Belmont joins me. Our muscles constrict, and our limbs spasm. We hold on for dear life until the sensations subside.

"Love you," he whispers warmly in my ear and kisses it.

"I love you too."

The car stops at a light, and I climb off Belmont's lap. Once I'm seated, he slips his hand between my legs and rubs my soaked slit. I rest my head on his shoulder and gaze at the pinnacle of a skyscraper that rises beyond the triangular gable of a rustic Dutch-style building. I've noticed Chicago, like Manhattan, fuses vestiges of its Eastern European roots with modern architecture, keeping alive the spirit of the past.

"I spoke to Maya." I moan when his fingers find what they were looking for.

He grunts disparagingly.

I thrust my head back. "It's not as bad as you think."

"I still can't believe you're friends with her again."

"I forgave her," I barely say.

Belmont jabs his fingers deeper inside my slippery pussy. I tense up because I wasn't expecting that.

"I'm lucky you're so forgiving," he says.

Moans escape me. I couldn't stop them even if I

wanted to. He's rousing spots inside me that he has studied and committed to memory.

"She didn't convince you that we were better off apart did she?" he asks.

"No…" I say, screwing his fingers.

"Your pussy is the eighth wonder of the world."

"That's what you always say…"

His chuckle is sensual. "Are you going to forgive me for leaving?"

I squeeze my eyes to bear the sensation spasming through my pussy. Suddenly Belmont is on his knees, and my legs are draped over his shoulders. His tongue prods me, and he sucks me softly. I whimper like a puppy.

"After you come, I'm going to fuck you like there's no tomorrow," he says.

His tongue rounds my clit. Belmont is impatient. He's getting right to the point. The way he's groaning… His fingers dig into my hips… Faster… Faster… He makes me scream. He tugs me off the seat and sets me on all fours on the soft rug. His dick breaks through my slippery sugar cave from behind. Belmont says shit over and over as he pounds into me. He moans as he ejaculates.

"Slayed too soon," he says with a laugh.

Although his dick has gone soft, he's still trying to prod me. After realizing he's not going to rise for a while, he lays me down and sucks and bites my nipples. One morning, Angelina complained she couldn't wear a bra because Charlie had murdered her tits. Belmont liked how sexy that sounded, and he adopted the habit of murdering mine. He keeps doing it until he's back up and inside me. This time, he takes it nice and slow, letting our souls make love to each other. The car stops and goes, turning corners, speeding up and slowing down. We're neglecting the sights.

"I miss this, baby," he says in my mouth.

"Me too…"

"Then you forgive me?" He grunts. He's ready to blow.

"Always," I whisper.

He murmurs a string of indecipherable words as he pins me to the floor and lets loose. I've let Belmont fill me to the rim tonight. My emotions have overpowered my reason, just like they did when we first met.

I yawn. Belmont pushes a button and tells the driver to return to my place. His dick is barely hard enough for him to steep inside me. We kiss as the skyscrapers slip past us. If only I could pay attention to them. Every now and then my hazy gaze falls over some interesting detail, like domed tops, saucer-like balconies, and pointy pinnacles.

Belmont lies beside me, and his strong hands knead my flesh. It feels so good. Then he stimulates my clit until the car stops in front of my place. His free hand presses a button, and he tells the driver not to open the door yet. He wants me to come first, and he doesn't rush it. I rest my hand on his shoulder. He kisses my forehead. I pant, and he works harder to get me off. Finally, orgasm pulses through my groin. I cling to Belmont until the sensation passes. He smiles, proud of himself. I flex my eyebrows to say thank you. After one last long kiss, we fix our sex-scented clothes.

"We're ready," he tells the driver.

The door opens, and the driver studies me. He must've heard everything. I hurry up and get inside as Belmont gives the driver his final instructions.

Once Belmont's inside, he takes his jacket off me, strips me out of my shirt, and grabs two handfuls of my ass as we ride the elevator to the third floor. His mind may want to screw me, but his penis is down for the count. The doors slide open. Belmont refuses to take his mouth and hands off me as we walk to my room.

"You're not sleeping in the master bedroom?" he asks.

"I prefer this one."

He wrinkles his eyebrows for a moment then lowers me onto the bed. We take a break so that I can take off my leg warmers, and he takes off his pants and shirt. We slip under the covers.

Belmont draws me against him. "Don't mind me. I'm going to paw you all night."

"Don't worry. I've had plenty of nights like that."

He chuckles. "It's your pheromones. They were made to turn me on."

I think I feel him getting hard again, so I reach back to touch it. "Really? You just came."

"It's you, not me."

I sigh. I'm damn sore. He's so big and thick and firm. "I have work tomorrow, you know."

"You still want that job?" He swirls his tongue around a sensitive spot on my back.

"Yes…" I sigh.

"I want you to take me back," he says.

"Don't you always get what you want?"

Belmont stops circling that spot. "Regarding that… Why the hell did you compare me to Hubbell Gardiner?"

I draw a blank. "I did? When?"

"You don't remember? The last time we were together."

I frown, trying to recall what I said. "Oh, right. I called you entitled."

"Yes, you did."

"Did that bother you?" I ask.

"It did. I'm not entitled."

"If you say so."

"If I say so?" He turns me onto my back and gets on top of me. "Why do you think I'm entitled? Be specific."

"Well… you fly private, no matter what."

"That's not entitled. I've earned the benefit to fly the way I want. If I could only afford coach, then I'd fly coach."

"Okay. If you want me to do things your way, then you'll pay to make it happen."

"You could say no."

"I never say no."

"You should try it. Baby…" He parts my legs and touches me to see how moist I am. When he finds me dripping wet, Belmont moans. He slips his dick inside me. "You have all the power. You're the entitled one."

I let my lips meet his. We let passion orchestrate

our kissing and love-making. The sun is rising, and we still haven't stopped.

OUR CELL PHONES CHIME IN UNISON. I BLINK MY eyes open. The room is bright. I'm wrapped in a blanket lying against Belmont, who has no covers over him as he snores in my ear. I pick up the phone nearest me.

"Hey," I say, expecting it to be Dexter.

"Who's this?" It's a woman.

"Daisy. Who's this?"

After a long silence, she says, "Check your email, *Daisy*," and hangs up.

I look at the phone in my hand. It's Belmont's. He's out like a match. I check the time. It's a little after noon, and we just stopped having sex two hours ago. Going into the office feels like a burden. Being in Belmont's arms feels like my destiny. I turn around to kiss his forehead, but he's too tired to know.

Why would a woman who called Belmont tell me to check my email? I slip out of his arms. He stirs a little but doesn't wake. We haven't made this much love in one session since before Joella was born.

I tiptoe to the office to turn on my computer. I definitely owe Dexter an explanation. I try to think of what I should tell him as I click on my email. The first message is from Stacy Pruitt. The subject reads, "Friend and Lover of Jack Lord."

My chest tightens. I open the message. One sentence reads, "I want him too—and he wants me." Below that are a lot of photos of Belmont and Stacy. She's giving him a blowjob. They're kissing on top of a bed, and he's groping her tits while they kiss. He's tasting her down there. She's on all fours, mouth open, as he humps her from behind. There are a lot more, but that's all I can stomach.

"Shit," I mumble.

I want to run out of this condo and escape to another planet. He did all of that to her? Seeing it, I feel as if a piece of my heart has been cut out. I take deep breaths to keep myself from crying. My legs are weak. I recall my last conversation with Maya. I'm big on running away from my problems, but I don't want to do that anymore.

I slog back to the bedroom and squat to study Belmont's face. He's snoring again. Recovering from this heartache seems light years away. His hair is graying, but it's always been so light that I couldn't tell until now. The skin under his eyes is dark. Whatever business he's doing in Chicago seems to be taking a toll on him. This is the face of the only man I can ever love. Ten years from now, when he's remarried and making love to another woman, I'll be alone because my heart will never again feel what it had before those photos broke it. I want to sweep my fingers down his cheek one last time, but instead I go to the closet and put on a robe. Our love nest has fallen off the branches.

"Belmont," I say, shaking him awake.

It takes a moment, but he opens his eyes and seizes my arm, pulling me to him. "Come here."

"No." I take back my arm. "You come here."

He frowns as if he's alarmed by my response. "What is it, babe?"

"You should come take a look."

He's blinking, waking all the way up. "Take a look at what?"

"Stacy Pruitt sent me an email."

He leaps out of bed, frowning. He touches my hip on the way to the office, and I recoil.

"Daisy, what's going on?"

We make it to the office.

"You should see for yourself." I point at the

computer and step back.

Belmont glares at the screen. "What the fuck?"

"I want a divorce. For real this time."

He turns around and looks at me as if he's unable to comprehend what's happening. "Daisy…"

I raise a hand. "Don't."

"These aren't real, baby."

"That isn't you with her?"

"It's me, but they've been taken out of context."

"Have you ever put your dick in her mouth? Have you ever put your dick inside her? Have you ever put your mouth on her pussy? I would've never betrayed you like that," I say.

"Daisy?" Belmont sounds defeated. "I already admitted that I had sex with her."

"You said you hadn't had sex with her since you met me. She time stamped them, see? Sure looks like after we met to me."

He sighs.

"I want a divorce," I say.

"Not yet. I want you to calm down, then we'll talk."

"And say what?"

"You should at least hear me out. Please?"

I stare into his eyes. I don't see how we can recover from this.

"For better or worse," he says, holding my gaze.

"Okay. I'll call you when I'm ready."

"That's all I can ask."

I fold my arms. "You should go."

Belmont catches a tear that's rolling down my cheek. He kisses my forehead and nose. I turn my face before he plants one on my lips. I stand in the office and wait until he goes and puts on his clothes. I can feel him standing in the hallway watching me.

"I love you," Belmont says.

I don't answer.

"We're going to talk, and I'm going to handle this," he says.

I shake my head. Finally he gets in the elevator. I stand here for at least another ten minutes, until I know for sure that he's gone.

BELMONT LORD

Belmont took a cab to the hotel. He felt as if he was carrying a pile of bricks on each shoulder. The look in Daisy's eyes haunted him. Her despair was visible. He never thought he'd be the one to make her feel that way.

He stopped at the front desk to see whether Stacy had checked out. She had. That was a smart move on her part. Belmont didn't know what he would've done to her if she had stuck around to bask in the glory of her victory. She had ruined his happiness! Of course, he'd had a hand in it. Out of context or not, he had let himself be intimate with another woman. What he'd done was inexplicable! Inexcusable!

Belmont made it to his room and showered. He had planned to spend the day in bed making love to his sexy wife. He wanted to ask her to blow off that job. Belmont didn't want her around Dexter Frampton. He knew Dexter wanted her and would fuck her whenever the opportunity presented itself. Belmont knew that because he knew his species.

Water sprayed over Belmont as he fought the urge to call Daisy and beg her to forsake her obligations and fly back to Malibu with him. She was angry and had probably lost a lot of respect for him, but if they lived in the same house, he could make sure they came out on the right side of this catastrophe, which had started the day he made the mistake of walking out on her.

He hadn't known that Stacy was recording their interactions. One lesson he'd learned over the years was never to tell more than necessary. That rule applies to everyone, even to those he trusts. So Stacy didn't have much incriminating shit on him, but she had enough to do more damage than what she had already done.

Belmont considered rubbing off to memories of making love to Daisy last night, but since he didn't have her erect nipples in his mouth and supple body beneath his, he took his hand off his dick and got out of the shower. He put on a suit and a tie before calling Herald Standard. Herald would contact the appropriate parties to leverage the information Stacy had acquired. Stacy had done a good job on the Voyager project, but she could consider that her last job for him or anyone else. From that point on, Belmont set out to destroy her.

7

WHAT HAPPENS NEXT

DAISY LORD

"*I* was with Belmont," I say and fight to keep myself from crying. I want to say, "my husband," but would a true husband do what he has?

What I saw in those photos wasn't news to me. He's been taking her to personal events, and he already admitted to having sex with her. But to see it—his passion for her was more than I could bear. His eyes were closed as he kissed her, and it showed in the way his hands grasped her. Not to mention the blowjob. Doggy style? It didn't look as if he'd had a problem keeping it up.

"Are you coming in today?" Dexter asks.

I clear my throat. "Yes. It's only a short walk over the bridge. I'll be in soon."

"You don't have to if you don't want to. It'll be nice to see you, but you can work from home."

"It'll be nice to get out of the house. I'm on my way."

"Okay!" He sounds chipper about my decision. "I'll order lunch. Unless you've already eaten?"

"I haven't, and I'm starving."

"Good. Are you on the California-bird diet?" he asks.

I snicker. I'm happy he got me to laugh. "Not today."

"Then I'll order pizza. The big, thick kind with lots of cheese."

I tell him that's fine. I'm pressed for time, but in order to get through the rest of the day, I must take a relaxing bath. Once the tub is full, I slide in and close my eyes.

I remember the first time I saw Joella. I felt a deep sadness because deep down I knew I had to say good-bye to her. I had a dream, or maybe a vision, the night she was born. I was heavily sedated, so it comes back to me in pieces. It was pitch black, but I heard Daniel say, "I have this, Ella. Just hold the other side and watch your hand." I can't see "Ella," but I know she's my daughter.

I get out of the tub, put on a stretchy flower-printed jersey dress, and rush into the humid, eighty-something-degree weather. There's a parade of strollers being pushed up and down the sidewalks. I see lots of dog walkers and people running off their nonexistent fat. I remember what Dexter said last night about the scene being jarring. *I get it.* There's too much of one thing.

I make it to the office. Kristin is sitting in front of Dexter's desk when I arrive. She looks at me with a grim expression. At least Dexter is smiling.

"Hey, sit down," he says.

I sit next to Kristin, and she musters up a weak smile. Whatever issues she has with me are her own.

Dexter hands me a plastic folder. "Here's the script. Reword it if you like."

I read the first page. "Wow. You've pulled the dialogue straight out of my book."

He smiles. "Thanks to your writing, it was easy to do."

I want to smile, but I can't. "Okay. I'll call my contacts and let them know I'm coming."

"Wait," Kristin says. "I was just talking to Dexter about this. I want to arrange a test shoot since you don't have any on-camera experience."

"Oh." The thought of performing in front of a camera just got real. "If you have any doubts that I should be the host, then by all means, recast."

Kristin raises an eyebrow. I wait for her to say something, but she doesn't. I don't think she expected me to relinquish the role so quickly. I really, really, *really* don't want to do it.

Dexter taps the desk. "You're the host, Daisy. And there won't be a test shoot. I was telling Kris that Ted and I had our own conversation."

Kristin snorts. "Okay, but I still have concerns." She touches my arm. "Not in your ability, Daisy. You've been great as a producer."

Dexter and I wait for her to say more, but apparently that's all she has to say. I had hoped she wouldn't give up so easily.

The team assembles in the conference room as the pizza arrives. When we compare notes, I'm thankful for the team. They've made all the broad strokes. Making TV is what they do for a living, and now all I have to do is shade in the space between the lines.

There's still a lot to be done, and I welcome the distraction. At the end of the day, I decline Dexter's invitation to grab a drink, and I turn off my cell phone when I get home. Belmont has been good about not contacting me, but I'm expecting calls from Angel and Maggie once they get word of what happened.

I make baked fish tacos and sit alone at the table, forcing myself to not cry. Being idle makes me remember my heartache. I get up, put on my workout clothes, and hit the home gym. I run on the treadmill until my legs turn to jelly, until I can't breathe, until I'm drenched in sweat. Then I stop and do rounds of exercises that Belmont taught me. Three months after we lost Joella, I started joining him in our home gym. He taught me how to combine cardio and strength exercises to decrease my workout time while giving me better results. Of course, we always made love afterward. He's always so consumed by me. I would've never guessed he could have intimate relations with another woman. I guess I was wrong.

I take a shower instead of sitting in a warm bath and then revisit my notes from my trip to Africa. Javar Les accompanied me. We had a good time eating, dancing, and taking thrilling, and oftentimes dangerous, excursions with locals off the beaten path. I couldn't include a lot of our destinations in the taxicab series because we also used buses, trains, and rented cars. To further distract myself, I start writing an article on South Africa. I remember the touches, the smells, the sounds, and the feelings of our trip.

At one a.m., I start making calls to my contacts in France. Regardless of my unpolished French, I convince them to sign release forms to be on the show. I don't mention that I'm the host because the jury is still out on that. By the time I turn in, I'm too exhausted to be haunted by images of Belmont and Stacy. I go straight to sleep.

My biological alarm clock wakes me at eight a.m. on the dot, but I'm as drowsy and dreary as the cloudy day. I get dressed quickly, grab a bite to eat, and head out. I decide to leave my cell phone on the dresser because I'm not ready to take calls from my family. As soon as I get to the office, I finish compiling the contact list and email it to Damien so that he can work on the releases.

I work with Braden on finalizing segment content. The camera crew will capture establishing shots, and I'll accompany them, along with the director, whose name no one seems to know. Apparently he's European and knows the French countryside like the back of his hand. I decide to work during lunch because I don't have much of an appetite. My desk phone rings.

"This is Daisy."

"Daisy, it's Angel. What's happened between you and Jack?"

I stifle a groan as I collapse on top of my desk. "How did you get this number?"

"Maggie. Are you okay?"

"So you know about the photos?"

"I do, and I'm so sorry," she says.

"Why are you apologizing for what he did?"

"Well, I'm just… disappointed. I knew there was something about that woman."

"She's not the one who's married."

"Jack said the pics were taken out of context."

I lower my voice. "His penis was in her mouth. What other context is there?"

"Oh, I know. It's just a wakeup call. I never thought Belmont would… on you. Charlie can't keep his hands off me. Would he cheat too?"

I roll my eyes. She has such a flair for the dramatic. "Don't internalize this, Angel."

"I'm not. It's just you can never know. But then what? Is it over now?"

"I don't know."

"Did you delete the pictures?"

I sigh. "No."

"Are you going to delete them?"

"I don't know."

"You should."

"I guess so."

Angel sighs. "Gosh, Dais. Charlie and I definitely have to rethink some things."

"Rethink what?"

"Just some things. Like our engagement party. You're still coming aren't you?"

"Oh shoot!" I pull up my calendar on my computer. "I'm supposed to be in Provence."

"You have to be there, Daisy."

"I'll try, but—"

"Don't try. Promise me you'll be there. This is *me* and Charlie, for goodness' sake!"

I roll my eyes. She's being dramatic, but how can I deny her? "Maybe I can arrange a private flight."

"You could use Charlie's service."

"Okay. I'll talk to the team, and I'll see you the week after next."

"Wait. No, it's next week."

"What?"

"I gave you the wrong date," she says. "It's next Saturday."

"The seventh and not the twelfth?"

"Yes."

"You're killing me, Angel."

She chuckles. "Don't worry. I'll make the trip worth your while."

"It's just…" I close my eyes. "I don't think I'm ready to see him yet."

"Oh, Jack won't be there."

I frown. "Oh?" The Belmont I know would never miss his only brother's engagement party. Perhaps he has changed for the worse.

"He said he's going to Oslo on business."

"Really?"

"Yep."

It sounds fishy to me, but I'm too exhausted to push for further details. "All right then."

I actually feel much better after talking to Angel. Maggie calls fifteen minutes later. She wants to know how I'm doing and considers immersing myself in work the best form of therapy.

"By the way, I told Jack he's an asshole," Maggie says. "I have my own problems with a chick who wants to bone my boyfriend. Emily," she says mockingly.

"Who's Emily?" I ask.

"Oh, she's his ex-girlfriend. They were in love in high school."

"And Vince hired her?"

129

"Robert hired her." She sighs dreadfully. "It's a long story, Dais."

"Yikes," I say. "This is not the season for love. What's her job?"

"First it was executive PR. Then after I quit, very embarrassingly…"

"I heard," I say.

"Yep… They wanted to slip her into my time slot."

"What's a time slot?"

"I meant my old job," Maggie clarifies.

"Oh! Well, is she qualified?"

"Not even close, which is why she's back to executive PR."

"Whoa."

"She likes executive PR better because now she's stuck to Vince like white on rice. It's complicated between them because what happened between Vince and I, and she and Vince, and… more."

I flinch. "There's more?"

"Gosh, Dais. I have to get you caught up."

"Soon," I say.

"Yeah…"

"Fourth of July?"

"Martha's Vineyard." I'm smiling, and I know she is too.

"Although Emily and I are like night and day. She always does herself up as if she's on her way to shoot a magazine cover."

"Oh, she's a magazine girl?" I ask.

"In more ways than one."

"And how is that?"

"She's just not real. Or she's real but has no depth. What you see on the outside is all she is."

I nod. "Ah, right. Maybe we can hire her to be the host of our show. I sure don't want to do it."

"What? Wait? You're the host?"

"Um-hum."

"It won't work, Dais. Viewers don't want to tune in and see you, in all of your sexiness, being uninhibited and carefree. It's like a trim woman saying, 'Buy this bathing suit, but only if you have my body.' Get it?"

"No…"

"Frampton is thinking with his second head," she mumbles. "Tell Frampton to get a ruggedly handsome and brash male host. Okay?"

"Okay…"

"Anyway, I have to go, but I love you, and Jack

will always love you. You're the one for him. So try to find a way to forgive him?"

I nod. "Okay. I'll try."

"That's all I can ask."

Maggie says she'll see me at the party. After we say our good-byes, I feel the dread of convincing the team that I have to fly back to the states in order to attend an engagement party only a day after we arrive in Paris. Considering the enormity of my responsibilities as the talent and a producer, I jump out of my chair and walk over to Dexter's office. The receptionist is sitting at his desk, legs crossed and giggling.

He stands as soon as he sees me. "Hey."

"Hey, can we talk?" I ask, ignoring how disappointed the receptionist is to see me.

"Talk to you later, Melissa," he says.

"So we're still on for dinner?" she asks him.

"Sure, why not," he says.

"Excellent, I'll make the reservation." She scurries out of the office without looking at me.

"I just learned two things—her name and why she treats me the way she does," I say.

"How does she treat you?" he asks as we sit.

"Rudely. Nasty. Not very welcoming."

"Why didn't you say something?"

I shrug. "I can handle it. Don't say anything to her. You're taking her to dinner? You must like her."

"A bunch of us are going to this pop-up restaurant on Wabash Avenue. Want to come?"

I shake my head. "Nope. But I do want to talk to you about a few things."

He narrows one eye. "Like what?"

"Well, I have to attend a party next Saturday."

"A party? In France?"

"No, in Louisiana. My sister and brother-in-law are having an engagement party."

"Did you say sister and brother-in-law?"

I sniff a chuckle. "Yes, Belmont's brother is engaged to my half sister. We're keeping it in the family."

"Wow, that's something."

"Yeah, but Charlie and Angel are not like us. They're destined to make it. I'm pretty sure we're going to get a divorce." I can't believe I revealed that.

"Oh… Sorry to hear that."

"Well… it's a pitiful spot to be in." I nod through the awkward silence. That was definitely too much information. Suddenly, I remember my conversation with Mags and finally understand her analogy. "Oh, I don't want to be the host, nor should I be."

He balks. "Oh? Why not?"

I channel Maggie. "It's not what I do. Plus, viewers don't want their women as adventurous as I am. Maybe in an article but not in person."

He chuckles. "And what makes you think that?"

"Well, you're not trying to make a sexy show, and my taxicab series has a pinch of sexiness in it."

"We."

"We what?"

"*We* are making a show."

I smile. "Okay—we. Unless we're only going for the L.A. and New York demographic, then for exploration and adventure, we need a male host. Someone ruggedly handsome and brash."

Dexter sits back in his chair and rests his chin on his steepled hands. He studies me with narrowed eyes. "That's exactly what Kristin said. She said you're too sexy, but damn, your voice in those articles… I want to manifest it."

"Then *man*ifest it."

He sniffs. "Nice pun. Are we really still that backward as a society?"

I shrug. "What about Javar Les? He's handsome

and rugged and self-assured. I gave you his number and—"

He throws up his hands. "He's our director, Daisy."

I nearly choke with shock. "What?"

"He wanted to surprise you."

"Well, surprise!" I shake my head. "Is Javar the reason you reached out to me?" I don't know how I feel about that. I thought Dexter was really a fan of my work.

"Perk up." He smiles convincingly. "After reading your book, I was more on board than he was."

I study his expression. It would be easier to ditch this entire project. As far as Javar is concerned, it sounds like an elaborate scheme to get me to sleep with him. I sort of feel as though I should give Javar what he wants just to get even with Belmont, but that wouldn't be me at all. "I'll continue working on the show, but we're going to get a male host."

"I like your suggestion. Javar is the next best option."

"He was my trip companion throughout most of Europe."

"And the two of you never had a..." He narrows one eye.

"No, we never had a..." I copy his facial expression.

Dexter laughs as he stands. "I'll update Kristin. She's going to love this." His desk phone rings, and he answers it. His eyes expand before he hands the receiver to me. "It's for you."

I'm taken aback. "Who is it?"

"Your father."

I'm stunned. "Jacques?"

JACQUES HAS INVITED ME TO HIS PERFORMANCE ON Saturday night at a venue near the Riverwalk on Dearborn Avenue. Kristin becomes nicer to me after she finds out that I've relinquished my role as the host. Alone in a bathtub is the last place I want to be tonight, so when Dexter asks me to join them for dinner, I say yes.

We go out in a large group of mostly unfriendly women and their men. The chef is cooking Italian cuisine, which is one of my favorites. A lot of conversations take place around me, but I smile and pretend I'm paying attention. Kristin, Kate, and

Emma are planning a couples' kickball game this Saturday. Kate suggests Lincoln Square Park, but Kristin says it's too big and crowded on the weekends.

"What about Lakeshore East Park?" Emma says.

"Where's that?" Kate asks.

"That's right outside your front door, isn't it?" Dexter asks me.

I'm suddenly hot under the collar. The girls intend to exclude me, and I want to be excluded. I didn't even think Dexter was listening to them since Melissa has been monopolizing all his attention.

"Is it? I don't know. It's my parents' condo, so..." I say.

Then I hear, "Aren't you married to Jack Lord?"

I feel as though my head turns in slow motion. When Emma asks the question, everyone at the table acknowledges my presence. I like it better when they are deliberately ignoring me. I clear my throat and square my shoulders as if I'm readying for a showdown. "I am."

"Is he in town? You two can come to the kickball game together."

I fidget. "He's in town, but we don't play kickball. Thanks for asking." My tone is icy.

"You two are divorcing, no?" Kate asks.

I spear the salty pasta on my plate. In all the hours we've worked together, they haven't mentioned Belmont since that night at karaoke, at least not in my presence. I can sense their curiosity and know they have been talking about me behind my back though.

I'm not used to mean-girl tactics. I'm the outsider, and they have continued to treat me that way. Emma and Kate are Kristin's friends, and that's how they got their jobs. That's why she's always giving them assignments. Damien and Braden where hired after a rigid interview process. They do all the heavy lifting, and they're the associate producers I usually work with.

So I show the mean girls how we deal with stupid people like them where I'm from. I continue eating and pretend as if she never asked that question. After a while, the conversation slowly turns back to kickball, but I'm still mad as hell. Dexter keeps flashing his smile and bright blue eyes at me. I give him a weak smile, and Melissa works harder to maintain his attention.

I check my watch. Thirty minutes have passed since Kate asked the offensive question. I calmly set my fork on my plate and take my napkin off my lap and lay it on the table. "Well, I've had good time. See you all tomorrow," I announce to whoever's listening.

I rise to my feet, and Dexter joins me.

Melissa is caught off-guard. "Are you leaving?"

I wave, signaling him to sit back down. "No, stay. I'll just walk up Wacker."

"It's fine," he says, walking in my direction.

"I'll go with you guys," Melissa says.

Dexter holds up a hand. "No, we're fine." He doesn't give her a second look.

I shrug as he puts his hand on my back and walks me out. The tension follows us out the door. I shiver as soon as the cold seizes me.

Dexter drapes his overcoat across my shoulders. "Better?"

"You didn't have to leave, you know."

He shrugs as he blows into his hands to keep warm. "I was bored."

"You seemed to be having a good time. You should take your coat back if you're cold."

"I don't want it back. And you seemed to be having a bad time."

"I can't believe Kate asked that. I'm aware that the girls on the team don't care for me, but she crossed the line."

"You handled her pretty well."

"Thanks," I say. He blows into his hands again, so I curl my arm around his waist. "Better?"

He pulls me closer. "A lot."

We cling to each other as we cross the bridge over the lake. I admire how the city lights paint the surface of the water.

"You want to grab a drink?" he asks.

I smile wryly as I shake my head.

He smirks. "What's that face for?"

I shrug.

"What?"

"Are you flirting with me?" my voice rings with curiosity.

He laughs. "A bit, but I'm a flirt."

"Yes, you are."

"You're beautiful, Daisy. You don't seem to care about that, which makes you even more appealing. But if I make a move on you, Javar would…" He runs a finger across his neck.

I roll my eyes. Javar's infatuation with me is so insane. I haven't the slightest attraction toward him. He's not unattractive. He's simply not my type. "How do you know Javar anyway?"

He stops us in front of Houlihan's. "I can answer that over a drink."

It's still too early to go home if I want to avoid thinking about Belmont. I gesture toward the door. "After you."

"After *you*," Dexter says.

He opens the door, and we're lucky to find two empty stools at the crowded bar. Dexter orders a whisky, and I get a glass of Merlot.

"So you were going to say?" I ask.

"Ah, Javar. He's my sister's husband's brother."

I grin. "He's such a cocky son of a gun. I wonder why he never told me he has a brother."

"You two are that close?"

"He taught me how to swim the seas."

He looks at me askew. "And you never sealed the deal?"

I take a sip of wine. "No. I had a boyfriend that I didn't love, or like, but nevertheless, I made a commitment to that jackass." I latch on to Dexter's hearty laugh.

"And now you have a husband," he says.

"And Javar knows this, right?"

"He knows. He also knows you're on the rocks."

"Oh yeah?" I sigh. "He's like Belmont, and you. He's tall, good-looking, and walks as though he expects the whole world to fall at his feet."

Dexter nearly chokes on his whiskey. "Who me?"

"Maybe not."

"You think your husband's arrogant?"

"I wouldn't say arrogant. He's not used to rejection, and neither is Javar. When I first met Belmont, I rejected him, and he just couldn't stand it. He's constantly chasing me because I'm always pushing him away. I don't do it on purpose. I used to wonder if I just gave in and became exactly who he wants me to be, would he retreat?"

"Who does he want you to be?"

I shake my head. "Hell if I know. But what do men like you want? I mean, you say I'm beautiful, but so what? If the standards of beauty changed tomorrow, then I wouldn't be beautiful and neither would you." I'm lightheaded, and my lips are loose. "Real people who feel human walk with the slightest hunch." I curve my shoulders to show him. "Like this."

Dexter's expression beams with amusement. "I walk with a hunch."

I shake my head. "No, you don't. You walk like… you know."

"Like I know?"

"Yeah… like you certainly know."

"Like I know what?"

"You're at the top of the pyramid. You have

your choice. And so does my husband. *My husband…*" I consider taking another drink. The wine is strong, and my tolerance is so low that not even an ant could reach it.

"So you think I'm beautiful?" he asks, smiling impishly.

"Very."

"Well, Jack Lord's an idiot."

"No." I shake my head vehemently. "What he did was inexcusable, but I have problems. That's why I walk with a hunch. I have problems, but I know that. He has problems, and he doesn't get it."

"I have problems. Ask my ex-wife."

I raise my glass. "You know what? It just came to me. My husband wants me to really want it."

Dexter frowns, confused.

"He wants me to show him who I really am," I say.

"Then who are you?"

I put on my best Jack Nicholson sneer. "Here's looking at her… Wait, that wasn't Humphrey Bogart." My head is spinning.

Dexter laughs and signals the bartender, who comes right over.

"That never happens," Dexter mutters.

The bartender points at me. "Wine and whisky?"

"I'm cut off," I say.

"A wine and a whisky," Dexter says.

"Got it." The bartender turns away before I can object.

"I'm not drinking it," I assure Dexter.

"Let loose. I'm not going to take advantage of you. You're safe."

I sigh deeply and rest my head on my palm. "It's not about letting loose. I don't like feeling inebriated. I love being in the moment. Where do you live anyway?" My brain is scattered.

"I'm staying in a brownstone on the north side. They call it the Gold Coast."

I perk up. "One of those beautiful brownstones with the big windows and come-hither lighting inside?"

"I like the sound of come-hither. Have you been to my neighborhood?"

"The other night. We went for a drive." I try to erase my memory of Belmont's touch, smell, and how he felt inside me.

"We?"

"My husband and I." I take a healthy gulp of wine.

"Oh?" he says.

"Is the brownstone yours?"

"It belongs to a friend of mine. He's in New York. He wants me to buy it though."

"Are you going to?"

He shrugs. "I don't know. I can give you a showing if you like."

"Well, you're living in it now."

"That's okay. Do you want to see it tonight?"

I snicker. "I thought I was safe with you?"

"I only want to show the house, not my bed. Plus, I don't like being alone, and I like hanging out with you."

I tap the rim of my glass. I feel the same way. It's as if he and I are kindred spirits. "You have coffee?" I figure why not throw caution to the wind? Belmont certainly has.

"Plenty, and a fancy machine to make it," he says.

I hop off my stool and stumble into his chest. He steadies me.

"Then let's go." I say.

"Goddamn, woman, no more wine for you."

We laugh. Dexter holds me steady as he pays the tab, then we walk out into the night. He hails a cab, and I rest my head on the seat and close my eyes. A familiar song is playing, and Dexter is singing along. For some reason, I know the chorus. I sing along with him. When I open my eyes, he's watching me with a smile.

"Who sings this song?" I ask.

"It's 'Baby Come Back' by Player."

"Jacques used to play this, and a million other songs I know the lyrics to. But I don't know who sings them or the title."

"Then you should've been better at karaoke."

I groan. "Don't remind me of that stupid pastime."

"You hate it that much?"

"Yes, I do."

"Well, guys like to see beautiful women like you murder a song. It makes you seem mortal."

"So is that what karaoke's all about? Taking the edge off?"

He chuckles as the car turns down a most enchanting street. "It can be an aid to getting laid."

We laugh as the car stops, and we slide out. The iron streetlamps are old-fashioned. The leaves of trees sway over the streets and sidewalks. I'm still woozy. Dexter takes my arm and leads me to the steps.

"One second." I stop before we reach the top. "Let me…"

I want to savor the details. The building is made of white stone. The tall oblong windows, which are upstairs and downstairs, protrude, and the large wooden doors are like the kind in old movies. I notice the lantern-styled light fixtures, the lines etched into the walls, the crown molding, and the cute balconies that are only wide enough to set flower pots and herb gardens on.

"Gorgeous," I remark.

I grab on to the sound of his breathy, "Yeah."

One by one, I climb the steps. My feet are heavy. Dexter retrieves his keys from his jacket that I'm still wearing. We giggle when he fondles my hip. What a silly night we're having. It's fun. Once we're inside, I plop down on the white leather sofa. Dexter kindles the electric fireplace. My gaze rolls around the room. The floors are hardwood, and all the furniture is contemporary.

"Are these the original floors?" I ask.

"That would be a yes."

"Nice."

"Should I put in an offer for you?" he jokes.

"Not yet…" I grin and sink deeper into the rigid

cushion. "I have to see the bathroom and kitchen first. Maybe you can take me on that tour."

He rises out of his squat. "You'd move to Chicago and live in this place?"

"No. Yes. Probably not. But I still want to see all of it."

"I'll show it to you, but first I'll make coffee so you don't stumble down the stairs and crack your head open." He chuckles and trots off into the kitchen.

I hear him banging around. He's such a nice man. Not only that, but he's good-looking and hardworking. Why would any woman divorce him?

"Belmont is nice too…" I whisper.

I think about how he used to massage me from head to toe every night while I was pregnant. He swore it relieved my swelling. When New York City started to cave in on me, he picked up our lives and relocated us to California without a quarrel. He tolerated my pushy mother while I was in the hospital, even while she drove me to the brink of insanity. He never seemed to notice all those unappealing consequences of pregnancy—even the gas. And he made love to me each time as if it were the first.

"Here you go," Dexter says.

I take the cup of coffee from him. "Thanks."

He sits across from me and gets just as comfortable as I am. "So two days ago you were with your husband, and now you're not. I've been wondering why."

I figure after he's saved me from the lonely walk home, gotten me tipsy, and made coffee to sober me up, I owe him the truth. "He cheated on me with an ex-girlfriend. She emailed me pictures just so I could be tormented by visuals."

"Holy fuck. Ouch."

"You said that right."

"I slept with an old girlfriend when my wife and I separated."

I open one eye. "You did?"

"Yeah," he says remorsefully.

I wonder if he could provide the answer to a question that has been vexing me. "Why did you go back to a previous lover?"

"She was available. Her name was Nadine. She heard I was getting a divorce, one thing led to another, and it happened."

"Did you think you were cheating?"

He hesitates. "I knew I was cheating."

"Did you care?"

He rubs his eyes as if he's tormented by the memories. "Daisy, you can't compare my circumstances to yours. My ex-wife and I were over. Our differences were irreconcilable. We didn't take car rides together while we were separated."

"I guess you can imagine what went on in that car."

"Oh, I already have."

He and I laugh. We change the subject and talk about Javar's latest girlfriend. He was dating a burlesque dancer when I last spoke to him, but now he's graduated to a ballerina.

"He goes through these spurts," I say. "It's like, 'This month I'll collect dancers and next month fashion models,' and on and on… I wouldn't be surprised if he has a creepy collection of stuffed women in his basement." When Dexter laughs, I realize I like making him laugh.

"He wants you though," he says. "Warning you in advance."

"I can handle Javar."

"Can I ask you something?" he says.

"Sure. What?"

"Why does he think he still has a chance with you?"

"Because he's arrogant! The minute I sleep with Javar, he'll be over it. I've considered doing it just so he'll move on." I sigh. "Maybe I will the next I see him."

Dexter pipes up. "Oh, that'll make his year!"

After another cup of coffee, I'm sober enough to check out the four bedrooms and bathrooms and the kitchen. The only bathtub is in Dexter's bathroom, and it's tiny. But at the end of the showing, Dexter makes me an offer I can't refuse.

"Why don't you move in with me while you're in Chicago? There's plenty of room, and I could use the company," he says.

"Is tomorrow soon enough?" I reply without hesitation.

8
A NEW PLACE

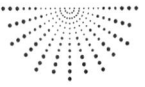

DAISY LORD

I move into the brownstone on Thursday. Dexter and I don't mention our living arrangement to anyone at work. They'll never believe we're just friends, and I don't want to create more tension between the other women and me. My bedroom is big enough. I have a view of the tiny courtyard and a stone cherub that spits water out of his mouth. I don't have a bathtub, but the shower is large enough and has ceramic tiled walls. I like it.

Kristin already has prospects for our new host. I notice that every time Javar's name is brought up, she rolls her eyes slightly, so I ask Dexter if she and Javar ever had a thing. He confesses that they were together for a year, but Javar cheated on her with all her attractive friends. They broke up before he could get his hands on Emma and Kate. Suddenly the behavior from the women on our team makes more sense. Dexter and I finalize the first script while on a conference call with Javar, who invites himself to town next week when Dexter informs him I'm staying at the brownstone.

"Why?" I ask. "The advance team is going to in Paris next Thursday. Aren't you the director?"

"Daisy, I'll see you on Monday," he says in his English accent before hanging up.

Dexter chuckles on his way out the office. He stops at the door. "By the way, I have a date tomorrow night. Do you have any plans?"

"Oh… do you want me to go somewhere so you can be alone? I can go back to my parents' place."

"No." He appears bothered by what I just said. "But do you have plans?"

"No."

"Do you need company? Because I can reschedule."

I fling my wrist. "No way. I'll be fine. I'll veg out on TV and popcorn or something."

"Is that what all the beautiful women do on a Saturday night? Why don't you come hang out with us?"

I look at him askew. "Are you seriously inviting me to be a third wheel on your date?"

He opens his mouth but then closes it. "That would defeat the purpose, wouldn't it?"

"If you're trying to get laid, it would."

He sniffs a chuckle. "Never mind." He walks away.

On Friday, we receive word that our four episodes have been cut to two. So we meet as a team and choose Malta as our second destination. Kristin and I work late into the afternoon, completing the shooting script. She doesn't digress from the task at hand, which I prefer. Before calling it a day, I watch the new host's test shoot that Kristin emailed me. His name is Scott Whistler, and he's an archeologist and world traveler. Kristin did a solid job casting him. He's obscure enough. He'll win the audience over with all the things women like about men and men like in their irreverent, unflappable adventurer.

Unlike yesterday, I leave work by myself. It's a half an hour walk to my new home. The evening is warm, and bulbous clouds usher in the humidity. The sidewalks bustle with people returning home from a day at work or wasting away some hours.

I'm stopped by a traffic light and take the

opportunity to switch on my cell phone. I've had it off since Tuesday. It dings and buzzes with messages. I look over the list of callers: Dexter, Maggie, Dexter, Maggie, Maya, Angel, Maya, Angel, Mom, Jacques, Unknown, Unknown, Mom, Maya, Mom, and Belmont. I gasp and force myself to try to feel an emotion that's fleeing. Could it be love? Perhaps it's trust.

People bolt across the street before the light turns green, and one guy narrowly misses colliding with a car. I listen to Belmont's message as soon as it's time to cross legally. He says my name and that he's sorry, then he hangs up. He sounds miserable, and that doesn't make me happy. If only I could get over it.

I stop at the market to grab a few salads, a bag of popcorn, and some fruit. I greet some of the neighbors who are walking their dogs before I lock myself inside for the evening.

I go to my bedroom, strip out of my clothes, and slip on Belmont's oversized Martha's Vineyard sweatshirt and a pair of knee-high socks. The house is icy because the air conditioner has been on all day. I turn it off. I wrap my hair in a bun, climb in bed with my salad and popcorn, and flick through the TV.

I end up watching a show on Showtime that links into the world of Bram Stoker's *Dracula*. As soon as the episode ends, I find the series on On-Demand and watch all the other episodes. The content is perfectly gory and suspenseful and keeps my mind off Belmont. I also try to catch up on this season of *Game of Thrones*. Belmont and I watched the last season together, never missing an episode. I fall asleep before I complete the season.

Much later, I hear a girl giggle and the front door slam. My eyes expand. Did Dexter bring his date home? Thank goodness there's a bathroom attached to my room. I take a shower, brush my teeth, and crawl back into bed. I close my eyes but reopen them as soon as I hear the sensual sound of a woman moaning. Dexter is definitely pleasuring his date. The noise doesn't bother me.

A memory makes me smile. Charlie, Angel, Maggie, and Vince once joined Belmont and me in Martha's Vineyard for an intimate New Year's gathering. At the end of the night, we retired to our rooms, which were too close for comfort. Angel was the first to cry out, then Maggie. Belmont and I were pretending we weren't on the outs, but we made love that night too. When he made me come, I came hard, and I screamed.

Charlie grunted. Vince grunted louder. Belmont just yelled. Then we all started laughing. We always have the best time together. It would be a shame if the six of us ever allow breakups to tear us apart. I fall asleep right after Dexter grunts.

My cell phone chimes and wakes me but only halfway. I fall back asleep as soon as the chiming ends. A while later, someone else calls. I flip over and continue dreaming about something that makes no sense. Then there's knocking.

"Hey, sleepyhead?" Dexter says.

I have to force my eyes open. I turn to see him standing in the doorway, fully dressed.

"Hey?" My voice is scratchy.

"It's after twelve."

I clear my throat. My head hurts. I groan and hide under a pillow.

"Are you okay?" Dexter asks.

I reemerge. "I don't know." I press the back of my hand against my forehead.

"Let me do it." Dexter puts his hand next to mine. He looks serious about the examination. "You're fine."

I roll my eyes. "Thank you, Mr. Doctor."

"You're not hot. So you're not sick."

Actually, I feel better already. "You brought your date home." I flex my eyebrows.

"Were we too loud? Sorry about that."

"Believe me, I've heard louder." Then I groan because I remember something. "I have to go to Jacques's performance tonight."

His eyes expand. "Jacques Blanchard is playing in Chicago tonight?"

"Yes, and surprisingly, he asked me to come. He never does that."

"Do you need a plus one?"

I balk. "Really?"

"Hell yeah."

"Well, sure, but aren't you taking the girl you brought home last night out on a second date?"

He drops his face and snickers. "Not tonight. Are you hungry?"

"Starving."

He tilts his head. "You're not going to ask me?"

"Ask you what?"

"Who I was with?"

I shrug. "It's none of my business."

"It was Melissa."

I gasp. That wakes me right up. "Our Melissa? You like her?"

"She's cute."

"Well, you'll definitely see her again."

"She promised no strings attached."

"Ha! Darling, there are always strings attached with women like her."

Dexter frowns as if what I said bothers him. I hop out of bed, and his eyes nearly pop out of his head. I forgot I'm wearing a tank top, no bra, and panties.

"Oh, shoot!" I scurry to the bathroom and close the door.

"I'll be back in thirty," he calls.

"Make it fifteen," I shout.

Dexter and I have lunch on the crowded patio of a restaurant on Rush Street. Never at a loss for words, he tells me he grew up in Milwaukee, Wisconsin. He wanted to become the puppet master living in the television set, which was why he majored in media studies at Perdue University. After graduating college, he returned home and worked at one of the local networks as an assignment editor. A year later, he married his now ex-wife.

"That's a mistake I wish I never made," he says.

"What do they say? Hindsight is twenty-twenty?"

"What does that make foresight?"

"Blind," I say.

We laugh.

"But didn't you love her?" I ask.

He takes a moment to reflect. "You see, there was this war going on in my head. In the back of my mind, I knew all the fun I was having in college had to end. That's why I used to drink and fuck like there was no tomorrow. I was supposed to marry a good girl with the values I needed to whip me in shape. I knew that was bullshit, but I couldn't stop the fucking programming, you know?"

I nod. "I know. It's kind of like being raised with religion."

"Exactly! Here's her trope—small-town wait-ress, virginal, good girl. Here's my trope—wild college boy returning home to saddle himself with the 'American dream.' It was just fucking good TV!" He shakes his hands dramatically.

"I wasn't raised to follow any tropes. My mom used to say that nothing in this world is real. It's all made up, and she made a career of reinforcing the shit people want to believe." I shake my finger and mimic Heloise. "'So don't you believe a fucking thing, *ma fleur*, unless you know for certain it's true.'"

"Who's *ma fleur*?"

"My mom and Jacques call me *ma fleur*."

"My flower?"

I nod. "Um-hum." I chew on my sandwich.

"I notice you don't call Jacques your father."

I frown. "I don't?"

He's amused. "You didn't realize it?"

I shake my head. "No, I didn't. Although when I think about him, I don't feel all warm and fatherly fuzzy."

"That sucks for him. I want my daughters to feel all warm and fatherly fuzzy when they think of me."

"Are you close to your daughters?" I ask.

"As close as a divorced dad can be."

"How much time do you spend with them?"

"I'll have them for the summer. That's why my friend wants me to buy the house. If the network picks up the series, we'll be headquartered here in Chicago. If the network doesn't green-light us, then I'll move back to New York."

"Jeez." I scratch my head, conflicted. I stop once I realize that it's a habit I picked up from

Belmont. "I don't know if I want to live here full-time."

"Me neither. I prefer New York."

"I prefer Martha's Vineyard."

"Yeah?" He's intrigued.

"It's where Belmont and I met. He has a beautiful house there, and I just like the island as a whole."

We smile at each other. He says he's happy his ex-wife chose to stay in Manhattan. His daughters attend private schools, the kind where the girls smoke in the bathrooms and hook up with boys from the school across the street.

"You're not afraid they'll fall down the wrong path?" I ask.

He shakes his head resolutely. "I'm not."

"Why not?"

"When Mariana was six—"

"Beautiful name," I interject.

"Thanks. She's a beautiful girl, but Luddie and I don't harp on it."

"Understandably."

"But when she was six, she was playing with something of mine. I can't remember what it was—maybe it was my watch. She used to like to play with anything that wasn't a toy. I took it from her and scolded her. Then it clicked—I should've given her the choice to give it back. I handled it differently the next time."

I'm on the edge of my seat. "What did you do?"

"She had my wallet. I told her it was very valuable to me. If I lost anything inside of it, then that would make things harder for all of us. I told her I didn't want to yell at her, but I wanted her to do the right thing. I asked her what she thought the right thing was."

"What did she say?"

"She didn't say anything. She handed me back my wallet and never messed with my shit ever again."

"Impressive," I say.

"My daughters know that life is about choices. That's it. They can make good ones or bad ones, right ones or wrong ones. There are always consequences attached."

"Not always," I say, smirking.

"Always, Daisy. There are even consequences for not believing in consequences." He winks.

I ruffle my eyebrows, pondering all the consequences of every choice I've ever made. Somehow Dexter ends up telling me the reasons why pot should and shouldn't be legal. He thinks it's a win-lose situation, and he wants to know what I think.

I frown and shrug. "I really don't care."

"Why not?"

"I don't smoke it, but if you do, then it's your business."

"You've chosen to be unaffected."

"I don't know if I've chosen it. Plus, I've been watching a news show on HBO. As my husband would say, 'We're fucked!'"

"Quoting Jack Lord? Javar's fucked!" He laughs.

I reprise the story of how Javar and I met. I start from day one and end with the last time we hung out, which was during the Cannes Film Festival nearly four years ago. Dexter has no comment. He asks if I want to go yachting on the lake with him and a few friends after lunch. I decline the invitation because I've been craving a long, hot soak in my parents' infinity tub. We agree to meet at the house at nine so we can head to Jacques's concert. I make the two-mile walk to my parents' condo to take that bath.

DEXTER FRAMPTON

Dexter hadn't expected Daisy Lord to be so fascinating. She hadn't tried to seduce him, but he found himself standing in line behind Jack Lord, which made him the improbable winner. Javar was no competition at all. The more time Dexter spent with Daisy, the more he understood why Javar could never seal the deal. He's too superficial, though not in a bad way. All of Javar's cards were spread out for the world to see. Dexter figured Daisy was the kind of woman who was attracted to enigma and depth. Dexter had laid awake trying to figure out what was it about Daisy that made him feel that something extra. What was her allure—other than the obvious? Why did she stand out?

Melissa was adequate. He'd gone out with her to prove to himself that he wasn't that into Daisy. He feared he'd made a mistake bringing Melissa home last night. She kept asking who lived with him after seeing Daisy's shoes by the door. He was positive Melissa had recognized Daisy's black heels. He had asked Melissa to quiet down during sex, but instead, she got louder. He couldn't see them getting any mileage out of a relationship. Melissa was good for a different kind of guy. He was an idiot for boning her.

Dexter boarded his friend Grey Lansing's luxury yacht at a restaurant along the riverfront. Grey had a reputation as a party boy who lived off his dad's cash. He did claim to have a career, but what it was, hardly anyone knew.

Dexter had met Grey at a fashionable party in the Hamptons last year. Dexter had been invited by a model he'd met in a bar in the West Village. Luta had lots of friends there and had left him alone while she circulated. He didn't mind because he wasn't that into her, although he did sleep with her at the end of the night—and a few nights after that. But while she socialized, he planted himself on a stool at the bar, and like most men in his position, he waited for something to happen.

Grey Lansing had squeezed into the space next to Dexter and mumbled, "Fucking models."

"Tell me about it," Dexter replied.

That broke the ice, and they'd started talking about how easily they got sucked into the model trap. Grey invited him to another party and promised there would be no models present, only desperate co-eds. Dexter declined with a laugh. They'd exchanged contact information after Dexter told him that he was an independent television producer. Grey never said what he did, but Dexter had heard whispers that Grey was involved with Internet investigations, obtaining legal and illegal information.

Grey was in Chicago for a few days, and when Dexter agreed to ride out on his yacht, he wouldn't have guessed Jack Lord would be on the boat with them.

"Hello," Jack said. His entire demeanor was frosty.

Dexter started sweating and couldn't look the man in his eyes. "Hi." He cleared his throat to say it with more confidence. "Hello."

Dexter only breathed easily when Jack followed Grey to the bottom deck. It was too late to abandon ship. Plus, leaving would make Dexter look guilty. So he lounged on the upper deck and drank beer as he listened to two men lament the changeable temperament of the stock market.

After losing interest in the men's conversation, Dexter focused on a group of pretty girls in bikinis dancing on the sky deck. There were a lot of scantily clad girls onboard, but most of them were in the Jacuzzi on the lower deck, griping about the lake being too cold to swim in. Dexter had made eye contact with at least three of them. They weren't his type. He was into women like Daisy. Her body was amazing, all curves and ass and tits, her pussy print in those panties… He'd grown wood after she'd climbed out of bed half naked. He would give a finger and a toe to make love to her one momentous, fantastic, and exciting time. But Dexter needed to convince himself and Jack Lord that that was not the case.

He finished his second beer and walked up to the sky deck to stand beside a pretty brunette with short hair. She was much shorter than Daisy but had the same killer curves. He said hello and commented on the ocean. The girls around her grinned and batted their eyes, hoping to divert his attention. If only dating were that easy in New York. He and the brunette talked about the cold lake and when it would warm up and the hot spots in town. She invited him to another party that night at a bar that was supposed to have the best beer and crowd. He asked if she drank a lot of beer.

She pumped her fist and said, "Hell yeah!" She smiled as if she expected him to find her response endearing.

He didn't, but he smiled at her anyway, mainly because she was easy. He could skip the concert and opt for a drunken night out, punctuated by riding the killer curves of the girl whose name he'd already forgotten. He asked for her number just as Jack Lord walked up the stairs.

"Can we talk?" Jack asked.

Dexter told what's-her-name that he'd be back.

"Okay," she answered, watching Jack Lord with stars in her eyes.

Just for that, Dexter decided he wanted nothing more to do with her. He followed Jack to the bar on the main deck. Jack made himself at home by pouring them both a glass of whiskey.

"How did you know I prefer whisky?" Dexter asked, trying to hide his nervousness.

"Who doesn't?" Jack lifted his glass and took a drink. "My wife has been living with you. Can I ask you something?"

Dexter threw up his hands. "Sure." He tried to sound as if he had nothing to hide.

"Are you fucking her?"

Dexter choked. "No. She liked my place. I have four bedrooms." He cleared his throat.

Jack's scowl deepened. "Do you talk to her?"

"We talk. We work together."

"I'm referring to personal shit."

"Oh…" Dexter shifted in his seat. "No." He couldn't believe he had lied.

Jack nodded as if he accepted that answer. "How's she doing?"

"She's okay. She sleeps late."

Jack glared at him. "Is that so?"

"Um…" *Shit.*

"Listen, Dexter, I'm going to need your address."

"I don't know… Daisy's still pretty upset."

"Then you *do* talk to her about her personal shit?"

Dexter was in the hot seat. "She didn't give me the details."

"But you talk to her?"

He shrugged. "Well, we live together."

The look in Jack's eyes indicated that he wanted to toss Dexter into the icy lake. "Right. So how's the project going?"

"What project?"

"The TV show."

"Oh…" Dexter sighed, relieved by the change of subject. "It's good. Daisy's not the host anymore."

"No? Why not?"

"It was her idea. She said the audience wouldn't want to watch her be adventurous."

"I'd watch her."

Dexter stopped short of saying that he would too. "I agreed with her. She's smart."

Belmont nodded. Dexter wondered what he was thinking. Did he think Daisy wasn't smart? Maybe that's why they weren't together. Belmont was probably one of those rich pricks who'd rather have a woman who's seen by his peers, fucked by him, and never heard by anyone.

They stayed on the subject of the TV show. Dexter was impressed by how familiar Belmont was with Daisy's work. He even made suggestions for future episodes. After the next round of whisky, Dexter asked Belmont why in the hell he was separated from a woman like Daisy.

"What do you mean 'a woman like Daisy'?" Belmont snarled.

Dexter made himself more comfortable in his chair. "There's a lot to her. Just when you think you have her figured out, she hits you with something else." He probably sounded as if he was in love with the man's wife. The booze had compromised his inhibitions.

Belmont glared at him. "Sometimes we don't understand each other."

Dexter was surprised and slightly sobered by the answer. "My ex-wife and I understood each other perfectly, hence the divorce."

Jack shrugged. "And?"

Dexter scratched the side of his face. He couldn't believe what he was about to say. "I still think whatever the hell you did, it wasn't enough to make her lose interest in you. That's all." There was no use mentioning that he knew Jack had cheated.

Perhaps Jack wanted to say more, perhaps not. But Grey joined them, so they changed the subject to how hot the women were onboard. They never got back around to talking about Daisy, and that was fine with Dexter. He found another girl to pay attention to. Hanna was her name. She was super thin with long blond hair, the exact opposite of Daisy. He made sure Jack saw them exchange numbers, but Dexter didn't plan on ever calling her.

9

PAPA MAY HAVE

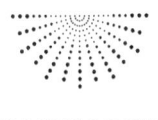

DAISY LORD

I knock on Dexter's bedroom door. "Are you ready?"

He opens it. "I am now." Dexter is wearing a blue shirt that matches his eyes and white-and-tan-flecked pants.

"You look good all dressed up," I remark.

"So do you," he says.

"Thanks," I mumble. I haven't put on any makeup, and I just threw on a little black dress and the heels I'd left by the door. There was no use in going all out since Belmont wouldn't be there. "The cab is waiting."

Dexter puts a hand on my hip. "You're the one who's supposed to make us late, not me."

"You couldn't have known that I'm a decisive

dresser." I laugh as he walks me to the door. I apologize to the cabbie and thank him for waiting while Dexter locks up. Once we're on our way, I ask, "How was the yacht?"

He shifts uncomfortably. "Fine. How was the bath?"

"Very much needed," I say.

He chuckles. "And that's all you did today?"

"I worked on a new article."

"Humph."

"Humph, what?"

"You're thinking about leaving us?"

I sigh. "I'm with you now. Can't that be enough?"

"Hell no. Do I have to make you sign a contract?"

"I'm not going to sign a contract."

Dexter blows on his palm and holds it out for me to shake.

"Did you just spit in your hand?" I ask.

He laughs. "Just a little. Put a little on yours."

"You want me to spit on my hand?"

"A little, not a lot."

I lick my palm, and he's entranced by the act. I wonder if I went too far by doing that. Belmont always warns me about appearing sexy when I don't mean to. He says it usually starts something I may not be in the mood to finish.

"You don't wear makeup, do you?" he asks.

"Every now and then, but not often."

"You're that confident?"

"I wouldn't say that. It was something Heloise said once."

"Your mom?" he asks.

"Yes, my mother. I think I was fourteen. I went to the Beverly Center with a friend, and we got our faces made up. When I got home, my mom was on the phone. She studied me and told whoever she was talking to that she'd call them right back. She said, 'Come here, *ma fleur*.' Then she lifted my chin, turned my face in different angles, and asked, 'What have you done to Jacques's and my masterpiece? The one beautiful thing we made together.' She shook her head and returned the phone call."

Dexter grins, appearing amused.

"So I went into the bathroom, wiped the makeup off, and stared in the mirror, searching for my parents in my face. And I saw them. Since then, I hardly wear it." I grunt thoughtfully. The enlightenment is slightly unsettling. "I guess I like looking in the mirror and seeing Heloise and Jacques."

"You look good with or without it," he says.

I hold up my palm. "It dried."

He weaves his fingers between mine. "Don't lick it again. You're with me now. I'll take that."

Traffic is thick on the streets and sidewalks, as though the whole world had decided to visit Chicago tonight. I'm nervous about seeing Jacques. I've never attended one of his concerts. I've never been acquainted with his musical side, but Angelina has.

A week after Belmont and I confirmed that I was pregnant, we flew to L.A. to see Jacques. He was very leery about our relationship, and granted, he should've been. But instead of voicing his concerns, he was rigid and cold. Perhaps if Jacques had said something, then I would've never married Belmont. I knew our relationship was happening too fast, and I'd even questioned whether or not I was the marrying kind. I sensed Jacques had the same reservations, but he had better things to do than correct my mistakes.

However, I saw a different side of him after Madame Beauchamp, Angelina's mother, died. He had loved a woman and his daughter. The woman wasn't Heloise and the daughter wasn't me, but at least he had the capacity to care. For some reason, that gave me hope in myself. I always knew that I was more like Jacques than Heloise, so I thought if he was capable of love and making a stable home for his family, then maybe I was too.

"Hey, are you shaking?" Dexter asks. He massages my shoulders as though I'm a prized fighter getting loose for a bout.

I look at my trembling hands. "I'm nervous."

"What's there to be nervous about?"

"I told you Jacques and I aren't that close. I've never heard him play live. I mean, other than at his mistress's funeral."

"Did you say mistress's funeral?"

"My sister's mother. Don't get me wrong, I harbor no bitterness toward either of them. I used to blame Jacques and Heloise for their farce."

"What was the farce?"

I sigh. The list is long. "Not loving each other, ever."

"Why would they get married if they didn't at least think they loved each other?"

I snort. "*Think* they loved each other?"

"That's how it all starts."

"When I was a kid, I never saw two people in love. I believe they liked each other. They used to throw these parties. They would send my brother and me to a neighbor's house. Her name was Mrs.

Crawford, and we used to wait until she fell asleep in her chair, watching the news. Like clockwork, at 11:58 p.m., she was out. Then Daniel and I would sneak out and go back home to see what they were doing. The first time, it was shocking. Jacques was getting a blowjob from another woman, and my mom was banging some guy who looked like Jesus Christ Superstar. The room was smoky. Naked people were in the swimming pool, screwing each other. It was an orgy of the gods."

"Damn," Dexter says. "Sounds like fun."

I chuckle. "Yeah, they were having loads of fun. And a lot of those people weren't strangers."

"Shit, you'd seen them before?"

"Yep."

"How old were you?" he asks.

"Ten or eleven."

"And what did you do the next morning?"

"I couldn't look either of my parents in the eyes, but my mom went on with business as usual, and Jacques locked himself inside his studio as though they hadn't made our home into a love den. I guess I believed mothers and fathers should be Carol and Michael Brady."

"Like on *The Brady Bunch*?"

I chuckle. "I even told Heloise that. She said,

'People like me are paid to make that shit up, *ma fleur*.'"

Dexter chuckles. "So the orgies made you conclude that your parents didn't love each other?"

"Oh no. I realized that when they started bringing some of their guests home during the day, and sometimes at night. They would disappear into their offices to"—I draw quotes with my fingers—"'discuss business.' Heloise and Jacques stopped sleeping in the same bedroom. They only spoke when discussing which series she wanted him to compose a theme song for or her using her contacts to finagle hard-to-land projects for him. They were in it for the benefits. Still are!"

Dexter shrugs. "Hell, Daisy, their shit is only shit if you look at it as shit. It sounds like your parents had a partnership. And hell, it worked. Look at them!"

"I know. I don't hold their mistakes against them—not anymore."

"Who said it was a mistake? They made you."

I roll my eyes and shake my head. "But they lost a son. I used to think they would have rather have lost me instead of Daniel. Then I believed they wouldn't have cared if we'd both gotten hit by a car. I still believe that. Don't get me wrong, I have a good relationship with my mom now, thanks to Belmont, but I'm nonessential in their lives."

Dexter furrows his eyebrows. "I don't know about that."

My frown deepens.

"You've said a lot about what your mom taught you when you were younger," he says. "It's a lot of the same things I want my daughters to learn. And I would thank my lucky stars if they grow up to be like you."

I smile coyly. "Thanks. And you're right. I used to look at it as Heloise messing with my head, but she was merely teaching me her philosophies."

"My mom knows how to fuck with my head too, but that's not always so bad. Look at you." He sniffs me. "You smell like life."

I gaze into his bright blue eyes, which are extra vibrant because of his caramel skin. I feel as if we should kiss or something, but I look at him and remember how it feels to have Belmont's mouth on mine, especially while he's thrusting into me. I look away to catch my breath. I think I'm getting horny for my husband again. "Thanks. So do you."

The car stops in front of the venue. The building has a strange shape, like something between a gray tongue and a horse's saddle. We're at least thirty minutes late, so the line is short. Dexter opens the door, and I slide out behind him. He pays the driver and holds my hand as we head to the box office. It doesn't feel like romantic hand-holding though; it's friendship hand-holding.

When we get to the window, I tell the girl behind the counter that I'm picking up tickets for Daisy Blanchard. Her eyes expand, but she still manages to look at me as though she hates me. This sort of unfriendliness is common with the females I've encountered in this city, and it's strange. However, she gives us our passes.

An attendant escorts Dexter and me inside. The lights are down, and the venue is crowded. The attendant clears a path for us to the front of the pit. Jacques is center stage, playing the trumpet. The crowd is so tight that Dexter has to stand behind me and wrap his arms around me. He's grown wood. I guess I can't hold it against him. It's a nice, hard, heavy load though—quite impressive.

"Oh hell," Dexter says.

I get not only my temperament from my father, but my height too. He's tall and lean, and he has the most incredible stage presence. I've never been this close to him while he's playing. As a voyeur, I'm searching for something new about him, something I could've missed along the way.

"Want to dance?" Dexter asks.

No one else is dancing, but I want to bury my face in someone's shoulder and think about what the hell is going on with me at the moment, so I nod. Dexter rocks me slowly to Jacques's sensual music. I rest my cheek on Dexter's chest and gaze up at the music man. *That's my father.* I close my eyes, hug Dexter tighter, and bury my face in his neck. He doesn't smell like Belmont, but he smells good in his own way.

I remember my dad walking past the pool on his way to the guest house, where he spent most of his time. He's wearing the same white loungewear he always wears when he works. He waves at Daniel and me. We're building another doghouse for our nonexistent pet. Heloise and Jacques wouldn't let us have a dog because they were positive we wouldn't take care of it, and they sure as hell wouldn't do it for us. They were probably right. Daniel and I were never home. But we wave back at our father. Then we look at each other for a long moment, and I continue holding the plywood while he hammers a nail through it. I wonder what Daniel had been thinking. What had I been thinking? I can't recall.

Tears roll from my eyes as Jacques plays the final note. The crowd applauds. I wipe my eyes and sniff back the rest of the tears. The spotlight turns off, and when it cuts on again, the beam is on Dexter and me.

"Look who's here," Jacques says.

I smile at him and wave.

"Isn't she something?"

The audience applauds and whistles. A few guys shout, "Yeah," and "She's hot."

"Watch out now… That's *ma fleur, ma belle fille*. My beautiful daughter, Daisy," Jacques says.

There's more applause. The floodgates have reopened, and my tears are unstoppable. Thankfully, I'm still holding onto Dexter.

"A man…" he says and waits for complete silence. "A man never knows how much he can love something until he has his first *belle fille*. There ain't much I love more than you, *ma fleur*, and that's for sure. This one's for you, baby."

Jacques announces Betty Moreland, a renowned nouveau soul singer. A curvy woman in an emerald gown with fluffy hair strolls on stage, and the audience goes wild. Betty Moreland is probably in her fifties, but she looks as if she's in her late twenties.

She waves at the audience and sings a few bars of "I Love You Too."

"Where is she, Jacques?" she asks in a soulful voice.

The spotlight points me out.

"Oh, wow… You would have another gorgeous daughter. Daisy?" She gazes at me. "Oh my Lord, glad you got a man, girl." She points at Dexter. "Is she yours?"

Dexter grins. "We're friends!"

"Um-hum…" She twists her mouth as though she's not buying it.

He laughs and shrugs.

Betty's smile is infectious. *"Ma fleur*, this is from your papa to you."

Jeez. I hadn't called Jacques Papa since I was fifteen. Jacques winks at me. He gives his horn to a stagehand in exchange for a saxophone. The stage is set. My father raises the instrument to his lips as if he's about to kiss his lover. He closes his eyes, and I see the transition from Jacques Blanchard into the music man. It's "God Bless the Child." Dexter wipes my tears with the back of his hand. I shake my head, because I'm upset with myself for being unable to control my blubbering.

"It's okay," he says in my ear.

Betty sings so beautifully. The emotion in the notes of the saxophone stirs my soul. I focus on Jacques through my tears. This is so surreal. I have been seeking the perfect moment my entire life, one that had some staying power, a life-altering one. That moment has finally come.

When the last verse is sung and note played, I look at my father with puppy-dog eyes. Jacques hops off the stage, and we hug.

He kisses me on both cheeks and says, "I love you."

"I love you too, Papa," I say, kissing him back.

We embrace tighter. As the concert continues, Dexter and I dance. I've never danced like this— not even in Louisiana at Madame Beauchamp's repass. Those people danced, sang, and played music until the next morning. Before the last song ends, an attendant asks Dexter and me to follow him backstage.

"That was cool. After what we talked about in the cab and then this?" Dexter says.

"I know. I had no idea."

"Are you better?"

I smile. "A lot better."

Dexter and I stare into each other's eyes just as we did in the cab.

"I know I don't have a chance in hell to be with you…" he says.

Applause erupts, and he stops to wait for it to simmer. My heart is pounding. The way he prefaced what he's about to say has me worried. I'm having a fantastic night with him. I've leaned on him in ways I probably shouldn't have, which is out of character for me. I do believe some sort of mutual attraction has been the catalyst to our friendship. The noise dies down.

"But will you let me kiss you?" Dexter asks.

My breaths accelerate. His robust boner has been poking me all night. I've let him grind me in the ass, fondle me here and there. I want his kiss. So I nod and brace myself for what comes next. His hands are against my lower back. Our bodies merge. Our eyes connect. I hear my father's voice, and we both step back.

"Ah, *ma fleur!*" Jacques walks in our direction. "Who's your friend?" Jacques extends a hand toward Dexter.

"I'm Dexter Frampton," Dexter says, shaking my father's hand.

"Nice to meet you, man. I'm glad you came tonight," Jacques says to me.

I smile. "Me too."

"Let's head this way and talk. Can you give us a bit, Dexter?"

"Oh, yes." Dexter sounds as if he's willing to give my father whatever he asks for.

Dexter and I give each other a look before I walk off with Jacques and round the corner. At least I now have time to pull myself back to reality. A minute ago, I would've broken my cardinal rule and let Dexter have sex with me if he wanted, which I'm sure he does.

"You were enjoying yourself," Jacques says.

"I had a good time."

We go inside a dressing room, and he closes the door.

"Sit," he says.

I take a seat on the edge of the sofa. I wonder if he saw Dexter and me about to kiss in the hallway. I won't ask, but I'm awfully nervous—until he pours himself a glass of ginger ale.

"Ginger ale?" I ask.

"Your sister finally convinced me to cut back on the sauce."

I chuckle. "She got to Belmont too."

Jacques grunts thoughtfully. "Are you and Jack Lord calling it quits?"

"I don't know." I sigh wearily. "I can't find a way to forgive him for what he's done."

"What the hell did he do this time?"

I feel as though if I tell my father what happened, then maybe he can magically make it better. "He had sex with another woman. She even took pictures and emailed them to me."

"Now that's some wicked shit."

"Yes, but he's the one who made a vow."

Jacques gets the vodka. "I need a real fucking drink after that. *Ma fleur*, vows don't end because you fucked somebody else."

"We're still married, so apparently they don't."

"What about you and Dexter?"

"We're work colleagues and friends—that's it."

He narrows one eye. I comprehend what he's suggesting.

"I'm not going to defile my marriage bed," I say.

"Why not? He's a good-looking cat."

"Oh my God!" Talking to him is like talking to Heloise.

"One outside fuck, and then you call it even. I'll admit I didn't like Jack Lord when you first introduced us. I thought, 'Why the hell is he here with you to talk to me about our shit?'" My dad gestures wildly. "I pegged him as a controlling cat, and I gave him a good three months before you got the hell away from him. But you stayed. I got to know him on our ride to New Orleans. I had to bend his ear some."

"Oh," I say. "You told him to give me space?"

"I told him to give you a football field of space."

I sniff a chuckle. "Thank you, I needed it."

"I know you did. I know you, *ma fleur*. You don't think I was watching, but I was. If you'd fallen down the wrong path, I would've been there to reset your feet. But you always had your shit together, and you still do."

"I do?" It sure doesn't feel like it.

Jacques takes my chin and lifts my face. "Yes, you do." He kisses my forehead.

I smile. "Okay, but I'm not going to defile my marriage bed. I don't care what you say."

"Defile your marriage bed?" He's mocking me. "Who the hell did you learn that from?"

I roll my eyes. "Papa, stop."

"All right, but here…" He gives me the ginger ale. "Have a drink with me."

Dexter joins us. My father runs down a list of family I should visit when I go to France next week. My mother's parents are included.

"I have a house in Bordeaux. I want you to stay

there for a little while. The fields and lakes and wine will help you get your mind right," Jacques says.

"But I have to return to Chicago after we finish shooting."

Jacques shakes a finger. "No, *ma fleur*. You stay in Bordeaux."

Dexter looks at me with raised eyebrows, but he dares not raise an objection in front of Jacques Blanchard. My father goes on to invite Dexter to one of Karina's parties in Iberia. Soon a handful of Betty Moreland's band members join us, and they tell Jacques what happened on their recent road trip with a boy band.

It's after two a.m. when we say good-bye to my father. Funny, he never mentioned Angelina and Charlie's engagement party. I kept waiting for him to mention it, but he never did. There's something strange about the whole ordeal. I decide to call Angelina in the morning to get to the bottom of it.

Dexter and I get in a cab to head home.

"So…" Dexter says. "Jacques wants you to ditch me."

I chuckle. "Yeah, I guess so. A few weeks, months, a year in Bordeaux wouldn't be a bad thing."

"You'll walk away from our show just like that?"

I take a moment to ponder. "You want the truth?"

"Lay it on me," Dexter says.

I shrug. "Yes, I would."

"Fuck…"

"You don't need me in the flesh to make the show successful, Dexter. You want me." I meet his gaze.

Dexter licks his lips. "About that kiss."

I snicker, remembering my father's suggestion. I couldn't guess in a million years that Jacques would say *that* to *me*. But then, what else could he say? After all, my father always practices what he preaches.

"What's funny?" Dexter asks.

"Just something my father said when we were alone."

"Was it about me?"

"Um-hum."

"What did he say?"

"He said you were a good-looking *cat* and that I should fuck you."

Dexter laughs. "He said that?"

"Yep."

He nods for a while. "That would be fun."

I elbow him playfully in the ribs.

"But I'll settle for a kiss for now," he says.

I offer him my lips.

He shakes his head. "Not like this. I want you in my arms, like this." He gestures as though he's hugging me tightly.

I chuckle. "Okay, then after this kiss, does the nature of our involvement change?"

"Not if you don't want it to."

"But do you want it to?"

He slides a finger down my cheek, gazing into my eyes. "Javar warned me that I would fall for you."

"And did you?" I'm holding my breath.

"I did, but not in the same way he did. I like your father, and I want to go to this house in Iberia. You're cool to talk to. I can tell you my philosophical bullshit, and you take me seriously. You're damn easy to work with. The fact that you're easy on the eyes is the cherry on top. I don't need to have you in a sexual way. I just want my damn kiss. Oh wait…"

I frown curiously as he takes a small tin container out of his pocket.

"I want our kiss to be minty fresh," he says.

I laugh as he pops a mint in his mouth and offers me one too. I take it, and we squeeze each other's hand. As soon as the car pulls up to the house, he pays the driver. Once we're out, he tugs me against him. Our kiss is soft and deep, and he does taste minty fresh. His hands massage my back, and his dick is so hard, I consider taking my father's advice.

"Hey…"

I panic. It's dark, but I recognize that voice. We both look behind Dexter at Belmont. He's dressed up in a pair of black trousers and shirt as if he's been to a party.

"Belmont?" I'm not sure I'm not hallucinating.

He shakes his head and scratches the back of his neck. "I want to punch you, guy, but I'm not going to."

"What are you doing here?" I ask.

"I gave him our address today," Dexter says. "I'm sorry, Jack. It was just a kiss."

My frown deepens. "What?" He saw Belmont today? When? Where?

Belmont stomps to his car. I contemplate running after him, but he's walking faster than I can process what just happened. Did he really catch me with my tongue in Dexter's mouth? His car speeds off as I take my first step toward it. Dexter and I look at each other, confused.

"Let's go inside?" he says.

I nod tiredly. Once we're inside, I flop on the sofa, and Dexter recaps how he ran into Belmont on the yacht. It makes me wonder what would have happened if I had accepted Dexter's invitation. Belmont and I would've run into each other unexpectedly again. I'm not angry that Dexter didn't mention he and Belmont had had a conversation about me, but I am happy I wasn't stuck on that boat with them. That would've been awkward.

"But giving Belmont this address was just the wrong thing to do," I say.

Dexter strokes the nape of his neck. "I didn't think he would just show up out of the blue."

"Oh, he will. But…"

I recall the way he was dressed. I'm sure my father's concert had been advertised. I wonder if Belmont had been at the venue. Had he watched us all night long? Had he seen the way Dexter and I interacted? I know Belmont and that expression he'd had; a flash of anger didn't put it there.

I slap my forehead and fall back against the sofa. "He was there. He saw us dancing and flirting and touching each other." I wait for Dexter's response, but he's silent.

When I look at him, he's grinning. "You *were* flirting with me?"

I roll my eyes. "Dexter, this is serious. My husband saw us kissing."

"And you saw him fucking."

I sigh. "I know, but it's still bad."

"It's not the end of the world. It was just a minty-fresh kiss between friends."

I laugh. "Will you stop?"

"We did it. It's out of our systems. Now go to bed, because you're going to need your rest. Javar will be here in the morning."

I gasp. "What?"

"He wanted to surprise you." Dexter flexes his eyebrows twice. "See you tomorrow, *ma fleur*."

I groan and sink deeper into the cushion as he walks upstairs. This cannot be my life right now.

10
POKING THE SLEEPING BEAR

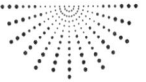

BELMONT LORD

*W*hat pissed him off the most was that Daisy had never behaved that way with him. The way Dexter had said nothing when Belmont asked if he had plans for the night, Belmont knew in his gut that the guy wasn't being upfront. So he asked the girl Dexter had pretended to be interested in if Dexter had made plans with her. She said he was going to a concert. Belmont did an Internet search, and *voila!* Jacques Blanchard was performing in town.

Belmont knew in his gut that Daisy would attend. He planned to run into her on purpose. She'd had a week to cool down, and they needed to talk and make love. So Belmont put on his most persuasive outfit and cologne. He purchased a ticket at the box office and positioned himself at the back of the nightclub. If Daisy had arrived before the lights were lowered, then she definitely would have seen him. The longer he waited, the more he questioned whether or not his instincts were right. Maybe Dexter hadn't planned on attending that particular concert with Daisy.

Belmont had decided to sit through two more songs before calling it a bust. He had a lot of work to get done before his meeting with Matthew Silver. Belmont had had a packet sent to Matt, and Matt was finally ready to have a serious conversation about how they should proceed. But just in case what he sent wasn't enough, he'd hired Grey to dig deeper. Belmont had heard Holden Reece was involved in insider trading. If that was true, then Grey had methods of finding the evidence.

Daisy finally showed up, and Belmont felt the relief of a hunter who had spotted his prey. He studied the way she moved toward the stage. Her hair was stacked high with stray strands fluttering around the edges. The carefree way she styled her hair had always turned him on. She wore that one black dress she often threw on whenever she didn't want to put too much thought into her outfit. So many times he had peeled the garment off her, sliding his hands up her body and sucking her breasts as the dress went up and over her head. Belmont didn't like how Dexter kept his hand on Daisy's waist. A gust of jealousy seized Belmont. He was just about to go steal her away when she and Dexter started to dance. Suddenly Belmont's feet wouldn't move. All he could do was watch.

The song had ended. Jacques made a big to-do about Daisy being there, and she cried. Dexter wiped the tears from her cheek, and Belmont wanted to break his neck. Then Betty Moreland sauntered on stage. When she'd asked Dexter if Daisy belonged to him, Belmont wanted to raise his hand and shout, "She belongs to me!" Dexter had said they were friends, but he didn't say it as if he meant it. Betty Moreland didn't believe Dexter, and neither did he.

Belmont had folded his arms, seething as he watched to see how far Daisy would take things with Dexter. She rubbed her ass against his dick. He had his hands all over her body. They would often stare into each other's eyes. Belmont wanted so badly to break them up, to take Daisy back to her place and fuck her until they were both clear that no one touched her but him. He despised that she was having a good time and not at home crying her eyes out over their separation. Belmont was on his way to collect Daisy when a girl bumped into him.

"Sorry," she had said, smiling. "Like your shirt."

Belmont had said thank you and continued to push through the crowd. He stopped when an usher beat him to Daisy and escorted her and Dexter away from the stage. Belmont was going to follow, but he remembered Daisy saying that he always got what he wanted, and not in a good way. She'd made him feel guilty for being himself. But even he was touched by Jacques's tribute to his daughter. It was Daisy's father's turn to make amends with her.

When the concert had ended, Belmont instructed his driver to take him to the address Dexter had given him. It was a brownstone just like the ones Daisy had admired during their night out in the limousine. The driver found a space to park down the street, and Belmont kept his glare fastened on the house. Hours passed. He wondered if they had decided to extend their night out. As far as Belmont was concerned, he and Daisy were more even than they were before she'd teasingly rubbed against Dexter during the concert.

Finally a taxicab had stopped in front of the house. Dexter held Daisy's hand as they flowed out of the car. In one unexpected moment, Dexter tugged her against him and shoved his tongue down her throat. Belmont blinked a few times. He could hardly believe what he was seeing. Dexter grabbed her ass and worked his way up to her tits. Daisy was into it. Belmont came to his senses and bolted out of the car to break them up.

"Goddamn it," Belmont muttered.

He was staying in an office suite on Dearborn near the riverfront. No one but Grey and Herald knew his whereabouts. The information Belmont had sent to Matt Silver and Holden Reece was explosive, and there was no way it couldn't be tracked back to him. He thought it best to keep a low profile until they met on Monday.

As the night replayed in his mind, Belmont couldn't fall asleep to save his life. Gaze pinned to the ceiling, he tried to figure out what the hell was going on between him and Daisy. Damn it, he wasn't prepared to see her in another man's arms.

His cell phone buzzed. He picked it up and looked at the screen. There was a message from Daisy: *"I'm sorry you saw that. I love you."* Belmont let out an earsplitting roar. A call came through before he could heave the phone at the wall.

He looked at the screen. "What?"

"Found it," Grey said.

"Is it solid?"

"As steel."

"Tracks?"

"As water."

"Harold will stop by." Belmont hung up and placed a call.

Stacy picked up on the first ring. "What do you want from me?"

"Are you still in Chicago?"

"You know I am."

Belmont ground his teeth to constrain the surge of anger. He said he would call her at seven a.m. to give her an address of where to meet him at eight. Belmont ended the call before she could say anything else. His phone buzzed again. It was another message from Daisy.

She wrote, *"I'm moving back into my parents' condo. I'll be there shortly. Just thought you might want to know."*

"Fuck!" Belmont shouted.

He texted her back, *"How are you getting there?"*

"Taxi," she replied.

Belmont didn't want Daisy calling a cab that late at night. *"I'll send a car."* He paused. *"I love you too. Always will."* Send.

"Ok," she replied.

That was it. Belmont was disappointed she

hadn't asked him over so that they could try to resolve things.

He spent the rest of the night battling the urge to drop everything and show up on Daisy's doorstep. It killed him that Dexter knew how her tight ass felt and how soft she was in a man's arms. He was relieved he'd stopped them before Dexter had grabbed her tits. Belmont wanted her succulent tits in his mouth. He tossed and turned, trying to find a comfortable position on the hard bed.

Seven a.m. arrived, and he hadn't slept a wink. He sent Stacy the address and made himself ready to meet her at eight. The security detail he'd hired patted her down before she entered his office.

"Really, Jack? You're going to treat me like a common criminal?" she groused.

He walked up to her, eased up the hem of her tight dress, and slid his hand under her panties. He touched a recording device at the top of her ass crack and snatched it. "You were saying?"

"That was for my protection."

Belmont grimaced. He'd always figured Stacy would be the last person he could *never* trust. "Did you read your mail?"

"I read it. I made a mistake. I'm sorry. I'm sorry.

I'm sorry! I made a mistake!" She turned hysterical. "What are you going to do? Destroy me for it?"

Belmont remained composed. "Me? Destroy you? Your troubles aren't my doing."

"The hell they aren't," she snarled.

"Just like the rest of your clients, I was warned that you utilized illegal search tactics." Belmont squinted curiously. "The memo said you had hacked financial data from top corporations for clients like, say, Reece Holdings?" He shook his head as if that was the worst thing he had ever heard. "You're in deep shit."

"You don't have to do this, Jack. I let my emotions get the best of me. It won't happen again."

"I just want to know if there's anything I can do to help. You're going to be facing some serious charges."

Stacy composed herself and sat in the chair in front of Belmont's desk. "I do not want to be your foe. I knew I'd be burned to ashes the second I crossed you."

He snarled, "Then why did you do it?"

"I said that I let my emotions get in the way."

"She's my wife!" Belmont roared.

She slapped her chest. "It's my heart! I had a moment."

Belmont sat across from her. "You had more than a moment. You've been recording our interactions from the start."

"I record all of my interactions with my clients. I record our fucking, our eating, and if we had taken a piss together, I would've recorded that too. I do what I have to do to protect myself."

Belmont rubbed the nape of his neck. "What frightens me the most is that you knew I wouldn't be happy when I found out you'd recorded our interactions, and yet me making love to my wife is what made you expose yourself. Fuck, Stacy, I can never trust you again."

Stacy released a long sigh. "I'm just a woman who made the mistake of treating you like someone who was merely a man."

Belmont studied her for the longest time. He'd possibly crossed the line the moment he had used her companionship to relieve his yearning for Daisy. Stacy was the only reason he'd made it through four months straight without Daisy.

"She's my wife," he said emphatically enough for her to catch his drift. "You don't call her. You don't send her emails. I don't ever want to learn that you spoke to her face-to-face."

"I will never fuck up like that again," she said.

Belmont nodded once.

She raised her eyebrows. "Then you forgive me?"

"As long as you realize that I'm not just a boy."

"What about the heat on my ass?"

Belmont smirked. "I'll find some ice for it. But workwise, we're done. Friends-wise, I apologize for my part in this shit. I should've known better."

Stacy raised a hand. "Don't… You're making it worse." She stood and smoothed her skirt. "Thank you for the ice."

Belmont watched her leave. He hoped letting her off the hook wouldn't come back to bite him in the ass. At least he knew how to destroy her if necessary.

Monday's meeting would be riskier. Belmont was on the verge of changing his mind about acquiring the riverfront property. The memories he'd made in Chicago so far weren't pleasant, and Matthew Silver wasn't Stacy Pruitt. Once Belmont bit a chunk out of Matthew, Matthew would require the same pound of flesh, if not more. Belmont had always walked a dangerous line between legitimacy and corruption. Threatening to out Reece Development for buying city, state, and federal officials to bypass policy, codes, and regulation was dangerous business. Especially once someone surreptitiously started naming names and leaking information to the press. Heads would roll, and there was a twenty percent chance one would be his.

DAISY LORD

The night Belmont caught Dexter and I kissing, I laid in bed, unable to sleep. Belmont had never run away from me that way.

About an hour after Dexter and I had settled in for the night, he'd crept past my door whispering, "I'll be right over," in the tone a man uses when he's horny.

I felt a pinch of something. I didn't know if it was jealousy or if I felt disrespected. I'd risked my relationship by kissing him, and he ran out to screw another woman?

He'd chuckled and said he couldn't wait to see her either. His feet pounded the stairs, and his keys rattled as he locked the door behind him. I thought he wanted me to hear him. I punched the pillow to make it more comfortable and to get out my frustration.

I thought, "What in the world am I doing lying in bed in some guy's house?" In addition to that, Javar was on an airplane flying into Chicago. I wasn't in the mood to deflect his constant advances, so I decided to pack my things and return to my parents' overpriced condo on the other side of town. I texted Belmont and informed him of my plans to leave. I didn't want him to think that the kiss Dexter and I had shared would be followed by a night of hot, steamy sex.

I'd wanted to invite him over so that we could, as he said, "fuck until we forget our issues," but then I looked at the photos Stacy had sent. Each picture pulled at the scab over my heart. By the time I deleted the email, my heart was bleeding again. I whimpered throughout the night. Eventually I fell asleep, and when I woke up, whatever had plagued me on Saturday morning had returned with a vengeance. My nose was congested, and I could hardly breathe. I was sneezing, coughing, my throat ached, and I had chills. I turned off my cell phone and remained in bed, fading in and out of sleep all day Sunday.

On Monday, I call in sick. I feel like a car, a train, and two busses have run over me.

"Have you told Dexter already?" Melissa asks when I call in.

"If I'd told Dexter, then I wouldn't be calling *you*." I'm out of patience for her nastiness.

"Well, you live with him, so…"

"Goddamn it, just tell him," I growl and end the call. What a bitch.

I've run out of tissues, but I'm too weak and achy to walk to the drugstore to buy more. I drag myself out of bed, find a roll of toilet paper, crawl back under the mounds of blankets, and go to sleep. Every now and then, I wake up to use the bathroom. Daytime and nighttime are trading places.

"Miss," a woman with a thick Spanish accent says. "Miss, are you awake?"

"Yes." I emerge out of the blankets. I see a tiny woman with black hair. "Are you the housekeeper?" It takes a lot of energy to speak.

"Yes, miss," she says and looks over her shoulder. "She is well."

I hear footsteps.

Javar Les appears in the doorway. "Daisy, what the hell!"

I groan and pull the covers back over my aching head. He turns my cell phone on, and it chimes and vibrates, alerting me that I have messages and missed calls.

"Get the hell out of bed," Javar says. "Our flight leaves in four hours."

"What?" I can't believe he thinks I'm getting on an airplane in this condition. I bury the side of my face deeper into the pillow.

Javar rips the blankets off me. "Oh shit."

I'm only wearing panties. "Just shoot the show without me. I quit." I roll up into a ball.

"You cannot quit."

"Could you please give me my blankets back and go?"

He sighs. "Your linens are grimy. I'll be back in a flash."

Moments later, I'm swept off the bed. Javar is carrying me.

"Where are you taking me?" I mumble.

"To the big bed. By the way, love your tits."

"Touch them, and I'll bite you."

"Where?"

I groan as my clammy skin makes contact with

dry, fresh sheets. Not too long after, a cold compress is placed on my forehead.

"Thanks, Belmont," I mumble.

It's early November. Belmont and I are on Martha's Vineyard, swimming off the beach near Lambert's Cove. The ocean, which is still warm from the past summer, is a cool but not cold sixty-something degrees. He catches me, and we swim to a boulder. Our mouths collide in a sensual kiss. I love him, but we've only just met.

"Daisy, will you give me your soul?" he asks.

His tongue takes an indulgent journey into my mouth. He shifts the crotch of my swimsuit, and his rock-hard erection impales me. I shudder as I'm immediately seized by orgasm. Belmont's thrusts are slow and explorative. Our eyes lock.

"Don't fight it, baby," he whispers. "You're going to get pregnant, so don't fight it."

I shove my hips against his dick. "I want whatever you give me."

He humps me faster. We cling to each other, moaning and whimpering about how good it feels. I'm about to come harder than I ever had. I scream before my orgasm detonates, and suddenly I'm in a hospital gown, standing on a cold floor in a shadowy hallway.

"Mommy," a girl calls.

My heart ties into a knot. "Joella!"

I race down the hallway and stop once I enter the room. My pulse is racing, my heart pounding. The incubator is in the middle of the room, and *ma fleur* lies inside it. She's full of life as she giggles and shakes her legs and arms as I approach. I open the container. Her bright eyes welcome me. My eager hands reach for her. She smiles as I lift her and press her against my heart. Her sweet odor... Her softness... She's warm with life. I weep uncontrollably, thanking God for my second chance with her.

"Hold it tight, Joe, and watch out for your fingers," Daniel says.

My baby is out of my arms. I whip around. I'm out of the hospital room and in my old backyard. Daniel's sandy-brown hair glistens under the sun. A little girl is helping him build one of our many doghouses. She's not me, but she's ours—Belmont's and mine. She looks happy. He looks happy. I wave at them. They both smile and wave back. My heart is content, and I'm satisfied.

I'm lying on top of our bed in Malibu. The sliding glass doors are open, and the Pacific Ocean breeze coats us. Belmont is behind me, slamming my hips against his as his dick goes in and out of me. I try to squeeze a pillow, but it has the consistency of water. I'm moaning, and so is he. My orgasm is like never-ceasing billows of waves that pound the shore.

"Daisy!" He sighs when he comes.

I wake with a stop. The ceiling looks different. I scramble to sit up. Tree branches canopy over a patio where two chaise lounges surround a hot tub. Steam rises from the aqua water. I'm in a white tank dress that I left in the closet in Malibu. Why the heck am I wearing it? Am I dreaming? I squeeze my eyes shut, and when I open them, nothing's changed—this is real.

"Daisy?"

I scramble to turn around. It's Belmont, and he has a black eye and a bruised cheek.

11

THE PLANNING

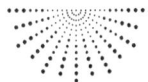

ANGELINA BLANCHARD

ONE MONTH AGO...

"*T*hat's not a bad idea," I say.

I'm sitting on the rail of the balcony, watching Charlie pull up the ugly yellow ceramic tiling. We're replacing it with wood. He's sweaty, shirtless, and on his hands and knees. He's so sexy that it's almost distracting.

He glares at me. "Babe, can you get off the rail? You're going to fall and break your neck."

"No." I shake my head. "I won't break my neck. I'll turn two flips and land on my feet like Catwoman."

"Ha!" Charlie jumps to his feet and draws me into his arms.

I giggle as he nibbles my neck. "Listen, I think we should do it."

"Me too…" He reaches through the side of my overalls and frees my tit.

I sigh as the stinging sensation of sensitivity is replaced by his sensual tongue on my nipple. "No, I mean lock them up and make them talk."

He stops working on my nipple. "You're talking about Jack and Daisy?"

"You said it, not me."

"That's crazy, Angel."

"No, it isn't. I can talk to Luc."

"Dr. Luc Calvet?"

I smirk. "You were listening."

"I listen to everything you say." Charlie's mouth finds my other nipple.

"Charlie," I whine, "I want you to take me seriously."

He sighs and presses his forehead against mine. "Babe, what you want us to do is crazy as hell."

"I think it's the only way they're going to get back together and stay together. They've been medicating their problems with sex."

Charlie sighs. "I know you think Jack is perfect—"

"I don't think that. I think you're perfect." I grin.

Charlie unlatches my overalls, leaving me topless for all our neighbors to see. "You're perfect too, baby."

He takes me inside. Once we're in our room, he devours my nipples as he lays me on the bed.

"Charlie?"

"Humph…" He's pulling off my clothes while maintaining contact with my breasts.

"Are we going to do this or not?"

"I'll do what ever you want," he says and sucks my nipple into his wet, warm mouth.

He kicks my overalls off from around my ankles, frees his erection, and gives it to me good.

I let Charlie murder my tits for as long as he likes. When he's had enough, I call Dr. Calvet, who asks me a lot of questions, including if Daisy and Jack have agreed to treatment.

I say, "Not yet."

He wants to know if they will undergo in-person treatment.

I say, "I'm not sure."

"Angelina, my darling—"

"I know, Luc, but I have to ask you to break the rules for me. It's for Jacques's daughter. Don't you love us?"

He tsks but tells me to give him the details once I have them. I call Maggie and convince her to get onboard. She'll fly into town and meet us at the Westport Lounge on Saturday night.

I help Charlie rip up the rest of the tile, then we drink wine and take a stab at writing lyrics. He's been hired to write two songs for a pop star named Sheena Riley. By the time we finish, we're tipsy and sweaty. We take a shower and make love until we fall asleep.

I plan Daisy and Belmont's sessions with Luc between rehearsals for a Broadway show at Harrah's that my dad helped me book. Charlie and I hardly see each other during the day, but we make up for the missed time at night in our bed.

ON SATURDAY NIGHT, CHARLIE AND I TAKE A CAB to the lounge to meet Maggie, who's late. I'm beat, but I have a solid plan that reads like a movie script. It even has alternative measures built into it.

Charlie reads through it with a wry smile. "You're prepared to go all the way, aren't you?"

"Did you read your parts?" I ask.

"I'll try to convince Jack to see Luc Calvet. If that doesn't work, then I'm supposed to have Stanley drug him?" He laughs.

"Isn't he an anesthesiologist?"

"Yes, babe, but he can't just knock Jack the hell out by sneaking up on him and sticking a needle in him."

"How do you know?"

"Because I know," he says.

"How?"

"You've been watching too much TV."

"I hardly ever watch TV. Charlie, you can't know until you at least talk to him. Just present him with a scenario."

Charlie sighs. He knows he can't win this battle. "All right, I'll see what he says."

"That's all I'm asking." I grin.

Maggie still hasn't shown up, so Charlie heads over to say hello to the guys gigging here tonight, and I go chat with a group of dancers from the show. They're letting their hair down since our stage is dark for six days. After a while, my gaze gravitates to Charlie, who's stroking a bass guitar.

Delia, one of the dancers, watches him too. I'm never the only woman in the room with her eyes on him. Charlie looks up from his instrument, and his hooded gaze penetrates me. I smirk. I love that I'm the only woman in the world he has a thing for. We break eye contact when Maggie gusts into the restaurant as though she only has five minutes to give us before her next important meeting.

Charlie gives the bass guitar back to a musician named Rick, and I say good-bye to my colleagues. We sit at a table for four. I'm alarmed by how beat Maggie looks, and I can tell Charlie is concerned too. Her already milky skin is three shades whiter, and the whites of her eyes are pink. I haven't seen her since Curtis's wedding two months ago, and she had been at least ten pounds healthier then.

"What the hell. Should we take you to the hospital?" Charlie asks.

"I'm okay. I had a long flight." She covers her mouth as she yawns.

"The way you look didn't happen over a course of a flight. You look like shit," Charlie says.

"So do you," she snaps.

I tap Charlie on the shin with my foot. He stifles a sigh. He's concerned about Maggie, as he should be.

"But, Mags, you don't look like your usual self," I say.

"Where's Vince?" Charlie asks.

She closes her eyes and shakes her head. At least now we know who's the source of her problems. Charlie and I give each other a look. He's shaking his leg, which means he's ready to bash Vince's head in for whatever he may have done.

"Let's just get down to business. Have you guys ordered?" Maggie asks.

"Not yet." I take Charlie's hand under the table. I want him to stay calm. We can discuss what kind of jerk Vince is at home while Maggie sleeps in the guest room downstairs.

Charlie waves our waitress to the table. We order, and Charlie asks her to put a rush on it. Exhausted or not, Maggie's brain is sharp. Before we're halfway through dinner we have a key and contingency plan in place.

Then Vince unexpectedly shows up. Maggie's eyes water as she watches him like a deer trapped in headlights. He appears stunned by her physical condition as they hug. I wonder what in the world has been going on between them.

"Don't say anything, babe," I whisper to Charlie.

"I won't," he mutters, but he's clearly not happy about keeping quiet.

I stand to give Vince a hug, and Charlie shakes his hand. Regardless of how frail Maggie looks, it appears Vince can't resist her sex appeal. He continuously massages her shoulder as I fill him in on the entire scheme. Like Charlie, he's hesitant but not resistant.

BELMONT LORD - HIS CAPTURE

Belmont met with Matt Silver in an office on Columbus near Randolph. It was neutral ground. Herald Doe, Belmont's right-hand man, accompanied him. Matthew had two colleagues with him. The fact that neither side greeted the other indicated that the meeting wouldn't be cordial. They sat around a small table. There were no secretaries or coffee or muffins.

"You'd better make damn sure you want to take it there before you take it there," Matt said.

"I have no idea what you're talking about," Belmont said.

Matt sniffed disdainfully. "This morning, I offered Voyager a bonus on top of our initial offer."

"Great, because I'm not offering them a penny more than my initial bid," Belmont said.

The men stared daggers at each other. Belmont noticed how old Matt looked, but they were nearly the same age. Perhaps doing the bidding of a dirty bastard like Holden Reece put those extra lines on Matt's face. Holden didn't mind getting blood on his hands in order to grab the next dollar. Belmont had never backed down from a tussle with a man like Holden Reece, but the last time he had been forced to take it this far, he wasn't married. He had to be careful and read the clues to see just how far he could get with option one. Option two would knock Reece Holdings out of existence, and Belmont would only be that ruthless if Daisy's safety was at stake.

"Where did you get your information?" Matt asked.

"You're assuming I'm the one who dug up your dirt?"

"I heard about your tactics, Jack. You've gotten away with it by hiding behind your daddy's name."

Belmont clenched his teeth. "My father's dead."

"I think you want to join him."

Belmont narrowed his eyes and held his composure. "If that's how you want to play it, then one of us just might."

"That would be too bad for your wife. Didn't she lose her brother? I heard he was playing in a busy street and got run over by a car. He must've forgotten to look both ways."

Belmont stared daggers at his opponents. He hoped his expression conveyed to all what he refused to say. Matt had just made the mistake of jabbing an angry bear with a spear. There would be no absolution from that moment forward. If Matt were an intuitive man, then he would've seen his demise in Belmont's stone-cold expression.

Matt broke eye contact with Belmont to glance nervously at his partner. "Listen, Jack, this doesn't have to get ugly. Give us twenty-four hours, and we'll let you know what we're going to do next."

Belmont shook his head. "No need. You've convinced me. I'm out." He stood, and Herald, who looked thoroughly confused, did likewise.

Matt also appeared astonished. "You're backing out of the bidding?"

"I am," Belmont said.

Matt stood. There was distrust in his eyes, and there should have been. Belmont had found his next big project: the destruction of Matthew Silver and Reece Holdings. Belmont held out his hand to shake on it.

"That's it?" Matt asked.

"That's it."

Matt chuckled. "Then I'll be expecting to hear from Voyager."

Belmont nodded. "You will." Belmont seethed as he and Herald walked down the hallway. Before they walked into a crowded elevator, Belmont said, "We're going Grey."

Herald nodded. He knew exactly what that meant. "When?"

"Immediately."

"I'll get on it."

They parted ways on the ground floor. Belmont exited the rear of the building to meet his car, but it was nowhere in sight. His cell phone dinged before he could call the driver. The message read, *"Traffic control instructed me to park in Level P6. The car will be waiting by the elevators."*

Belmont grumbled and headed back inside. Before he entered the elevator, he caught sight of Matt and his team leaving through the front revolving doors. Belmont remembered that Daisy was supposed to fly to Paris that afternoon. He wanted to see her first, perhaps delay her a bit. Belmont shuffled through his contacts as he walked out the elevator.

Someone grabbed him from behind and shook him. It took Belmont a second to realize he was actually being attacked, then he head-butted his assailant in the face. The guy shrieked, but Belmont didn't see the second assailant, who landed a punch on his jaw.

Belmont stumbled a bit, but he recovered and threw an uppercut at the masked man. The man stepped back as if he knew that would be Belmont's next move. Belmont followed up with a straight punch, catching the guy in the jaw. The attacker stumbled backward. Just as Belmont was going for the disabling blow, he got hit in the eye, hard. He saw white. He felt a prick in his neck and collapsed.

One of his attackers cried, "Fuck. I think he broke my nose!"

Belmont was about to say something, but everything turned black.

PART II
VIVE LA FRANCE

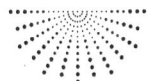

12
CAPTIVITY

BELMONT LORD

*B*elmont sat up and shook the cobwebs from his head. He had been lying down, tucked under warm blankets, in a cold room.

He looked at his chest. "What the…?" Someone had attached nodules to his chest, the kind that monitor the heart. Belmont ripped them off as he glared at the blue waterproof walls. He recognized them. He'd had them built to protect himself from the destructive forces of nature that affect islands in that tropical region. He was on the private island he owned in the Bahamas, and he sure as hell hadn't brought himself there.

After Belmont confirmed that he was alive, it dawned on him that he felt like shit. The left side of his face, including his eye, throbbed, and something heavier than nothing weighed down his ankle.

"What the hell is this?" he whispered as he touched it. It was the type of ankle bracelet the courts put on criminals to track their whereabouts. Was someone trying to keep tabs on him? If so, who?

He examined the room, looking for some sort of clue to how he'd gotten there. A handful of his enemies would love to see him suffer, starting with Matt Silver and Holden Reece. Matt had made a backhanded threat against Daisy, and Belmont took that remark as a declaration of war. So Belmont had locked and loaded and fired back. He had a plan in motion that would expose Reece Holdings for insider trading. But they couldn't have learned that fast about the shot he took.

Belmont massaged his jaw. He had been heading over to Daisy's to make sure she was safe, and to seduce her, before he was assaulted. He'd needed her body—he still did.

Belmont frowned as he remembered the cry of one of his assailants. "Charlie…" He could pick his brother's voice out of a lineup of distorted voices. Why in the hell had Charlie accosted him in a parking garage?

Belmont slid off the bed. His body ached from throwing a barrage of unsuccessful punches. He went into the box-sized bathroom and studied his face in the mirror.

"Damn it," Belmont whispered. He had noticeable bruising around his eye and on his cheek and jaw. Charlie had gotten him good.

Belmont opened the medicine cabinet to look for the antibiotic cream before he remembered it was in the first aid kit in the master suite upstairs. He decided to treat the bruise then figure out what the hell was going on. Belmont rushed out of the bathroom, but when he smashed the button to open the door of his prison, nothing happened. Just to be sure, he tried it again, and again the door didn't budge.

He beamed in on the control console located on the wall in one corner of the room. Upstairs, there was a full control room that let him monitor and control every part of the three-acre island. The smaller panel was a substation of the larger room, and it was wired to remain on twenty-four hours a day, seven days a week. However, none of the indicator lights were on. The panel had been turned off. Belmont walked over to the machine and tried to turn it on, but it wouldn't power up. He checked the sockets—it was plugged in. Then he ran his fingers along the edge of the rectangular box and noticed a screw loose at the top.

"What the hell?" he said under his breath.

Someone must've rewired the system. Charlie was the only one who knew Belmont's safe room existed. He was also the only one who was aware of the complex wiring connecting that room to the one upstairs.

Belmont fumed. Fucking Charlie. He was going to wring his neck as soon as he got himself out of that jam. Belmont shook his head. Charlie must've forgotten that he was a first-rate electrician. Belmont believed that a man who bought and sold multimillion-dollar properties ought to know how to build a structure from the inside out.

He went on a rampage looking for a tool kit. He opened drawers in the kitchenette then headed back to the bathroom to check the drawers and cabinets. Sometimes he went overboard storing his things, often hiding them from himself. Daisy often watched and remembered where he put things. She was a big help. Unfortunately she wasn't around when he built the safe room. Belmont paused to calm down so that his memory could flourish. He hadn't been in that damn room in six years, since he'd installed a new camera on the western side of the island and had to hook up the wiring to the control panel.

That's it! Belmont smiled victoriously. He pushed the bed away from the wall and opened a hatch in the floor. Inside, he found a compact transceiver that he had stored in case he lost cell phone reception. His current predicament was worse than that —he had no cell phone at all. There was also a first aid kit, which was better stocked than the one upstairs. He kept digging until he found the small black toolbox that contained a ratchet set, a wrench, a set of pliers, extra wires, and a soldering kit.

Belmont sighed with relief. Things were looking up. Even though his face hurt, he went to work restoring the power to the control panel. Once he got started, he realized Charlie sure as hell hadn't rewired the panel himself. Belmont was undoing the work of a professional. Hours ticked by, and the longer it took him to finish the task, the further away from Daisy he felt. He missed her body, the sound of her voice, and her sensual kisses.

Belmont was convinced that he wouldn't be stuck in that predicament if he and Daisy had never hit that rough patch. While he was wasting away on the damn island, she was in Provence, France, traipsing off into the sunset with Dexter Frampton. Belmont tried to shake the thought of the two of them together out of his head. If only he could make Daisy as happy as he strove to make her. The only part of Daisy that still wasn't a mystery was making love to her.

Belmont tugged too hard at an essential wire.

"Shit," he muttered. He had almost destroyed it.

Suddenly his thoughts sent a surge of frustration through him. Hell, he had given Daisy everything he thought women wanted. Her every wish was his command. The only problem was she never asked for a damn thing! All she did was stew in discontentment while trying to mask her agony with a dull smile. Damn, he hated that smile just as much as he loved her.

Loving Daisy had never made much sense to him. She was nothing like the women he'd dated in the past. They loved his wealth and his status. They wanted to flaunt him every chance they got. They asked for what they wanted, and he had bought everything from boob jobs to BMWs to summer-long vacations traipsing around the world. He liked to give, and he only took infrequently.

But when he'd first laid eyes on Daisy, he knew

she was different. He knew she was *the one*. He just didn't think she would be so difficult to make happy. Belmont had hoped he could fall out of love with her, but the cells of his body loved the cells of her body. His soul craved her soul. His mind needed her mind to complete him. He had waited thirty-five years to find her. Daisy was the woman God had made for him and he was the man for her—that he knew for sure.

Belmont's glare rolled around the room. There were no windows, but the clock on the oven said he had been at his task for at least six hours. He had gotten a portion of the control panel working but not the part that controlled the safe room door. Belmont felt like road kill. He was so exhausted that he started mixing up wires. Charlie's electrician had added filters and control boxes that weren't part of the original design, so Belmont had to find workarounds. Then when he fixed one function, another function stopped working.

Belmont wanted to yell, but instead he kept his composure. He needed food and a bit more sleep. He opened the refrigerator. There wasn't that much there to eat. What did Charlie want to do? Starve him to death? Belmont took out one of the three turkey sandwiches wrapped in plastic and one of the three beers. Charlie knew he only drank beer when he was stressed.

The silence was getting to Belmont. He had to force his brain not to think of Daisy or all the work he was neglecting. He also had to keep himself from getting so pissed off at Charlie that he got careless with the box and made mistakes. Belmont hated being helpless, but there was no use in pushing himself to exhaustion. After he finished eating, he took two painkillers for his throbbing everything, lied down, and closed his eyes.

When Belmont woke, he was laying on his side, facing the kitchenette. The oven said it was nine a.m. He rolled up to sit. He had been asleep for almost ten hours. At least his head felt better.

Belmont brushed his teeth, washed his face, took two more painkillers, and got back to work on the control panel. Now that he could think more clearly, he figured out that he shouldn't try to remove the aspects Charlie's guy added—he should meld them into the existing wiring. More hours ticked away, but Belmont had finally fixed the last wire. When he pushed the button to open the door, it slid open.

He smiled and looked at his ankle monitor. It would only take a dig and turn in the lock with a flathead to free himself from it, but he wondered what the purpose of the damn thing was in the first place. So he left it on. Now that he had telecommunications back up, he wanted to call Charlie and insist that he explain himself. However, Belmont was too curious to put an early end to the madness. He would wait as long as he could to see what Charlie had planned. From the amount of food that Charlie left in the refrigerator, he hadn't expected Belmont to remain in the hole for long. At least, that was what Belmont hoped.

Belmont rushed up the stairs to the main control room. He had to make the main system the slave and the smaller panel in the safe room the master because an outside source had linked into the main system, giving that person the ability to control everything. Belmont didn't terminate their control, but he fixed the system so that he could lock them out if he wanted. He powered up the massive surveillance system, but all he heard was white noise. Belmont rushed back downstairs to activate the override function, and this time when he activated the system, the TV monitors showed various shots of outside and inside the property. The timestamp on the corner of each monitor said it was Wednesday afternoon.

"Damn," he said under his breath. It had been Monday morning when he was accosted by Charlie and his buddies.

Belmont rewound the video until he pinpointed the moment of his arrival. He scowled as he saw himself, out cold and on a stretcher, being wheeled off a helicopter by Charlie, Vince, and another man he scarcely recognized.

Belmont took a closer look. "Stanley Roswell?"

Stanley was Charlie's friend, and he was a doctor of some sort, which type eluded Belmont. A lanky middle-aged man met them at the front door. The stranger had already been in the house, which didn't sit well with Belmont. The men quickly shook hands and hurried inside.

Belmont switched to the interior cameras and rewound the video until he matched the timestamp from the outside video. Charlie and Vince sweated profusely as they wheeled him down the long hallway. When they reached the back of the house, Charlie flipped up the cover over the security pad and pressed his thumb to the reader. Belmont clenched his jaw, regretting his decision to give Charlie access to the secured room. The door slid open, and they took the lift down instead of the stairs. They entered the safe room, carefully lifted

Belmont off the stretcher, and put him on the bed. Belmont turned on the audio just in time to hear Charlie complain about "Jack's" dead weight. Vince agreed he was heavy.

"This is fucking nuts," Vince said.

Belmont could see the regret on Vince's face.

"We're already here now, so let's just get it over with," Charlie said, also regretfully.

Stanley prepared a syringe. "He's going to bruise around that eye. This should help." Stanley injected Belmont with the serum.

"What's that you're giving him?" Charlie asked.

"Something to accelerate the healing."

Charlie nodded, but Belmont noticed Charlie's stressed expression. "I think he knows it was me."

"Well, he can't retaliate in this condition," Stanley said.

Vince nervously scratched the back of his neck. "When is he going to wake up?"

"Three or four hours." Stanley shook his head. "I don't like leaving him unattended."

"Me neither," Vince said.

"He'll be fine. Right?" Charlie asked the unidentified middle-aged man who was strapping the monitor around Belmont's ankle.

The man motioned to Stanley. "He is the medical doctor." He spoke with a French accent.

"That's right, and if anyone finds out I did this, I'll lose my fucking license," Stanley said.

"No one's going to find out," Charlie said.

Belmont sneered. Charlie was always sure the foul shit he chose to do would have no consequences, but there were always consequences. Belmont had bailed him out of all of them.

Belmont shook his hands. "I could've died, you nitwit!"

Stanley shot Charlie a skeptical glance then placed nodules on Belmont's chest. "I'll monitor him closely. If his vitals become concerning, then you fly me back to this fucking island, and we put an end to this shit. Got it?"

Charlie didn't respond.

Stanley gave Charlie a look that said he meant business. "Or I'll wake him the hell up."

"Jack will be fine," Charlie said as if he were trying to convince himself. "He always is. Plus, he's going to want to kiss the ground we walk on when his better half gets here."

"Daisy…" Belmont whispered. *So she would be arriving.*

"Yeah, but he won't be able to touch her." Vince shook his head. "That's sinisterly cruel…"

"It won't be forever," Charlie said.

"I still don't see anything wrong with how much they do it. You do it a lot. So do I. It's healthy," Vince said, looking at the lanky man for corroboration.

"Their sexual relations are not excessive. I will use sex as an unconditional stimulus," the lanky man said.

Vince and Charlie looked as if they were confused by the man's clinical speak. However, Belmont understood him. The lanky man was a doctor, and he was planning to keep them apart sexually and only let them fuck as a reward. Belmont sniffed. *In his fucking dreams.*

"Whatever," Charlie said. "The point is, Dr. Calvet knows what the hell he's doing. Jack and Daisy are going to be fixed when he's done with them."

Belmont bit down on his back teeth. He'd heard that name before. *Dr. Calvet.*

"These methods *are* inordinate. I too am risking my reputation, but I am doing this as a favor for a friend," Dr. Calvet said.

Suddenly Belmont remembered Charlie had

asked him to call or meet a marriage therapist who was a Frenchman. Belmont had said he'd think about it but never gave it another thought. He scrutinized Dr. Calvet, who had finished activating the ankle monitors.

"Tuck him in," Stanley said. "Jack will be lethargic when the anesthesia wears off. He won't be fully awake until tomorrow, but other than a little soreness from the bruises on his face, he'll feel like new."

Vince and Charlie seemed fine with that prognosis. Belmont watched all four men file out of the room. Another helicopter arrived with food, and they stocked the refrigerator in the main kitchen and the one in the room where he was being kept. One of Charlie's electrician buddies was on the copter, and he tested the control panels to make sure Dr. Calvet had complete control from his home in France, which explained the extra wires and filters in the safe room. The guy was good, but his work was rushed and sloppy.

After he watched both helicopters lift off, Belmont touched his ankle bracelet. It didn't bother him, but at least Charlie's shenanigans weren't more sinister. The entire plan had Angelina written all over it. She had a flair for the dramatic, one of the many ways she differed from Daisy.

Unfortunately, all of their planning would go up in a ball of smoke, though not immediately. He liked the idea of him and Daisy fixing their relationship. Something was definitely wrong. They had never been on the same page, but Daisy just wouldn't give him anything to go on. He needed something, but hell if he knew what that was.

Belmont flipped between cameras to evaluate the lay of the island in real-time. The speedboats had been removed from the docks on both sides of the island, and not one caretaker roamed the grounds. On average, six workers stayed on the island to tame the brush and wipe back the dust in and around the six guesthouses. Each had its own swimming pool, which also had to be maintained.

Belmont had initially intended to turn the island into a vacation resort, but he fell in love with the terrain. He had paid top dollar for a deserted island with sloping bluffs with flat planes, which made it good for building. The main house was built on the highest point of the island, facing west. The sunsets were therapeutic. Belmont had never named the island. He had been waiting for something remarkable to happen in his life, an event or person he wanted to memorialize. Why hadn't he ever thought to name his piece of Heaven Daisy?

All of a sudden, one of the cameras showed a helicopter hovering over the helipad. Belmont smirked. Daisy had arrived while he was thinking of her. That confirmed it. He would name the island "Daisy's Heart." Belmont held his breath as Stanley and another guy carefully unloaded the stretcher with Daisy on top. She was out cold, and he didn't like seeing her that way. She looked dead, lying there with an IV drip feeding her the knockout drugs.

Belmont was taken aback when he saw Angelina step out of the helicopter, carrying a suitcase. The pilot took the suitcase from her, and she clenched the handrail of the stretcher. Belmont tried to recall if he had ever seen that strained look on Angelina's face. Angelina and all the men carted Daisy into the house, down the hallway, and into the room he called the mouth because the trees that surrounded the patio furniture looked like lips, and the furniture resembled teeth. Belmont hadn't planned it that way—it just happened.

The mouth was one of the only rooms Belmont hadn't installed cameras in, so he couldn't watch what was happening. He kept his gaze fixed on the monitor showing the doorway. He was eager for everyone but Daisy to leave.

Finally, one attendant walked out of the room. Three minutes later, Stanley and Angelina left. Angelina was wiping away tears, and Stanley had an arm around her shoulder. As soon as the helicopter lifted off, Belmont heard a click. Someone was using the control center. He decided to let them keep their access for the time being. He ran out the door to Daisy.

DAISY LORD

I sit on a black leather sofa in a room that reminds me of a TV station control room. Belmont has just filled me in on where we are and why we're here . We're on his privately owned island in the Bahamas. I feel as if I'm living in a dream. It would be a nightmare without Belmont. However, the shock collar around my ankle feels as if it's around my neck, choking me. It's already made me break out in an itchy rash.

"Babe, you have to stop doing that," Belmont says when he catches me scratching my ankle.

I look at him solemnly. "But I'm itchy."

He takes a step in my direction but doesn't come closer. "Take some deep breaths. It'll help."

"I don't see how that can help."

"The discomfort is in your head."

"No, it isn't. It's around my ankle."

Belmont and I gaze into each other's eyes. I hate getting huffy with him, especially while under duress. Maybe he's right. I take a couple deep breaths. Plus, I'm willing to try anything.

"What happened to your eye?" I ask.

"Charlie and Vince had to fight me to bring me here."

I shake my head in disbelief. "Does it hurt?"

His gaze caresses me. "Not anymore."

My heart skips a beat. That one long, sensual look is enough to make me get a grip. I drop my foot off the seat. "Okay, I'll stop scratching."

Belmont smiles faintly, and so do I. He powers on a sizable system of television monitors, electrical control boards, and switches. A man with mildly graying hair around his temples fills the screen. He's sitting in front of a bookcase stacked with psychology books.

"We're here. Now what is this about?" Belmont growls.

The man takes a moment to appraise me. "I am Dr. Calvet."

Suddenly I hear Angelina's voice speak his name in my head. "You're Luc Calvet, the psychiatrist?"

He straightens his posture. "I am Luc."

"You're a friend of my father's."

"Jacques and I are good friends."

"But Angelina put you up to this?" I ask.

"Angelina asked for me to help."

"Does she know about the shock bracelets?" I snarl.

"May I call you Daisy?" he asks.

"Sure." My tone is gruff.

"The ankle monitors are part of your therapy."

The word therapy resounds inside my head like a shotgun blast. "Therapy? I did not agree to therapy. And if I were undergoing therapy, then I'm at a loss as to how outfitting us with ankle monitors as if we're criminals will help." My skin turns hot as it does when I'm angry.

Belmont holds up his hands. "Calm down, babe."

"Mr. Lord—" Dr. Calvet says.

Belmont grimaces at him. "It's Belmont."

"Belmont, does your wife's discomfort make you uncomfortable?"

The question seems to catch Belmont off guard. He parts his lips as if he wants to speak, but he's lost for words.

I feel as if I have to say something to save him. "You don't have to give us shock therapy to keep us away from each other. We're adults." I make sure to use a less contentious tone.

"I do agree with you."

"Great, then how do we get them off? I feel like there's a noose around my neck."

"The keys are buried in the sand."

Belmont and I look at each other as if that's the most ridiculous thing we've ever heard. This whole situation is like something out of a B-movie, and Belmont and I are the talentless lead actors.

"Once you have progressed, I will send you the map," Dr. Calvet says.

I don't know whether I should laugh or cry.

Belmont's frown deepens. "Neither Daisy nor I have agreed to treatment. Don't think we will be bullied into this clusterfuck."

Dr. Calvet's gaze shifts between Belmont and me. "I see. You must choose my help. I cannot proceed if you do not agree, but I do hope you agree, because I can help you."

Belmont and I glance at each other. I don't doubt that our marriage needs whatever assistance he can offer. I feel as if we're clinging to a buoy in a rough sea. We could hold on until we die, but we don't want our relationship to perish. We want to live, and Dr. Calvet is offering us a lifeline.

The problem is that we didn't choose this. Angelina and Charlie decided it for us. I still can't believe she let him outfit me with such a torturous device. She should've known better. I recall her being inside my bedroom in Chicago and how soothing her warm, moist hand was on my forehead. I was feeling a lot better, and I'd wanted to let her know.

"I'm sorry," she'd said.

I'd wanted to ask, "Sorry for what?" However, the next thing I knew, I woke up on a bed in a room I didn't recognize.

I remember Belmont and the woman in the purple dress, Stacy Pruitt. I see myself kissing Dexter and that look on Belmont's face when he caught us. I recall our stupid, stupid arguments. He accused me of being loveless. I accused him of being entitled and controlling—the two traits I hate most in a man. Yet I love him, and I can't picture a future without him. Dr. Calvet watches me as if he already knows what I'll say.

"Okay, I'll do it," I say.

Belmont smiles faintly. "Me too. I'm in."

13
THE LOST

DAISY LORD

*D*r. Calvet faxes over release forms. The massive system of machines prints them. Belmont winks at me before he signs. I know that look—he's up to something. I sign my form, and Belmont faxes them back. I hate that we're being forced to keep our distance. I avert my eyes from his figure. He's wearing a white T-shirt and a pair of green hospital scrubs. I can tell that being near me has already gotten to him because his bulge is firm. He's not alone in the *aroused* department. I want him too.

"Daisy?" Dr. Calvet says.

I bring myself out of my fantasy of being under Belmont and back into the moment. "Yes?"

"Tell me how you met."

I nod as I think back. "We met on Martha's Vineyard. I was an emotional wreck."

"And why is that?"

I feel Belmont's stare picking me apart. "My then-boyfriend and best friend had decided to get married without telling me they were even in a relationship."

"You felt betrayed?"

"I did at first."

"What do you mean?"

I glance at Belmont. He's watching me with that skin between his eyes puckered. "Well, I think the moment I got over what they had done to me was in the Stop & Shop, when Belmont asked if he could share my basket. I mean, that was the first time I really took a good look at him and saw…" My heart swells. "It was as if I had known him my whole life."

"I felt the same way but way before then," Belmont says. "It happened for me when I saw you walking off the docks."

"And so you fell in love?" Dr. Calvet asks.

Belmont and I say "yes" at the same time.

"That is good. Then there is no doubt that you were in love."

"Not for me," Belmont says.

Dr. Calvet looks at Belmont askew. "I see…"

I roll my eyes a little. "Belmont doesn't think I'm capable of love."

"That isn't true," he says.

"He thinks I'm in love with my brother, who is dead."

"I don't think you're in love with him. I think you haven't gotten over whatever the hell the two of you had."

I shake my head. That doesn't make sense. "I've done everything you wanted me to do. What else do you want from me? My soul?"

Belmont shakes his head out of frustration. This is the point where we always reach an impasse.

"What is your answer?" Dr. Calvet asks Belmont.

"You mean what do I want from her?"

"Yes."

Belmont stares at me intensely. "Every fucking thing she has to give, I'll take."

"Then you do want her soul?" Dr. Calvet says.

"Every inch of it."

The way Belmont looks at me when he says that makes my nipples stand at attention, and Belmont notices. I know for a fact that he doesn't mean my soul more than my body, which is the one thing I love giving to him without impunity.

"But that is not possible," Dr. Calvet says, seemingly unaware of the sexual energy between us. "Only the maker of her soul can claim her soul. Daisy, what do you want from Belmont?"

The way Belmont is still looking has me discombobulated. I'm drawing a blank. "I don't know."

"I see…" Dr. Calvet checks his watch. "This is a very good start. Tomorrow we can resume. I have an assignment for you. Tonight, tell each other what you would be doing this instant if you had never married."

"Tell each other?" I ask.

"Who else is there to tell?" Dr. Calvet replies.

I shrug.

"Daisy, I would like for you to share first."

My eyes meet Belmont's. I have actually thought about what my life would be like without him in it, but I could never decide whether it would be better or worse. However, we say goodnight to Dr. Calvet, and Belmont turns off the system.

The equipment stops humming, and now there's nothing louder than the silence between us. This is when we would typically hug and kiss and touch and rub against each other until we're hot and bothered and ready to make love. We would do it over and over until we forgot about Dr. Calvet's assignment. But neither of us wants to feel the electrical shock that occurs if we get within five feet of each other, so we maintain our distance.

"How have you been?" Belmont asks.

Before today, we hadn't seen each other since the night I kissed Dexter. "I've been fine."

"I was on my way over to your place before I was abducted." He snickers.

I touch the side of my eye. "So Charlie hit you in the eye?"

"Yeah, he did."

I want to make a joke about how Charlie has been waiting a long time to cold-cock him, but instead I bend over to scratch my ankle. "I can't believe Charlie and Angelina went through all this just to get us to see a psychiatrist. This is really drastic." Belmont doesn't respond, so I look up.

"Why does that bother you?" he asks, referring to the ankle monitor.

"Why doesn't it bother you?"

"It bothers me."

I sit up. "Well, there's nothing we can do about it. I just have to deal."

Belmont is watching me in a strange way. He's obviously thinking something.

"What?" I ask.

"What, what?"

"Why are you looking at me like that?"

He cracks a tiny smile. "I'm conflicted."

"Conflicted about what?"

"At least I'm stuck with you."

"I doubt that's what you were thinking, but I'll take it."

Belmont's sexy grin fades into a vulnerable expression. "What you said about that thing feeling like a noose around your neck…" He looks at the shock collar around my ankle. "Do you feel the same way about me, about us?"

"No, you're not a noose," I say earnestly and hopefully convincingly. It's not happening at the moment, but sometimes, too many times, I do feel as if Belmont is smothering me. But that makes him less like a noose and more like a pillow.

"All right," he barely says. He still has his doubts. I hear it in his tone.

"Well…" I stand. My head is groggy, perhaps from the anesthesia. "I'm going to take a bath and then cook something."

Our stares linger on each other. This is new—

being so close and being unable to make physical contact.

"It's been a couple of days since I bathed, so I feel grimy," I add.

Belmont gets that naughty look in his eyes.

I point behind him. "Okay, well, could you move five feet that way so I can pass without getting shock treatment?"

"You do know that I want you?"

I smirk flirtatiously. "Of course you do."

"I'm going to have you."

"Five feet, Jack Lord."

He raises his eyebrows. "You called me Jack?"

"You sound as if you like it."

"Let me try it on when I'm making love to you."

I roll my eyes again. "Stop it."

"You stop it."

I raise a hand. "Five feet, Jack."

Wearing a lopsided grin, Belmont takes two large steps backward. I chuckle and start toward the doorway.

"Daisy?"

I stop to look back at him. Gosh, he's good looking. It should be a crime to be so sexy.

"Where do you think you're going?" he asks.

"Back to the room I was put in."

"Sleep with me in the master suite," Belmont says.

I shake my foot. "Jack, we're wearing these. What if we roll within five feet of each other in the middle of the night? Think about how shocking that will be—pun intended."

Belmont snickers as his eyes lasciviously fall over my body. He and I are alone on what I suspect is a deserted island. Under these circumstances, all the stuff that pulled us apart gets stored at the back of the closet. I ignore those haunting photos of him and Stacy Pruitt. He tries to forget about my sensual kiss with Dexter. I forget that I have been keeping score, and on a scale from one to ten, his indiscretion was a ten and mine was a one.

"Right," Belmont says. He seems absorbed by his thoughts again.

"Okay."

"But use the tub in the master suite. It's bigger. You'll like it. If you don't want me to show you where it is, then I can tell you how to get there."

"What's wrong with the tub in the smaller room?" I ask.

"Nothing. It's nice, just not as big."

I cut a tiny smile. "You do like everything bigger."

"Not everything…"

I stifle a laugh. He just doesn't stop. He's referring to my pussy, which he constantly reminds me is tighter than average. But he knows I can't resist a luxurious bath. "Okay, I'll use the bigger tub."

"Out this door, make a right. Down the hallway, make a left, go up the stairs, make a right, and the master is on the right. It faces the ocean. It has the best view in the house, next to your tits and hips."

I roll my eyes. "Jack Lord, you're just working yourself up for something that can't happen."

"Right," he says, still grinning naughtily.

"Right."

"See you soon."

I grunt and shake my head, but I can't wipe the smile off my lips as I walk down the long hallway and follow Belmont's instructions to a T. Now that a lot of the stress I felt earlier has dwindled, I can get a better feel of this mini-mansion. The décor is so contemporary chic and in line with Belmont's pristine bachelor-pad tastes, even though he isn't a bachelor. I walk up the floating stairs made of heavy-duty glass then take the first right down a hallway with textile art on the walls. The sun is setting, and the lights turn on automatically as I go.

I make it to the master bedroom, and it's just as

grand as I knew it would be. The wooden head-board of the king-sized bed sits against a textured ceramic wall. Serious special effect lighting surrounds the headboard—it would make anyone sleeping in the bed appear to be the sun king or queen. Pendulum lights shaped like teardrops hang on both sides of the bed, and a white fur rug lies at the foot of the bed.

I walk over to the large windows and look out over the island. Belmont could never fully articulate this view. Tropical trees coat the hillside. Soft orange and yellow lights have been placed pleas-ingly throughout the brush. At the moment, I'm transcending our entire situation. I feel as if I'm on vacation or on assignment on a tropical island I've never explored.

I pull off my dress and figure out how to open the large windows. The island breeze consumes me. A full moon is rising, so the ocean is active. I would love to swim in those waters, but I would never do it without a guide. Tiger sharks are thick in these parts. I take a deep breath and one last survey of the land before I trot off to the bathroom to run a bath.

Of course the tub is to die for. It's oval shaped, sunken into the floor, and outlined by a smooth, rectangular-shaped layer of gray slate rock, which is surrounded by warm gray stones. I easily figure out how to draw the perfect bath. Belmont has the same programing mechanism for the bathtubs in his homes in Malibu, Manhattan, and Martha's Vineyard. I order a sweet peach, creamy bubble bath, sit on the edge of the tub, and put in my freed foot as water fills it. I close my eyes to breathe in the delicious scent.

"Don't move. Stay just like that," Belmont says.

I open my eyes. There's something different about him. He's wearing shorts as he strolls confidently in my direction. What the hell is he doing!

I freeze, bracing myself for the shock of my life, but nothing happens. I look at his ankle, and my mouth falls open. "Where's your shock collar?"

Belmont smirks. "I threw it away." He stands over me. "I've been waiting to…"

I gaze up at him breathing heavily, wondering what he will do first. His hand travels down my neck. I gasp as his fingers caress my breasts. I brush my cheek against his bare leg. "How did you get it off?"

"I'll tell you later." Belmont lifts me, and I clamp my legs around him. Now I've gotten him all wet.

My head feels as if it's floating as we kiss. Belmont's lips release mine, and I sigh when he nibbles his way down my neck. His erection is as hard as steel and pressed against my slipperiness. Belmont moans, frustrated, as he sucks on the hills and slopes of my breasts. His tongue and lips are soft and warm, but his grasp is tight.

"Damn it," he whispers. "I don't know what to do to you first." Our skin is so slippery. He bites my nipple, and I flinch. "What do you want, baby?"

I thrust my damp hips against his rigidness. "This."

He sighs. "Me too."

Belmont lays me on the bed. We don't relinquish eye contact as he steps out of his shorts. I can't speak, but the cells of my body beg him to hurry up and screw me. Finally, Belmont slides up between my legs. We both gasp as he breaks through my depths.

"Damn, you're so fucking tight," he mutters.

Belmont shifts his hips. His strokes are fervent. He's already shivering as he shifts slowly. Our eyes are locked. He seizes my hips and sinks his throbbing penis so deep, I feel him in my belly. Our lips are close to touching, and our breaths crash against each other. No words are needed. This is how we want to stay forever. This is bliss.

I forget how easy it is to stimulate him to the point of non-restraint, and I slide the tip of my tongue across his top lip. That's all it takes. Belmont pounds me as we smash our mouths against each other. I love Belmont's unbridled passion. I feel my insides pulse around his thickness, and I whimper as he makes me feel streaks of pleasure.

"Holy shit." Belmont crushes the pillow on both sides of my head and grunts as he blasts his nectar inside me.

I relish the taste of our kiss. Our lips smash and grab at each other. Our tongues slip against each other. I could do this all night, but at the moment, I can only think of one thing.

"How did you get that thing off your ankle?" I ask before his tongue rounds mine.

"I'm not easy to detain. You're the only one I'll surrender to."

I chuckle. "That was really cheesy."

"You want out?"

I furrow my eyebrows. "Out of what?"

"The noose around your ankle."

"You have no idea."

"Then you're going to have to…" He pins my

knees to the bed and trickles kisses down my belly until his wet tongue smashes my clit.

I wriggle against his mouth. Belmont never wastes a lick. His strong hand massages my thighs, and I suck air as his fingers fuck me. I close my eyes to feel everything he's doing to me. I gasp and bite my bottom lip to keep from screaming. Belmont is in complete control of my lower half.

"Belmont," I say breathlessly.

"Call me Jack."

"Jack!" I arch my back as my thighs quiver and my pussy spasms. His fingers dig deeper into all of the excitement.

I'm only able to open my eyes when the most potent, pleasurable sensations subside. Belmont watches me with a smirk. I so know what he's thinking.

"We weren't supposed to do that," I say.

"We can make love whenever the hell we want," Belmont says.

I laugh. "Humph. Was that making love or something much dirtier?" I flex my eyebrows playfully.

"It was a sweet symphony of both. But now…" He springs to his feet. "I'm going to free you, and we're going to eat. Then I'm going to eat you. Then

I'll make love to you. And at some point, we'll do the good doctor's assignment because I'm still in. What about you?"

I sit up on my elbows. My arms are still shaky from the potent orgasm I just experienced. "Yeah, of course."

He takes a decadent look at my body. "Then wait there."

"Okay," I say and press my head into the pillow as he trots off. Freedom is only a few minutes away. I still can't believe Angelina let the doctor strap those things around our ankles. I mean, what the hell was that about? I would never do this to her, no matter how bad things got between her and Charlie. Of course, they'll never have the problems Belmont and I have, and they're smug about it.

"Hey," Belmont says, standing in the doorway.

I beam at him. "Hey."

"You didn't move."

"Don't I always do what you say?"

He frowns, seemingly bothered by my carefully crafted jab, which I already regret. After a moment, he walks over with a toolbox and takes my foot. One by one, he sinks my toes into his warm mouth. The erotic sensation makes me moan.

"You know this is one of the few things you ever asked me to do for you," he says.

"I've never been high maintenance."

"I can afford it."

We look at each other. After Belmont realizes I have no response, he digs a flathead screwdriver into the keyhole of my shock collar.

"Give me a pillow," he says.

I hand him a pillow.

"Relax. I'll be gentle," he says.

I snicker. "Does everything have to have a sexual reference with you?"

"In your case, yes." He winks.

I shake my head and lie back. My foot is elevated. I feel him tugging and pulling.

"Am I hurting you?" Belmont asks.

I smile. "No. It feels kind of good actually."

I hear a click, then my ankle is as light as a feather. I sit up on my elbows. He's holding the offending device.

"Thank you, Jack," I say with a sigh of relief.

Belmont takes hold of my foot, throws the ankle bracelet on the floor, and slides up between my legs. His erection presses against my pussy again. My head has taken flight, and I indulge in my favorite flavor—the taste of his mouth. Each tangle of our tongues and melting of our lips makes me wetter and wetter.

"Belmont," I whisper between kisses.

"Humph," he replies without stopping.

"Aren't we supposed to keep our distance?"

He stuffs his erection inside me. "Like this?"

I gasp. I love when his dick gets so hard. His erection slips in and out of me. Belmont is on a seek-and-ignite mission. Each stroke is slow but firm, and my pussy pulses like an irregular heart-beat. His spontaneous whimper excites me even more. It's so honest. It lets me know that he's not screwing around. Making love to me truly gives him immense pleasure.

I can tell he wants me to come hard. He knows it'll take longer for me to arrive, so he has to force himself to wait. He aims a little to the right, and I shriek and hold him tighter. A little moan escapes him as he holds there and rotates his hips. The sensation builds. My breaths come quicker, and I wrap my arms around Belmont, bracing for blastoff. Then it happens. My walls quickens. I cry out and hold on tight as bolts of pleasure streak through my pussy.

Once all the tension falls out of my body, Belmont takes my hips and rams his penis in and out of me. His mouth catches one of my bouncing tits, and he sucks hard on my nipple. Then he nails me deeply as he whimpers and grunts. Our bodies quake in unison. I let the waves of pleasure and emotion rush through me. We love each other the most when we're doing this. Belmont rolls me on top of him, and we lie with our bodies pressed together. I haven't felt this relaxed in a long time.

"Daisy?" Belmont says.

I sigh and fall deeper into relaxation. "Yes."

"Can I ask you something?"

"Sure."

"Was that the first time you kissed Dexter Frampton?"

I knew we would have to talk about it sooner or later. "Yes."

We're silent, but I can feel him thinking.

"I saw you dancing with him," he says.

My father's concert in Chicago was just last Saturday, but it feels as if it occurred eons ago. I remember hugging Dexter on that emotional night. My father had dedicated a beautiful song to me, and my conversation with him after the concert was beautiful. I knew Belmont was there the whole time. I can always feel him when he's near.

"Yeah, well, we were at a concert," I say.

"Betty Moreland sang to you."

"Yeah," I whisper.

Belmont massages the round of my ass. At least he's still frisky. "He had his fucking hands all over you."

I try to remember it that way. I'm pretty sure Dexter did *not* have his hands *all over* me. "He was just comforting me, that's all."

Belmont snorts cynically. "He wanted to fuck you, and he still does."

"Well… I wasn't going to let him do that, so..."

"Did you quit your job?"

I lift my head off his chest and look him in the eyes. "Why are you asking?"

"It's an easy yes-or-no question. Did you quit?"

"No, I haven't, but I've been sick."

"Your body is still warm. How do you feel now?"

"A lot better." I smirk. "Probably because I'm on top of you."

Belmont's fingers slide down the crack of my ass, and he plunges two fingers into my wetness. "Um…" He flips me onto my back beside him and slides those fingers in and out of my pussy. "Is Dexter still expecting you to join him in France?"

I sigh. "Yes."

"Are you going?"

"How can I? We're stuck on this island."

"Baby, I'll never be stuck on an island, and neither will you. The doctor said he wants you to answer the question first. So why don't you tell me what you would be doing if you weren't married to me?"

I have to close my eyes to imagine a life without Belmont. "I would definitely still be living in my little cottage in Santa Monica. I miss it sometimes."

"You're not happy where we live?"

I sigh hard. "Eight bedrooms, seven bathrooms, and all those other rooms, but there are only two of us. Why did you ever need a house that big?"

"It's the first piece of luxury property I ever owned in L.A."

"Oh." I feel as though I shoved my foot in my mouth. "I'm sorry, I didn't know."

Belmont frowns. "It's no big deal."

We fall silent.

"What are you thinking?" I ask.

He shakes his head. "Nothing. So answer the question. What would you be doing if you weren't lying here with me?"

I shrug. "My father actually suggested that I ditch *The Lone Traveler* and spend some time at his house in Bordeaux. I'm not sure if things would be as good as they are between my father and me if there had never been a you and me, but if a different road had led me to my father's invitation, then that's where I'd be right now."

"Living in France?"

"I don't know if I would live there. However, I would stay there until I was ready to leave, which could be in two days, or a week, or a month."

"And who would be your lover?"

"I don't know. Some guy. No guy." I grin to lighten the mood.

Belmont pulls his eyebrows together. I'm waiting for him to respond with a witty quip, but the seconds tick by, and the silence grows louder.

"You should do that then," he says.

I tilt my head. "Do what?"

"Go to Bordeaux."

"Oh…"

"Tomorrow I can have a helicopter take you to Nassau, and I'll arrange a flight to Bordeaux for you."

I'm speechless and very confused. I look at his hand, which is now stroking my nipple. "But what about Dr. Calvet? We agreed to treatment."

"Fuck treatment. This will be our kind of treatment," he says as he tweaks my nipple.

I push his hand away. "Did I just make you angry or something?"

"No, baby, you didn't."

I narrow one eye suspiciously.

"I have business to attend to. I can't stay here past tonight anyway."

"But you want me to just go to Bordeaux?" I say.

"I want you to be happy."

"So is this you calling it quits?"

He shakes his head. "You can't get rid of me that easily." He gives me his lopsided smile. "This is *me* getting to know *you*."

I frown. "I'm confused."

Belmont slides his hand back between my legs, and strokes my clit. "Do you know why Dr. Calvet wanted you to tell me what you thought your life would be like without me first?"

"I figured it was ladies first."

He grins. "He knows I can't picture a life without you."

"Then why are you sending me away?"

"You can picture a life without me. I want you to live that life."

I shake my head. I have no idea what Belmont

is talking about. I still think he's upset about Dexter. Perhaps our lovemaking has conjured latent feelings of resentment within him. His reasoning is so off, but I look in his eyes and see that he means it. He really wants to put distance between us.

"Okay," I say, masking my pain and anger. Now that I think about it, I should be sending him packing! He's the one who had sex with another woman.

"But first…" He parts my knees, gets between my legs, and licks my pussy from top to bottom.

I nudge his head away from my sweet spot. "No…" I swing my legs over the side of the bed while the sensations Belmont's tongue has sparked subsides. "I'm going to take a bath." Neither of us is used to me denying him, but sex can't fix how I feel.

He hugs my waist. "Did I make you angry?"

I put on a fake smile. "No, of course not. It's just the bath is calling my name. I've neglected it long enough."

He kisses the small of my back and then lets go. "If you must. I'll make us something for dinner."

I want to make a joke about him never cooking, but instead I walk to the bathroom. The jets have kept the water warm, so I get into the tub, get comfortable, close my eyes, and try to forget all the pleasurable things Belmont just did to me.

Why didn't I insist on staying with him? I could've said that I'd go to Malibu, Manhattan, Chicago, Martha's Vineyard, or wherever his business took him. But the truth is, I'm tired of chasing Belmont. I think that's why I chose to take that job with the Travel X channel. Deep down I do want to go to Bordeaux.

Belmont was on the money about something else: my heart and soul have been numb since that car hit Daniel, my brother. Being numb was how I coped with the pain, then with life. My relationship with Adrian and my strained relationship with my parents allowed me to feel nothing. Then one day, the most gorgeous man I'd ever seen walked up to my table in a charming café.

If he hadn't been so determined, then I would've missed it—I would've missed him. His every touch, kiss, and lovemaking massaged my heart and soul back to life. But he didn't stop with himself. Would I have the relationship with Heloise that I now have if Belmont hadn't intervened? I should run out of this bath and into his arms and shout that I give up all my ambitions, passions, and wants just to stay close to him. But shouldn't I be completely happy?

Our problem is making "us" work. Belmont has been a bachelor for so long that he doesn't know how to integrate me into his life. His solution? Get me to conform to his universe. So that's exactly what I've been doing. But when the sex is over and endorphins settle and the oxytocin wears off, I feel like a loser.

Perhaps it's time to do what I want. Maybe that's what Belmont meant when he said that it's time for him to get to know me. Am I lost? I don't know. I sink all the way under the water. When I reemerge, I'm kind of excited about figuring out the answer.

14
DESERTING THE ISLAND

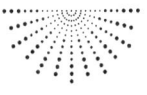

DAISY LORD

I dry off and put on a stretchy white slip dress. Angelina must've packed my clothes. A nice collection of garments that I normally wear—comfortable, lightweight dresses, distressed jeans, and over-washed tank tops—hang in the closet. She's very observant.

A scrumptious scent drifts in the air. Belmont is actually cooking. Night has fallen. The heated pool on the patio is lit, and steam rises from its aqua depths. I just took a bath, but I'm tempted to swim some laps. Suddenly I feel Belmont's erection against my butt and his warm hands clutch my waist.

"Hungry?" Belmont asks.

"Starving. What did you make?"

"I warmed up chicken pot pies. The refrigerators are stocked with packaged crap that I would never eat otherwise. They were counting on us being here for a long time."

I bend my neck so that he can nibble on it. "So what are we going to tell Dr. Calvet?"

"Oh, I'll handle the doctor. I called your father and made arrangements."

Belmont's lips are so tender. "And what did he say?"

"He's having the house prepared for you."

"Him or you?"

Belmont spins me around to face him and slides his hands down my arms. "You're so soft." He kisses me. "Both of us."

I'm momentarily dazed. "Both of us are soft?"

He chuckles. "No, Jacques and I are making sure his property is fit for my wife."

I wrap my arms around his neck and devour his lips. He picks me up, and I clasp my legs around him. My stomach growls.

Belmont tosses his head back and groans. "Fuck! I'm going to have to feed you first."

I try to unravel my legs, but he keeps us knotted together. We keep kissing as Belmont carries me to the kitchen.

"So what's this business you have?" I ask as he sets me in a chair.

"Just business, nothing big."

His tone is always dismissive when I want to discuss his business, but this time I press. I want to know more.

"It sounded like something big to me," I say.

"Wait a sec." Belmont trots over to the gourmet oven. He uses a mitten to take out two pot pies on a cookie sheet. "I need to tie up loose ends."

"What loose ends?"

He looks at me curiously then scratches his eyebrow. "You're really interested in my loose ends?"

I smirk. "What's the big deal, Jack Lord? It's a simple question."

He smirks back. "I told you that I like it when you call me Jack."

"Then, Jack, explain your partnership with Harold Doe. I mean, is that even his real name?"

Belmont's smirk transforms into a scowl. "He's my business partner. What else do you want me to explain?"

"I get the impression that he works for you?"

Belmont opens a cabinet and takes out two

plates. "He doesn't work for me, and his real name is Harold."

"Harold Doe sounds too much like John Doe for it to be his real name."

Belmont puts the pot pies on the plates and takes two forks out of a drawer. "Yes, Harold Doe is his real name." He puts a plate in front of me and sits next to me with his plate. "John Doe had to come from somewhere. You know… The Doe family." He grins at his own humor.

I roll my eyes, smirking. "He never says hello, good morning, or anything. It's weird."

"If you'd like for him to speak to you, then I'll talk to him about it."

I grunt. "Don't talk to him about it. I don't care if he speaks to me or not—it's just strange that he doesn't."

Belmont rubs my inner thigh. "He's my business partner, babe, nothing more, nothing less. So eat…" His finger stimulates my clit. He sips air. "Damn it, I love the way this feels. It's hard and swollen. I want it in my mouth."

I should stop him, but I like it. I just don't know if I like the feeling or the fact that it's him who's touching me. I tilt my head back and sigh. Belmont's lips crash down on mine, and in an instant, I'm straddling his lap. He fishes his rigid penis out of his shorts. I lift up and come down on his throbbing girth. We exhale on impact and continue to do what we do best.

THE SEX SESSION ENDS. WE EAT. BELMONT EATS ME. I come hard—over and over and over again. We fuck in the warmed pool—twice. Earlier Belmont asked me to sleep in bed with him, and as usual, he gets his way.

"Are you on Viagra?" I ask.

I'm on top, and he's shifting my hips against his never-ceasing hard-on.

He does something between a gasp and a laugh. "I'm on Daisy Lord."

He grinds a hot spot, which makes me moan. "Is your business taking you back to Chicago?"

"No…"

"No more business there?" I sigh.

"Too risky."

"Risky?"

"Babe. You want to talk about this right now?"

A whimper escapes me. He's trying to pleasure me into silence, and it's working. He bounces me faster against his erection, hammering that spot. I wrap my arms around his neck. He's delaying his orgasm, waiting to hear me scream and for my pussy to pulsate. As soon as it happens, he jabs me deep and lets loose.

We pant and hold each other tight. My breaths come slower, my eyelids are heavier, and my body is fatigued. Belmont guides me in front of him, spoons me, and kisses my ear. Maybe we should stay on the island—like, forever. We should make love until we die. But for now, I fall asleep until he's ready to go again.

We sleep in because Belmont and I screwed all night long. All. Night. Long. I reach for his watch on the nightstand and check the time. It's 2:43 p.m. I blink until I'm more awake. Belmont's body is still pasted to my backside. No matter how hot body contact makes us, he hardly ever lets go of me during the night. So I'm sticky, and I have to pee. I carefully free myself from his grasp.

He stirs and pulls me back into him. "Where are you going?"

He always asks that. "Bathroom."

He lets go. "Hurry."

I scamper to the bathroom and pee. Today's the day. Belmont and I haven't talked about my trip to Bordeaux, and Dr. Calvet is expecting us to be tagged around the ankle and sitting in on his session.

Once I'm done, I crawl back in bed. What happens next isn't a surprise. Belmont moans and squeezes my breast. I feel his thickness rub against the entrance to my pussy. His slippery head circles my snug hole until I'm moist enough for him to break through.

"Shit," he mutters, and I gasp as he sinks his tongue into my ear.

He bobs my hips against his groin. I tighten my muscles around his dick to catch every sensation his thrusts have to offer. I climax before he does. Then he sets me on my knees and enters my pussy from my backside. He whimpers and mutters about how good it feels as he indulgently shifts in and out of me.

"Shit!" He rams his dick deep inside me and holds it there. "Stay still."

I turn to look at him.

He watches me with hooded eyes. "You're so sexy." He trails kisses up and down my back. I pitch my hips back against his cock, and he holds me steady. "Not yet."

Belmont is trying to delay his orgasm. He does this whenever he wants to double the amount of times we make love in a day and night.

He stays inside me as he pulls me against his chest so that we can lie down together. "Shit."

"What is it?" I pet his hair.

"I don't know if I can let you go."

"Then don't."

Silence lingers before he says, "I have to."

"What do you say that?"

"Aren't you tired of going around in circles?"

"Are you counting on absence making our hearts grow fonder? Because we've already had a lot of absence."

"Babe, I just want you to be happy. I need to learn how to make you happy because I've given you all I got."

I frown because he's not making any sense, but he's smart, and I trust him. Maybe he sees something I simply can't. "Okay. I'll fly to Bordeaux. It's time anyway. I haven't seen my grandparents since my freshman year of college. Then there are my *oncles* and *tantes, et beaucoup de cousins...*"

Belmont slowly shifts my hips against his dick,

toying with my pussy. "It turns me on when you speak French."

The very slow way his thickness slides in and out of me feels so good.

"My accent and pronunciation are so bad." I laugh. I twist my body to meet his mouth, and we kiss tenderly.

"Damn it. My dick is sore as hell," Belmont complains, frowning.

I chuckle. "You should've paced yourself."

He grabs my hips. "Stay still."

"You're a masochist!"

"I'm in love with you."

"You mean lust."

"Both."

"I love and lust you too."

He kisses my shoulder, licking, sucking, and gently biting me. "Shit." He bobs my hips against him.

There's loud beeping, and we both look toward the sound.

Belmont strokes me deep and holds himself there. "Is that the fucking ankle monitor?"

"I think so," I barely say.

"I guess it's time." He crashes in and out of me to the sound of the beeping until he blasts off inside me.

I HAVE NO IDEA WHAT BELMONT SAID TO DR. Calvet after we finished making love. I took a shower instead of joining the conversation. I just want to put the whole captivity aspect of our ordeal behind us.

An actual cook made our late lunch of seared scallops with sautéed peaches on a bed of ginger couscous with roasted yams and kale. Belmont was back on the telephone with Harold Doe as we sat at the table. Whatever Harold said seemed to agitate Belmont. As usual, he only responded with "right" and "I see" and "we'll talk later."

After he hung up, Belmont looked as though he wanted to discuss whatever was bothering him, but he kept it to himself. Instead, we talked about my grandparents' farm in Coutras. I recalled how Daniel and I went sheep herding with *Pepe* and washed our clothes with a washboard in a large pail with *Meme*. No matter how Heloise tried to bring my grandparents into the twentieth century, they wouldn't come. I haven't seen them since the turn of the century. I wonder if they've joined the rest of us yet. I told Belmont that I can't wait to see.

"Your eyes dance when you talk about them," he said.

"I didn't notice," I said and wiped the smile off my face. There was no use in admitting that after Daniel died, I gave up on my family. I felt as though everyone had betrayed us by continuing to live. It was stupid of me. What were they supposed to do? Stop living as I had? Stop loving as I had?

"So what did Dr. Calvet say?" I asked to change the subject.

"We'll call him in a few weeks to give him an update."

"Oh… do you think we'll have something good to report?"

Belmont gave me a lopsided smile. "Absolutely."

It's now later in the day, and I'm packing my things. Angelina put a lot of thought into providing for my captivity. She packed all the toiletries a girl needs, plus makeup I hadn't owned in the first place. Half of my clothes are short, sexy dresses, so she did think that, at some point, I'd be seducing Belmont. However, there will be no sexy dress for me today—the jet will be cold. I put on a pair of jeans that are ripped at the knees and thighs and a white V-neck T-shirt. All I have are sandals, which is fine. Belmont has three jets, and I store warm socks on all of them.

"Hey," Belmont says as I zip up the suitcase.

Seeing his beautiful face appear out of nowhere never gets old. "Hey," I say.

He looks at me from head to toe. "You can always make a pair of jeans and a T-shirt sexy."

"Back at you."

We smile at each other and look at the bed.

"Are you ready?" he asks.

I nod.

"I'm going to miss you."

"Ditto."

He walks to me. "The only reason I'm not fucking you right now is because he's sore."

I chuckle. "If he's sore, can you imagine how sore *she* is?"

Belmont frowns as he strokes my neck. "Have I hurt you?"

I look into his eyes. It's so quiet and still. He smells good. He's wearing that cologne I like. Out of nowhere, I'm flooded by new emotions. Has he hurt me? "You have hurt me. We haven't talked about it, but you've hurt me."

Belmont sighs gravely. "You're referring to Stacy?"

I nod as I try to keep from tearing up.

He holds my face to make sure I'm looking into his eyes. "Daisy, baby, I need you to believe me when I say that those pictures looked worse than what actually happened. I told you, I tried to…" He sighs. "I tried to have sex with her, but I kept having mental blockages."

"I know you love me, Belmont."

"I more than love you."

"Then why did you even *try* to have sex with her?"

He says, "Because…"

"Because?"

"Because loving someone else half as much as I love you would be easier."

I think he just knocked the wind out of me. "Why am I so hard for you to love?"

"You're so sad, Daisy. I love to see you laugh. I know if you're laughing, then you're happy, at least for the moment. I don't know how to make you happier. Well, I do, but I'm not God. I can't raise the dead."

I've swallowed his words, and they've choked me until I can't speak.

291

"Listen, babe, Stacy was a stupid-ass, knee-jerk reaction that brought me more misery than it did you. You're the only woman I want to love, make love to, fuck, or do anything else with. I'm going to figure out how to make you happy every goddamn second of the day even if I die trying."

We're staring into each other's eyes.

"It's just… you were intimate with her."

"I know. If I could take it back, I would. I'm sorry… I'm very, very sorry. You can hold my actions against me for as long as you need to get over them, but baby, don't ever leave me again."

I see Belmont's soul behind his eyes. He means every word he just said. "Then…" I clear my throat. "I forgive you."

"I love you," he whispers.

"I love you too."

Belmont's lips covers mine. We kiss as if we're rediscovering each other's tongue and lips. I whimper because I want him so much. Cool air hits my back as my shirt lifts. I raise my arms, and our lips separate momentarily so that Belmont can pull my shirt over my head. He unclamps my bra, and when my tits are freed, his mouth consumes one of my nipples then the other. I run my fingers through his hair as he makes me wet.

"This way," he whispers.

Belmont walks me to the bed and spreads me across the mattress. He snatches his shirt over his head and throws it to the floor. I smooth my hand across the ripples of his chest and torso.

A phone rings. We both look at his pants pocket.

"Is that a cell phone?" I ask.

"Yes."

"Did you have one when you got here?"

"No. I had one brought to me this afternoon."

I frown. "Oh. When did you start putting it in your pocket again?" I thought Angelina had convinced him to keep his cell phone out of his pocket.

Belmont takes out the cell phone and looks at the screen. "I normally don't. I forgot. It's the helicopter operator. He's ready for you."

I try to sit up, but Belmont's hand stops me.

He shakes his head. "He's going to have to wait."

Belmont works faster. He undoes my pants and snatches them off, along with my panties. I figure it'll be a quickie, but he smashes his mouth between my legs, and his tongue slides up and down my slit. The erotic sensation makes me moan. My moaning makes Belmont hornier, and he frees his stiff penis.

"Wait," I say and sit up.

I reach for his dick, but he takes my hand and shakes his head. "No, baby. I don't want you to suck me. I want to feel you." Belmont pins my knees to the mattress. He sucks air as he slowly slides inside me. "You're so wet."

I gasp. "And you're so hard."

We kiss as he shifts his hips. Our souls seek to become one.

"Your pussy is so hot," he mutters. "Baby, when was your last period?"

I frown. "Huh?" I can't believe he's asking me about my period right now.

He sucks air between his teeth. "You're extra hot."

I know what he's trying to insinuate. "I'm not pregnant."

"Says you," he breathes.

"I'm not."

He looks at me with one eye narrowed.

"I'm not," I assure him.

"If you say so." He thrusts into me. "Um…"

We stare into each other's eyes as his dick glides in and out of me. Last week, I would've died if I'd thought I was pregnant. Right now… it wouldn't be such a bad thing. I just don't think I am.

I didn't expect to get off this time, but Belmont hardly ever fails to deliver. I don't know how he does it, but the spark hits me, and I forget all about the word pregnant. I cling to him, and he agitates that hot spot. Our breaths come quicker. I lift my hips and concentrate on making *it* happen.

"Come on, baby," Belmont says.

He wants to hear when I climax. I tense when the most potent part of the sensation hits, and I scream. Belmont jams his dick against that spot, keeping the orgasm alive for as long as he can. I whimper, floating in a mist of pleasure.

"You're feeling it, baby?" he whispers.

"Yes," I sigh.

His dick crashes in and out of me. He shouts then jerks and shivers upon release. Unfortunately, we've made it to the finish line. We hold each other.

"Are you sure you want me to go?" I ask.

Belmont pulls out of me and kisses and licks my pubic bone. "I don't want you to ever leave me." He sucks my clit.

I pitch my head back and lift my hips. Belmont grabs my ass and shoves my pussy closer to his face. He groans, not letting up. I try to grab at something, anything, but nothing is stable enough. Belmont's tongue is ferocious, and all I can do is moan and bear it. When I reach the climactic moment, I feel as if an orgasmic symphony has played its final and grandest note. All I can hear is myself screaming.

Belmont comes up for a kiss and massages my pussy when he's done. "I'm going to miss *her*."

We chuckle and kiss more passionately. He thrusts his fingers deep inside me. I gasp.

"I'll finish my business, then we'll figure out our next step," he says.

I nod.

He pulls his fingers out and pins my arms over my head. He kisses and sucks me in as many places as he can think of until the helicopter pilot calls again.

FAMILY ON THE WALL

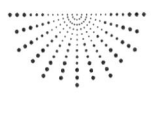

DAISY LORD

*B*elmont takes my luggage to the helicopter. We kiss one last time before I board. I'm positive that the happiest place on Earth for me is lying in his arms. We say our final good-bye; he helps me onto the helicopter and straps me in. Belmont gives me another kiss and tit grope and closes the door. We wave at each other as the helicopter lifts off.

I arrive at the airport, and a cart takes me to the jet. I look at my watch. It's six thirty p.m. I wonder where the hours in this day went. I feel as if Belmont and I just woke up. The sky is overcast, but it's still hot. I board the jet, and the cabin is nice and cool. I find my socks in one of the cabinets. I smile once I see that Belmont has added to my collection.

"Good afternoon, Mrs. Lord."

I turn to see Dan, the flight attendant. Dan is the only guy who isn't related to either of us that Belmont trusts to be alone with me.

"Good afternoon, Dan," I say.

"Would you like your usual coffee?"

I choose the pink socks. "Yes, please."

"Amaretto or French Roast?"

"I would like Amaretto."

"Will you be eating dinner?" Dan asks.

"Um, no, I already ate."

"Then I'll fix you breakfast at least two hours before landing."

"Why don't we play it by ear?"

He smiles. "You're going to have to let me do my job sooner or later."

I chuckle. I usually like to be left alone during my flight. That's the beauty of flying private. Other than a few cups of coffee, and sometimes a meal, I dismiss the flight attendant for the duration of my flight. "You are doing your job. I'm taking the coffee."

He laughs. "Fine, Mrs. Lord. Whatever you want. I'll have a cell phone for you shortly."

"Oh?" It hadn't dawned on me that I was without a cell phone until he mentioned it.

"Mr. Lord ordered it. It just arrived, but your data hadn't been downloaded to the device. Steve is working on it in the control room."

"Oh, he's our pilot?" I ask.

"Yes."

I nod. He's another of Belmont's employees who hardly ever speaks to me.

As soon as my socks are on and I have my coffee, I get comfortable. I don't have my computer, which sucks, so I pull up my subscription to *Point Destination Magazine* on the screen attached to the chair and catch up on all the articles I've missed. Thirty minutes later, the jet is speeding down the runway. It lifts off and gains more altitude as we go.

"This is for you, Mrs. Lord," Dan says as he hands me the cell phone.

I take it. "Oh, thank you."

"It's hooked up to the airplane's service during the flight, so you can use it."

"Great."

He asks if he could get me anything else. I say, no. As soon as I'm alone, I activate the screen. I have one electronic note. It says: *I miss you already. Love, Jack.* I beam as I read the message over and over. I press the phone against my heart and close my eyes, remembering his fingers sliding across my pleasure spot and his tongue finishing the job. I feel our bodies melting and his erection expanding inside me. I smell his skin, taste his mouth, and feel his warm breath on my ear.

The phone rings, and I jump. I fumble as I take it off the chair table. My head is woozy. I must've fallen asleep. "Hello." I sound spastic.

"Daisy?"

I grimace after identifying the voice. "Dexter?"

"Daisy, how the hell are you?" he asks.

"I'm good."

"Jav said your sister and cousin took you out of your apartment on a stretcher. I think her name is Maggie?"

"Oh, yes, Maggie."

"She wouldn't tell him where they were taking you. Are you back in Chicago with your husband?"

"No, I'm on my way to Bordeaux."

"France? What the hell?"

"I'm taking my father up on his offer."

Dexter's disappointment is clear during his silence. "Is your husband with you?"

I feel a pinch of disappointment. "He's not."

"You're on your way to Bordeaux, and your

husband isn't with you?"

He sounded judgmental. "That's what I said," I snarl.

"Do you know what's going on with him?" Dexter asks.

"What do you mean?"

"Then he hasn't told you?"

I roll my eyes. "Just spill it."

"He's been accused of using prostitutes to influence his competitors' bids."

I can't believe what I'm hearing. "What? When did you hear this?"

"Yesterday. It was all over the news."

"Well, he was with me yesterday. We were both exiled on an island."

Dexter goes silent. "You were on an island?"

"Belmont's private island. That's where I was taken. They want us to work on our marriage."

"Shit he has a private island too?"

I detect the bitterness in his tone.

"So is that the only reason you ditched us?" he asks.

I roll my eyes. "Yes, Dexter. I was planning to be on that flight with you and the crew."

"We're in Provence now. Just join us here, and we can keep the show on the road."

"I can't."

"Why the hell not? You're supposed to be here anyway."

I sigh. "I know, I know. And it's so unprofessional of me to just change my mind—"

"Hell, that's the shit you can do when you're married to a guy with Jack Lord's kinds of billions."

I flinch. "Was that a jab?"

"Is it?"

"You tell me."

He sighs forcefully. "Fuck, Daisy. You were supposed to do this with me. And now you're on your way to Bordeaux? I thought…" He sighs. "I thought we were getting somewhere with each other."

I'm speechless. I didn't believe Dexter had deep feelings for me, especially after his booty call on Saturday night. So heck, Belmont was right about him! But I'm more worried about the ordeal with Belmont than Dexter's feelings. Was what Dexter just told me the reason Belmont looked so severe while he was speaking to Harold Doe?

"Listen, I have to go," I say. I need to call Belmont.

"So that's it? You quit?"

"I'm sorry, but television production isn't where

my head is at the moment."

"Then where is it, Daisy?"

I'm hit by a brief dose of confusion. "I don't know…" I chuckle. "But I better find out, right?"

He grunts. "Where are you staying in Bordeaux?"

"At my father's house, but I'm not looking for any company."

"I'm not offering my company."

Awkward silence lingers.

"Okay, well… maybe we can meet one day. Have lunch or drinks," I say.

"You mean I have drinks and you have a drink?"

I chuckle. "Deal, then?"

"Damn it, Daisy. I can't stay mad at you."

I grin. "Good luck on the show. It'll be great. Don't hesitate to call me if you have any questions. After all, you're using my material."

"I'm going to hold you to that."

"You do that."

"Later, Daisy."

"Later, Dexter."

I hang up and call Belmont, but he doesn't answer, which never happens. He could be on the losing end of a sword fight and still take my phone call, so I'm sort of freaked out. I leave a message asking him to call me because a friend told me some disturbing news about him. No need to mention that that friend was Dexter.

I take a deep breath to settle myself and look out over the Atlantic Ocean. I want to ask the pilot to fuel up when we land and fly me back to the United States so that I can find Belmont and stay by his side, but it occurs to me that Belmont isn't the kind of man who needs or wants me to stand by his side. He's really an island. He invited me onto his island, but he's the ruler and I'm the resident—and that is our problem in a nutshell.

I relax and try to figure out the best way to approach this issue, which is a non-issue to most of the world. I'm exhausted from last night and this morning. Truthfully, I got more rest after we split. Belmont and I can go all night, no matter what sort of tension exists between us. I could never do that with Adrian. Whenever we argued, I couldn't let him touch me until we resolved the issue, which generally ended with him or me giving the other a half-hearted apology.

I sink into my seat, pull up my socks, and wrap myself in a blanket. I close my eyes, and soon I'm sitting on a checkered blanket near the edge of a stony hillside above the slow and murky La Dordogne River in Bordeaux. A tepid breeze blows against my face. Strong hands are massaging my shoulders.

"That feels good," I say and fall back into his fingers.

"You feel good."

I gasp and look behind me into Dexter's light blue eyes.

"Lay back," he says.

My heart pounds with panic. "What are you doing here?"

"We should finish our kiss."

"There's no kiss to finish."

"Oh yes, there is." He narrows one eye naughtily. "Come on, Daisy. Admit it. You want me."

I shake my head. "No."

"Then kiss me again."

"No."

"Mrs. Lord?" Dan says.

I gasp as my eyes open. The cabin is dusky. I scramble to sit up. Dan's hand is on my shoulder. "Yes?"

"Are you okay?" he asks.

"Um, yes."

He removes his hand. "We'll be landing in

about an hour." He still looks disturbed.

"Okay."

"Can I get you breakfast?"

I'm prepared to say I'm not hungry, but actually, I'm starving. "Yes, please." I take my cell phone out of the compartment on the arm of my seat.

"Oh, good!" He sounds surprised. "How about another cup of coffee, French Roast this time?"

My heart stops when I see a text message from Belmont. "Yes, please." I read it as Dan walks away. *Don't worry, babe. Everything is being handled. I love you. P.S. Who's this friend?*

My smile turns upside down. I know better than to tell Belmont I had a conversation with Dexter. I turn off the phone and wait for breakfast and coffee.

IT'S FRIDAY AT SEVEN A.M. WHEN I WALK DOWN THE ramp in France. It's cool, but it'll warm up later. Dan, who's behind me, carries my suitcase to a cab that waits off the tarmac. The driver is a tall, trim guy with brown hair that's pulled back into a pony-tail and brown bedroom eyes. I've met a lot of cabbies but never one as attractive as him. The driver leans against the hood of the car, studying Dan and me as we shake hands and say good-bye. I slip into the back. The driver sneers and trots around to the driver's seat. He turns on the radio, and we take off to avant-garde instrumental music.

I haven't visited Bordeaux in ages, so everything is new to me again. I like that the driver's slower speed gives me a chance to delight in a landscape that changes from a barren field with radio towers placed in a single-file line, to lines of trees that look like fat cotton balls on toothpicks, to muddy lakes, to petrol stations and communities of houses bunched together off the side of the road, to the lone but homey farmhouse peppered here and there.

"I am called Daisy," I finally say to the cab driver in French. I've been avoiding eye contact because I could feel him watching me with that pucker of skin between his eyes.

"I'm Anton," he replies in English. He grimaces as if it was a chore to tell me his name.

I smile anyway. "So where are you taking me, Anton?"

"We are going to Chateau Mes Fleurs."

I'm stunned. "A chateau?" A chateau is very different from a house.

"Yes, that is right. You did not know?"

"No, I didn't. A chateau has a vineyard. Does it have a vineyard?"

"Yes."

It dawns on me that the chateau is called My Flowers, and my father calls Angelina and me his flowers. Usually the name of the chateau is the same as its brand of wine. The gesture is surprising. I never believed Jacques had an ounce of fatherly sentimentality until the concert on Saturday night. Once again, he has taken me by surprise.

We pass fields of pine trees and more farm-houses with oversized windows, white shutters, stocky chimneys, and red brick roofs. I drink in the scenery.

"This is gorgeous. Do you live near here?" I ask.

He eyes me curiously. "I live close."

"And do you love it?"

"When I love life, yes."

I chuckle. "Are you in love with life now?"

"Today she is adequate."

"Yes, *he* is." I wink at him, and his eyes smile back.

The clock on the dashboard says we've been on the road for forty-one minutes, and according to a road sign, we've just passed Cercoux. Anton veers off the main road and onto a lonelier one. Fields of wild grass lie on both sides of us. I love everything about wild grass—the touch, the look, and the smell of it.

I'm fighting the urge to bait Anton into chauffeuring me around for my taxicab series, but I didn't come here to work. Hell, I don't even know why I came here, but I know it's not to work. Plus, Anton isn't a talker, so I would have to work extra hard to soften him up. I catch him leering at me again but not in a lustful way. He acts as if he's waiting for some sort of expectation to be met.

I ignore him and pay attention to the grass, which gives way to a murky lake. A lonely man wearing a light jacket and a dark cap rows an old canoe across the water. I twist in my seat, studying him until rows of grapevines layer the landscape, blocking my view. It appears as if we're now on the outskirts of a vineyard. I narrow my eyes to see how the fruits are growing. The clusters are thick, and the grapes are green and solid. The car rounds a corner, and the tires crunch dirt as we roll up a narrow path. The vines seem to go on for an eternity. We're moving up an incline, and I can see the lake again out the back window. I look for the man rowing the boat, but he's not in sight.

The car is traveling up a driveway. The lawns on both sides are cut, the shrubs are trimmed, and the trees give the grounds a mystical ambiance. I love the flower gardens sprouting here and there across the lawn, but nothing is more awe-inspiring than the chateau itself. It's a castle. It has a mansard roof with a tower rising on each side. Ornate details are carved into the walls, and an arched pavilion covers the front porch. I snort and shake my head. Jacques knew exactly what he was doing when he told me this place was a house. If I had known the estate was this massive, I would've never agreed to come here. I feel duped.

"You don't like it?" Anton asks.

I'm frowning. "It's just… huge. That's all."

"You don't like big?"

"Not necessarily."

Anton and I get out of the car. I can't take my eyes off the castle. The trunk slams.

"Are you ready?" Anton asks. He intends to carry my luggage to the front door.

"I got it. The suitcase rolls, and it's not that heavy," I say.

"Whatever you want." He looks me in the eyes as he hands me the suitcase. There's something familiar about him.

"Okay…" I open my purse and take out my wallet.

He holds up a hand. "No need to pay me."

I snort. "Right."

He narrows one eye. "What do you mean by 'right'?"

"My husband paid you?"

He looks at my right hand. "You are married?"

"Oh, yes," I say, realizing he's looking for the ring that I stopped wearing months ago.

"Me too," he says.

I look at his left hand. He's not wearing a ring. Is he mocking me? "Right." I refuse to get into an argument with a driver who has been sort of brusque thus far.

He smirks a little and trots to the driver's side of his car. "Is good to see you, Daisy."

"Nice to meet you too," I say, although he said, "good to see you." That implies he's seen me before.

The car drives off, and I watch until it's out of sight. Now there's no turning back. I stomp up the steps, bang the brass knocker against the door, and wait. A fly buzzes around my head. I swat at the fly, knock again, and continue to wait. I grow more frustrated. How I am I supposed to get into the house? I turn the knob, and the door opens. A sweet floral scent lingers in the air.

"Hello!" I call.

I stand still and count to ten before I take a few steps and look into the room to the left. It's a huge living room filled with modern furniture and the sort of abstract textile wall art Belmont likes. I would think this castle belonged to him if I weren't so sure it was Jacques'. The floating shelves, obscure trinkets, and angular furniture have man-taste written all over them. There's even a huge installation against the wall that looks like three pieces of torn metal. After I study it closely, I see the naked man in the middle with his head leaning forward and his arm behind him. The floors and fireplace look original, and the fireplace has been refurbished.

I take out my cell phone and call Belmont. My call goes straight to voicemail. I start to leave a message, then I end the call. I suspect he's trying to teach me a lesson on how it feels to be without him. I'm too frustrated to give Belmont's games much thought. I place another call, and it's answered on the second ring.

"*Ma fleur!*" Jacques sings.

"Hello, Papa, guess where I am?"

"I know where you are."

"Guess how surprised I was to see a mansion—no, a castle—instead of a house."

"Where are you?"

"France," I say as if that's obvious.

He chuckles. "I know you're in France. I meant what part of the house are you in?"

"Oh, I just walked through the front door. First of all, is this place haunted?"

Jacques laughs. "Are you afraid of ghosts?"

"No, but these sorts of dwellings always have something supernatural lurking in the walls, through the quarters, and in the old cellar. I know—I do a lot of traveling. So it's not a matter of me being afraid as much as a matter of me being on vacation and not wanting to deal with that right now."

"Baby, there's nothing lurking in the house. I promise you that," he says. "But that hallway you're standing in?"

"Yes?"

"Look straight ahead."

I sigh impatiently and do as I'm told. "I see a wall."

"It's not a dead end. Go ahead and walk toward it."

313

I roll my suitcase up the hallway. Without really paying attention, it's tough to see an option to go left or right at the end of the hallway. On one side is a door marked "Studio." It appears as if the room takes up the entire first floor. Of course Jacques would have a studio that big built into his chateau. I grin. That's one thing I've always liked about my father; he's mostly predictable. I see sunlight trapped in a room on the other side of the hallway.

The studio is to the left. "I should go right?" I say.

It takes Jacques a moment. "Yes, go right."

I follow his direction.

"Do you see the patio?" he asks.

I feel relieved. "I see it."

"That'll lead to the back," he says. "You'll see tall hedges on the other side of the courtyard. There are three private cottages behind it, but Anton is living in one of them."

"Whoa. You mean Anton, the driver?" I ask, surprised.

"He's your cousin. You don't remember Anton?"

"No! Why didn't he say anything?"

The phone crackles.

"I have to go," he says in a rush. "I had the

south cottage prepared for you. Meals are in the main house, but Inés is supposed to bring you bread and cheese every morning. Love you, baby."

"Okay. Love you too, Papa."

"That's what I like to hear. Call me if you need to."

"I will."

I walk through the garden patio, which has views of the valley, and through an alcove, which leads to the back of the house. The courtyard takes my breath away. There's a long swimming pool in the center of a healthy lawn, which is surrounded by shrubs cut into boxes, circles, and upside-down and right-side-up triangles. White jasmine flowers have been planted all along the red-brick walkway. The sweet fragrance makes me feel as if I've bitten into a piece of heaven. I can see the brick-shingled rooftops and chimneys of the cottages, but just as my father said, a thick line of shrubs hides their walls.

I fight the urge to strip off my clothes and jump into the swimming pool. I still can't believe Anton didn't say, "Hey by the way, we're cousins." I finally remember him. His father is Jean Luc, Heloise's younger brother. Anton and Daniel were better friends than he and I were. I remember his family visiting us in L.A. Heloise chastised Daniel and me for not welcoming our cousins and made us stay home to entertain them. I couldn't wait until the entire family left. I also remember Anton thinking I was a boy, though I didn't care to enlighten him. Back then, I thought the week they visited was the worst five days in my life.

I round the hedges and go up a cobblestone walkway. A plush green lawn fills the ground in front of the quaint cottages. Each house has a white french door entrance with views of the grape vines and the winery in the distance, and I walk inside the far south cottage. It's nice, cozy, and furnished in the French country style. I go into the living room and open the large windows. Fresh air flows over me. In the tiny kitchen, a cheese platter sits on a wooden table. Suddenly I'm starving, and I dig in. Oh, French cheese made of sheep's milk is one of the tastiest foods on the planet. I devour the bread and cheese.

I satisfy my stomach then head to the bedroom. I'll be sleeping on a four-poster bed set against an exposed brick wall. Sheer floral-patterned curtains hang from the rails. The bed is so gorgeous and inviting that not only do I want one for myself, I want to strip off my clothes, go into the kitchen for the rest of the cheese platter, and eat in bed until my belly is tight and all I can do is lay on my back and dream of the last time Belmont ravaged me. I should also think about my next article. I need to publish soon in order to stay relevant. I sit on the mattress and bounce a couple of times to test its comfort. *It's very comfortable.*

I go to the bathroom which, for me, is the most important room in any house. Actually, the bathroom is where my and Belmont's tastes find harmony. I love a decadent one. I have to step down into the bathroom in the cottage. The walls are made of frosted glass and red brick. A European-style bathtub is on a platform in the middle of the room, and it's calling my name.

"Oh my," I whisper.

I kick off my sandals, stomp out of my jeans, and snatch off my tank top. I run the bath water and find the towels, loofa, and jasmine bath soap. As soon as my bath is ready, I grab my cell phone and get in. There's another person I must speak to as soon as possible. So I find her name in my contact list and place a call to her.

The phone rings twice, and then, "Hello."

"Angelina?"

"Daisy? Is this you?"

I put the phone on speaker and set it on a wooden stand next to the tub. "It's me."

"Oh..."

I smirk at her surprise. "Did you think I'd still be confined to an island without access to my cell phone?"

"Are you? I mean, still on the island?"

"No, I'm not on the island anymore. Belmont saved us." I sink into the water until my shoulders are covered. "Although I have no idea where he is at the moment."

Angelina is silent.

"Angel?" I ask.

"I'm just… what about the ankle monitors?"

"Belmont took it off of me."

She sighs with relief. "Oh my God… I'm so sorry, Daisy. Tell me you're not mad at me."

"You were only trying to help. I just don't understand why you cooked up such an extreme scheme. It had to have taken a lot of planning to pull off."

"You have no idea. But I don't think you guys will make it without real help."

I'm silent as I look at my hands waving through the water in front of me. Belmont and I definitely need real help. Our problems aren't glaring. They can only be seen through a professional lens. "I understand. But how did you even do it?"

"At first we were just going to wait until the party."

"Your engagement party?" I ask.

"It wasn't a real engagement party."

I slap the water, splashing my face. "I knew it!"

"Are you taking a bath?"

"Yeah, I'm actually outside of Bordeaux. In a castle…"

"You're at Chateau Mes Fleurs?"

"You've been here?" I sound as surprised as I am.

"Many times."

"I'm not the only one here. I have a cousin on the premises. Anton…"

"Anton Bisset?" she says.

"You know him?"

"He's your mother's brother's son, which makes him and me unrelated, but Papa still considers him family, so I know him. Like *know* him, know him."

"Ha! No way!" I say.

"Yes way."

"Oh my God. He's strange. Do you know he never even mentioned we were related?"

"He probably thought you should've known who he was," Angelina says. "He's crazy like that."

"Crazy?"

"Crazy in a good way."

"How can one be crazy in a good way?"

"He's an artist—an exciting and tormented one."

"Tormented?" I ask.

"You know like, *tormented*." I visualize her putting her shoulder into the word "tormented" as she says it.

"Oh, got it."

"He dropped out of college and became hooked on drugs. Then he put his life back together, and now he's a well-known artist. He makes a lot of money."

"He said he's married. Is he?"

"I don't think so, unless it happened in the last two years."

"I figured he was just being facetious." I roll my eyes. "Whatever."

"I'm so sorry for putting you on that island. I regretted it the minute I left you lying on that bed. You were knocked out, and I just didn't want to leave you that way."

I sigh as I sit up. "Stop apologizing, Angel.

What's done is done, and you were only trying to help."

"But what would happen to all of us if you and Belmont get a divorce?"

"Who are the 'all of us' you're referring to?"

"Maggie…"

"Maggie is like family."

"Me and you…"

I'm taken aback. "Angelina, we're sisters. Nothing can tear us apart."

"I don't know about that. I'm the one who's always calling you."

"But I just called *you*."

"It doesn't happen often."

I frown and shake my head. I can't believe what I'm hearing. "Like I said, we're sisters. I'm not going anywhere. I love you."

"You say that now."

"I know I suck at relationships—well, healthy ones at least—but I'm getting better at them as I sit here and soak in this royal tub." I spread my hand across the withering suds. "My husband isn't answering my calls though. Have you heard from him?"

"No, I haven't," she says.

"What about Charlie?"

"No. I don't know if you've heard, but there are some stunning allegations against Belmont."

I sigh hard. "I heard, but he and I haven't talked about it. He sent me a text telling me not to worry."

"Well, Maggie's been working on clearing his name, and your friend is attached at her hip."

"What friend?"

"The English guy."

"Javar Les?" I flinch, splashing water all over the place.

"He was in the apartment when we came to get you, and he just sort of latched on to Maggie."

I shake my head. "Yes, because he's a human leech. Maggie's got to get him off her butt, or he'll stay there."

Angelina chuckles. "He's actually helping her a lot, and he definitely wants you to know about it."

I roll my eyes. "Then Maggie knows where Belmont is?"

"I don't think so, Dais. She would've called me and said something like 'Shit, take cover, they're off the island.'"

I smirk at her sarcastic humor. "Which didn't happen?"

"Didn't happen."

"Okay then..."

Angelina and I chuckle.

"I love you," I say.

"I love you, too."

Angelina agrees to call me as soon as the brothers make contact. I invite her and Charlie to the chateau, but Angelina doesn't think it's a good idea for her to see Anton. They apparently had a pretty steamy relationship.

I finish my bath and put on a purple spaghetti-strap T-shirt dress. I don't have my computer or my backpack, two things I never hit the road without. There's a camera on my new phone, so at least I can take pictures. I put on my sandals, stuff my mouth with more cheese and crackers, and head out. I walk down the grassy hill into the vineyard, snapping away. I love the way the soil feels under my feet. I squeeze the grapes, testing their ripeness. They're too firm to taste.

When I find the winery, I take a gamble and push the barn door, and surprisingly, it opens. I walk among the barrels, snapping shots. I'm the only one here, but I see a wine-covered rag on a bench, and it's pretty fresh. Someone was here not long ago, maybe yesterday or the day before. I take shots of the rafters and the lights attached to them.

I get a close-up of the brick pillars. Other than that rag, everything is so neat and in place.

To up the adventure factor, I exit out a different door, which puts me on a pathway. Three feet in front of me is a field of trees: pines, oaks, and other wild types. I succumb to my impatience and walk through the wild. Low brush scratches my calves. Dirt slithers between my toes. I glance back at the castle just to get an idea of where I am. It's not far away, but if I remember correctly, the lake is nearby. I cross the road and keep walking until I'm beyond the grapevines and looking out over the lake. The narrow waterway snakes across the valley. It was probably cut to irrigate the fields. I make myself a seat in the grass, hug my legs, and bask in this perfect moment.

I hear brakes squeal to a halt. I look behind me and see Anton getting out of a car.

"Hello, cousin," I say.

He grins and walks in my direction. I just noticed that his car isn't a cab, though perhaps it was at one time. The roof is painted black, but the body is a faded yellow. It's not the kind of car a man who makes "a lot of money" would drive. However, Anton doesn't strike me as the type who collects status symbols.

"You like lakes?" he asks.

"Only the muddy ones." I smile.

Anton scans the cliff that dives into the bank of the lake and the trees on the other side of the water. "To me, it's old. To you, it's new. Maybe that's what you like. The new." He sits beside me.

I snort. "Another man trying to tell me what I feel."

"Ah ha. Is that why you do not wear your ring?"

I wiggle my ring finger. "I would wear it if I had it. Peculiar circumstances landed me here without it or my husband."

"I see."

"Do you?"

Anton digs into the soil with the heel of his brown leather shoe. They're nice shoes. He's the kind of man who thinks about what he wears.

"You did not remember me," he says.

I snicker. "You spoke to Jacques?"

He nods.

"If you'd said something, then I would've looked closer and recognized you."

His chuckle is quiet. "I last saw you at your brother's funeral."

"I didn't see you, but that doesn't mean you weren't there. I didn't see anyone."

"This I know. You only saw your grief."

My memories want to carry me back to those days, but I won't allow that. "I do remember your family visiting us before then."

Anton tilts his head and studies me. "Home is for losers."

I snort. "Daniel's motto."

"My brother and I thought we were cool until we met you and Daniel."

"We didn't do anything that was particularly 'cool,'" I say.

"You were, as they say, laid-back. That was cool."

I chuckle. "All Californian kids are laid-back. It's the air we breathe."

"No, it was the freedom. When we came in, you and Daniel were leaving. You had skateboards, very long ones."

"Ah, our longboards."

He points at his head. "You wore *calottes*."

"Our beanies."

"You both had long hair."

"I remember you and Leon thought I was a boy," I say.

"You remember my brother's name?"

"I remember you both clearly. You don't look that much different now than you did then."

He laughs and rubs his face. "I look old, but you are very beautiful, Daisy. You are no more a tomboy."

"You don't look old. I think back then, I was trying to become Daniel, and Daniel wanted me to become Daniel."

He nods, grinning nostalgically. "You would have gotten away with ditching us if my mother had not asked Tante Heloise where you had gone all day."

I laugh as I remember why we got in so late from our excursion that day, which had started so early in the morning. "Daniel and I got separated because some guys on Venice Beach tried to steal my skateboard. We took off running in different directions to confuse them." I chuckle as the memories race through my head. "I jumped a rail and ended up on a patio bar. Even though I was under-age, they let me stay because I told them I was being chased. A pack of drunk guys realized I was a girl, and they went after the boys chasing me. It was the sort of crazy day Daniel and I used to always have."

"I never said I'm sorry, but I'm sorry," he says.

I flinch. "Sorry for what?"

"That my mother complained."

"Oh, I was a selfish little snot-faced kid. Daniel and I were just lucky nothing seriously bad ever happened to us. We teetered on the line of getting our butts kicked by punk kids every day." I smile. "But I pouted about being on house arrest longer than Daniel did. He had a way of making a bad situation go up in smoke."

He nods while smiling at the grass. "We had fun."

"Jumping off the skateboard and into the swimming pool," I say.

"You were daredevils…"

I chuckle, then we sit in silence. The memories fade into the distance, where they belong.

I smile impishly. "So you and Angelina?"

Anton laughs. "You have spoken to Angel?"

My eyes are lit by anticipation as I bobble my head.

He shrugs. "She is beautiful."

"Beauty's never enough, is it?"

"Her soul is beautiful. Her face and her heart are beautiful. Her dance is beautiful. Her body is beautiful. Her mind is…"

"Beautiful?"

He shakes his head. "Full."

I can't help but chuckle. Anton is as melodramatic as most artists, but so far, he's not as narcissistic.

"Is full a bad thing? Women shouldn't have *full* thoughts?" I ask.

"A woman's thoughts should not only be full but infinite. Women are men, and men are women. We dream together or not at all."

"Wow… deep."

"Not deep. True."

There's the arrogance. "And so who was the infinite dreamer: you or Angelina?"

"Angelina was the infinite dreamer. I was kicking a habit." He bumps his finger against his nose and sniffs, indicating that his addiction was cocaine.

"*Les enfants perdus de Bisset*. The lost children of Bisset," I say. "By the way, in case you're wondering, she's happy and in beautiful love with my brother-in-law, whom she's infected with her beauty."

"Infected?"

"I guess he let her make him beautiful too, because he was a hot mess when I first met him— but then, do people actually save people?"

Anton rifles through his pants pocket. He takes

out a pack of cigarettes and lights one. He doesn't ask if I mind, but the French never do. I do mind, but there's nothing I can do about it.

I stand. "I think I'm going to go home."

He looks at me with a grimace. "To the United States?"

I nod. "Yeah... it's time I get back to my husband."

Anton offers me his cigarette. I shake my head.

He snorts. "You almost made me believe you were a French woman."

I laugh.

He hops to his feet. "Stay. We can go to a party."

I pull back. "A party?"

"Yes. Do you dance?"

"Sometimes."

"You can stay, get to know me and I can know you."

I twist my mouth contemplatively. I'm dragging it out, but he's already convinced me. "A party?"

"Yes."

I narrow one eye. "It's not going be a tame, family, wine-and-kids kind of party, is it?"

"Kids? Like goats? We can have goats but *enfants* —no. We will, as you say, have a blast."

"Okay… then sign me up!"

"You said, yes?"

"That's a definite, yes."

Anton's smile matches mine. "I am happy. Come, I'll drive you."

This time, I take the front seat, and Anton drives us to the main house. We enter through the front door and are met by a plump French lady. Anton sweeps his arm around her waist, kisses her cheek, and asks her to make dinner taste special for ma fleur of Mes Fleurs.

"Ah…" The lady shakes my hand and tells me that her name is Inés.

"Je m'apelle Daisy."

However, Inés is done humoring me. She waves her tiny hand and tells us that dinner will be ready soon. Anton takes me on a tour of what he deems the only interesting part of the house. We climb the spiral staircase to the castle tower. The brick walls have been painted white, and portraits are tacked to them.

"Look. Pépé and Mémé," Anton says.

I move in close to get a good look at a black-and-white photo of our grandparents. She's in his arms, and he's spinning her as they dance. "They look happy."

"They are happy."

Our grandparents visit Heloise and Joseph once a year, but I've never felt the need to stop by to say hello. I'm too ashamed to admit that to Anton.

"Papa said they're in Switzerland," I say.

"You are a travel writer?"

"I am."

"Like you, they love to travel," he says.

"Maybe I inherited the bug from them."

"There is no doubt."

Anton continues my schooling. I like him. He knows I haven't seen our grandparents in over twenty years, but no part of him knows to judge me for it. We stop to admire photos of his parents, his brother, and his little sister. I've never met her. We stop at one of Angelina. Anton slides the backs of his fingers down her face and moves on without comment. There's a picture of my aunt who lives in Washington, DC. Her name escapes me for moment, but then it comes to me—Lorraine Nestor. There are my father's brothers: Cyprus, and Pey and Dongo, who are a set of extremely handsome twins. Gosh, I haven't seen them in eons. By the time we make it to the top, I feel terribly guilty but also curious. I'm not the only one who was left out of the hall of family—so is Anton.

16
ONLY THE COURAGEOUS

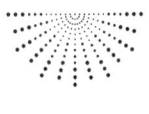

DAISY LORD

*A*nton and I talk about his work over chicken thighs sautéed in onions, garlic, mushrooms, balsamic vinegar, and white wine. We're on our second bottle of Mes Fleurs red wine, and I'm on my second helping of the mouth-watering dish Inés made.

"It's a… a… fucking lose-lose situation, love is. I eat what he wants me to eat. I live the way he wants me to live. I fly on his jet. I haven't published an article in a year. Nobody takes me seriously anymore. I'm the chick who gave up her *vivre* for a boy—no, a man. He's a man. I'm…" I gulp down the wine that's left in my glass.

Anton pours me another. I've already decided to drink until I can't.

"No, Daisy, you cannot disappoint me, your cousin. A long time ago, you had courage. You were a superhero, able to leap over a swimming pool on a skateboard—or die trying."

We giggle. I feel extra silly and uninhibited.

Anton simmers down. "But your husband, he believes what men have taught him, and you feel what God has made you. How do you resolve the difference?" He shrugs.

My head is spinning, but I want it to go faster, so I take another healthy swig. "You're asking me? I have no idea what you're talking about."

"Jacques says that you and I are alike. That means you understand perfectly. Try."

I slump deeper in my seat, close my eyes, and give it the old college try. "You're talking about people, right?"

He chuckles. "Look at me."

I open one eye. He's blurry until I manage to focus.

"I am one human. I am what's wrong and right in the world. Evil and good are human. They are people who make choices. They use their hands, their mouths, and their minds. Look at me, Daisy." Anton holds up his hands and spreads his fingers. "I am human only. I am what's wrong and right in the world."

Like me, Anton has had too much to drink, which in his case seems to make him philosophical Anton. His bedroom eyes are more hooded as he engages in passionate sex with his intellect.

I raise a finger. "I like that. Repeat it tomorrow when I'm sober. I want to remember it."

"I want to show you something. Can you walk?"

"Could you help me if I can't?"

"I can. Come," he says.

I polish off most of the wine in my glass. Anton grabs the bottle. I stand too fast and tumble over. Anton catches me, and I wrap my arm around his neck.

"You are steady?" he asks.

I take a deep breath. "Yeah… let's go."

Anton guides me out of the kitchen and down the dusky hallway.

"Four glasses of wine is all it takes?" he asks.

"Actually, it only takes one."

We make it to the patio, and shortly after, the cool night air collapses around my face. I take a deep breath.

"That is good. Breathe deep. It will help," Anton says.

I take more deep breaths, and the oxygen settles me. Anton sings in French about a woman who adorns herself for a man who's in love with another woman. Then he sings in a dialect I scarcely understand.

"What's that language?" I ask as we sweep past the swimming pool and around the hedges.

"It's Basque."

"Yes, yes, I've heard it before. Did you sleep with a Basque woman for seven years?"

"I fucked her for seven days."

"And that's all it took?"

"I'm a smart man."

I snicker as we walk up the steps to the middle cottage. "You're such an amusing bullshitter. I got it," I assure Anton.

"You can stand on your own?"

"Yes."

He carefully lets go of me, and I steady myself. At least for now, I'm in control. Anton opens the door, but he still helps me inside, which is a good call.

The living room has no furniture in it, only paintings on easels.

Anton walks me to one particular piece. "This is it…"

I open my eyes extra wide to focus on the design. It's a silhouette of a woman and man emerging from a grain of wheat.

"It's…" I whisper. I don't know why this one painting is arousing tear-provoking emotions within me, but it is. "What does it mean?"

"The man and woman are brand new. They have not heard humans tell them who they should become; only God has spoken to them. They are Adam, Daisy, and so are you."

Suddenly I understand, and I don't know why, but tears roll down my eyes. "I'm sorry," I say. And I do apologize for my reaction to his work.

"Your tears are one result I seek."

Anton and I stare into each other's eyes. My tears just keep rolling. He's showing me that I should never lose my independence, that Belmont and I are identical. We have to find a way to make his independence and my independence our independence.

"Now what am I to do?" I ask Anton.

"Do what is natural," he says.

I wipe my eyes. "Right."

"Or wrong."

I sniff back the rest of my tears and point at the bottle in his hand. "Let's just finish that."

He lifts the bottle. "Do you mean this one or those?" He points toward the table, where there are more bottles and an untouched cheese platter.

"As much of it as we can."

Anton tilts his head toward the table. "Okay, we drink!"

BELMONT LORD

After the helicopter carried Daisy away, Belmont felt the impact of her absence. When she actually had an answer for how her life would be without him, he knew they would be in trouble. Even though she'd said that she would be in Bordeaux, he pictured her at a nightclub called Divin in Paris. It was a place where the wealthy, and the women and men who were drawn to affluence, mingled. He imagined Daisy in a red dress made of a soft, slinky material. It was short and tight around her velvety thighs. Her hair was wild, just the way he liked it. She had split the aisle, strolling toward him. All the men desired her, but Daisy had chosen him to give her the world. He was willing to offer her the universe and so much more.

But then he realized something—he would've never run into Daisy in a place like Divin, or anywhere else he used to frequent to meet women. So he changed the scenario in his head to Daisy with a pack on her back, wearing a sleeveless T-shirt dress and worn ankle boots. Her wild hair was tied in a bun on top of her head, but loose strands had broken free. She was walking through a vineyard, snapping shots with her camera phone as she usually did. She didn't have stimulating a man's sex drive on her brain, but the way her dress rested against her firm nipples and the crease of her ass made him want to take her down in the grape fields and sink his dick into the tightest, warmest, wettest place on earth. He couldn't suppress his lust for her. He had hoped it would subside to a normal level after being married for nearly two year, but it hadn't, and he didn't think it ever would. If only sex was all they needed.

There was a part of Daisy that he couldn't understand, or perhaps find credible. Didn't all women want his wealth? As far as looks went, he was tops. He wasn't a jerk—he gave her what she wanted. Yeah, his favorite place for his dick to be was inside her, but he made sure it was pleasurable for her. So what the hell was he doing so wrong? He had to find out. He'd told her to go to Bordeaux because he planned to arrive shortly thereafter, but he did not lie to her. First, he had business to take care of.

The helicopter disappeared from sight, and Belmont hurried into the house. He headed back to the control room to contact Dr. Calvet. A few seconds after Belmont pinged him, Dr. Calvet answered.

"Belmont," Dr. Calvet said.

"You said we should have a session before I leave. Well, I'm here."

"It is good you decided to take my offer."

"Yes, well, you went overboard with the ankle monitors. I considered reporting you for that alone."

"I understand. I do apologize. When I was told that the sexual aspect of your relationship was excessive, I thought I might use sex as an unconditional stimulus," Dr. Calvet said.

"Excessive?"

"A lot of sex is good for your marriage. As it is said, the more the merrier. The question I want to ask you is the same one I asked you to think about. What do you, Belmont, want from Daisy?"

"I don't want a damn thing from her. I give her everything she wants."

Dr. Calvet raised a finger. "No. That is an answer from a man who has not given thought to the question. Take your time. So I ask again. Belmont, what do you want from Daisy?"

Belmont took a moment to consider his physical and mental state. His body was tense, so he relaxed. He was standing, so he sat. He pressed his temples to clear the anger and frustration from his head.

"I will rephrase the question," Dr. Calvet said when Belmont still didn't answer. "A husband and wife require parts of each other. What parts have you required from Daisy?"

Belmont didn't speak the answer that came to him, but he knew he had been requiring Daisy's soul. He wanted her near him. He wanted to smell her and taste her. He had found *the one*, and he wanted to possess her.

"I require her love," Belmont said.

"I see…" Dr. Calvet looked down as though he was writing something. "You grew up in Denver, Colorado?"

The tension rushed back into Belmont's shoulders. He rounded them to take out the tightness. "Yes."

"Tell me about your father."

Belmont snorted. The doctor had been talking to Charlie. "What about him?"

"When I ask this question of people who had a positive experience with a parent, they do not ask what you just asked me."

"He was a bastard. It sounds like Charlie filled you in on him."

"He was rich?"

"Very."

"You are a very rich man, no?" Dr. Calvet asked.

Belmont grimaced. "Your point?"

Dr. Calvet sighed wearily. "Belmont, you must make this easier. I am here to help you, not hurt you."

Belmont nodded. The man had a point. Belmont was a guarded son of a gun, and when he thought about it, Daisy had tried to make him realize that. "Okay, I'm wealthy. My father's rich too, but I never used a penny of that bastard's money to build my wealth. I used his name though. I earned it by putting up with the shit that comes with being his son. But his money? Never a penny of it."

"I see…" Dr. Calvet nodded. "We do not have the time we would have had if you and Daisy had chosen to stay, so I go straight to the matter. Use adjectives to describe your father, like nice, good, bad, etcetera."

"Bitter, cold, ornery, mean, controlling, bastard, hypocritical, weak."

"I see. What about your mother?"

Belmont started to speak but stopped. "Are you trying to draw correlations here? Because I'm nothing like my father."

"I asked about your mother, and you refer to your father?"

"Daisy's nothing like my mother."

Dr. Calvet looked at Belmont with a look that encouraged him to say more. "There is no need to anticipate my motives. My purpose is not to trick you."

Belmont sighed. He'd agreed to the session, so he figured he might as well be compliant. "Adjectives. Right. She was meek but flashy. I think she worked at it. She was sad." Belmont looked off. "Very sad. It was as though she wanted something that was too far to reach. She was oblivious, studied…" Belmont nodded. "She was kind. She felt sorry for us—it was as if she was trying to apologize for bringing us into this world and under that bastard's roof. He controlled her and tried to control us with his money."

Dr. Calvet waited until Belmont looked him in the eyes. "I have done my homework. I do believe you have acquired more wealth than your father, no?"

Belmont shrugged. "I don't know. I never counted."

"No?"

"No."

Dr. Calvet grunted thoughtfully. "Have you ever heard of post-traumatic stress syndrome?"

"Of course," Belmont said.

"Some children live in a home where their parents put a lock on the refrigerator. When those children become adults and can buy their own food, they gorge themselves. They become obese, and still, they cannot stop eating."

Belmont instantly made the correlation. His pulse raced, and his head felt as if it was floating while his soul took a nosedive. He had a lot to think about. "You're saying I have post-traumatic stress disorder?"

"All people who were raised by humans are

afflicted with this disorder—some are more severe than others. Some people let becoming a reasonable, studied adult heal them, but many people merge the symptoms of their disorder into their personality and never become healthy, so they develop personality disorders. You are one of the lucky ones, Belmont."

"I am? Why is that?"

"You are working to heal your condition."

Belmont nodded thoughtfully.

"Unfortunately, we learn from our parents even the things we don't like. So I ask you, what do you want from Daisy?"

"I want her partnership."

Dr. Calvet smiled victoriously. "Good! That is good. So—you have given Daisy all that she wants. What has Daisy given you?"

Belmont beat back the thought of being inside her. He would have to think beyond sex. "If it weren't for Daisy, I don't think Charlie and I would be in the good place we're in now." Belmont frowned so hard that his head felt tight. "But the truth is…" He scratched the back of his neck.

"What is the truth?" Dr. Calvet said.

"Now I understand why she sees me as a controlling motherfucker."

"You are not a controlling 'motherfucker.' As it is said, know better, do better."

Belmont nodded. "Right…" It clicked. Belmont knew what he had to do.

AFTER FINISHING HIS SESSION WITH DR. CALVET, Belmont touched bases with Harold Doe. Belmont knew for sure he wouldn't be able to return to Chicago to deal with Reece Development latest scheme to shame him. Plus, he had given up his plans to develop in Chicago. The headache was greater than the reward. Why the hell had he locked horns with the likes of Reece Development in the first place? They were small potatoes, and the stupid stunt they had pulled was proof. Belmont had plans to dismantle them, and when they were down to their last morsel of bread, he would force them to sell to him at base price. Then he would sell off their assets until the Reese name became nothing more than ashes in the desert. But did that make him the same vengeful prick his father was? If only Matt hadn't threatened Daisy. Belmont would live and let live, but to keep his wife safe, retaliation was required.

"You said Maggie's handling my corporate image?" Belmont asked Harold.

"Yes."

"How's she doing?"

"She's effective," Harold said.

"With your help?"

"Yes."

"Good. Then let her continue handling it. Did you get the data into the right hands?" Belmont asked.

"Yes."

"Are they making the right kind of noise?"

"The misconduct was discovered after a routine check."

Belmont smirked. That was Harold's way of telling him he'd made it look as if the intelligence had been discovered through a routine check of Reece Development's records.

"Keep your eyes open. Call me if shit goes awry," Belmont said.

After he ended the call with Harold, he called Audrey Summers, his PR person in New York for Lord & Lord Industries. He asked her to call Meg, his lead executive assistant, and work with her to arrange a wine festival for Saturday night. The event would take place at the chateau he rented in

Bordeaux, which neighbored Chateau Mer Rouge. The festival should be well attended by people who found value in meeting each other. He didn't want to be stopped every five seconds by someone looking to see what he could do for them. Daisy would be his only priority.

17

THE GIRL FROM CALIFORNIA GOES WALKING

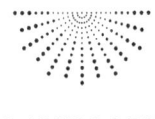

DAISY LORD

a door creaks. Light footsteps approach. My face is pressed against a hard surface, and my neck and shoulders ache. I slowly blink the tiny particles from my eyes. Two small hands pick up two empty wine bottles right in front of my face. Anton yawns and says good morning to Inés, who grunts. She's not happy about the mess we made.

"Goodness gracious," I say hoarsely as I massage the back of my neck.

"I put coffee and croissants on your table." Inés shakes her finger. "No more wine."

I'm shocked. I didn't think she spoke English. "Thank you." I rub my temples. "And I agree. No more wine for me."

She glances crossly at Anton as she takes a decorative envelope from her pocket and sets it in front of me. My name is written on the envelope.

"For you," she says.

"What is it?" Anton asks.

I shrug. Even raising my shoulders feels achy. I need a long, hot bath. I open the envelope. "It's an invitation to a wine festival."

Anton grins slyly. "Ah, a party."

"But you didn't arrange this. How could you?"

"No, no, I did not."

Inés swipes two more bottles into the trash bag with the others. The clinking sound makes my head thump extra hard. Last night, Anton and I drank like fish. If I remember correctly, we made up poems and dirty songs about our lives. I was in the middle of saying something when I closed my eyes, and now here I am.

I stand. "Well, I'm going to go, because I'm not a morning person."

Anton uses his palm to rub his nose. He looks worn out. "Wait. When is the party?"

I hold the invitation in front of me and blink until my focus improves. "Eight o'clock tonight."

"Which chateau?"

I narrow one eye suspiciously. "How do you know it's a chateau?"

"They are all chateaus. Which chateau, Daisy?"

It seems someone else isn't a morning person either. "Mer Rouge."

He nods. His bedroom eyes focus on me, and he smirks. "We had a good night, no?"

I nod. It was a good night. "I'm going to get that coffee and bath and more sleep." I head to the door.

Inés is still banging things around as she cleans.

I turn back to Anton, who's resting his head on the chair with his eyes closed. "Hey, Anton?"

He opens one eye. "Yes."

"There are no pictures of you in the tower. I mean, there are none of me either, but I know why I'm not included. But you've been around. Why aren't you in any of them?"

"Who says I have, as you say, been around?"

"Haven't you?"

He opens his other eye. "I have been lost too, Daisy."

Inés looks at both of us then continues running water in the sink.

"Are you still lost?" I ask.

He holds up his hands and smiles tiredly. "Haven't you found me?"

I sniff, amused. I like our ambiguous banter. We

haven't confused each other yet. "Wait, I need a dress for tonight. Do you know where I can get one?"

"I do. I will take you when we are sober."

I look at my watch. "How does noon sound?"

He rolls his eyes. "Noon's too early."

"He does not come out in the day," Inés says.

Anton and I look at her as if pigs just sprouted wings and flew. I didn't expect her to weigh in.

Anton throws his hands up in surrender. "Is true, I sleep during the sun and rise under the moon like a vampire. Not yesterday, because Jacques asked me to get you from the airport. But I know where to get the dress."

"And the party? Did you know anything about it before the invitation arrived?"

Anton measures the air between two fingers. "Only a little."

"My husband?"

"I don't know. Jacques only said there will be a party and you should go."

I nod. My father doesn't like to give details, so I totally believe that that's all Anton knows. "Okay then..."

Inés hums as she turns the water off in the sink. Anton and I widen our eyes at each other.

"Bonjour, Inés," I say as I wave good-bye.

"Bonjour," she says as she wipes down the counter.

I return to my cottage, take off my dress, and draw myself a hot bath. Naked as a jaybird, I pour a hot cup of coffee and add sugar and milk. I would try to call Belmont, but I've left my phone on the kitchen table inside the main house. I hope he tried to call me at some point during the night. I'll get my phone after my bath.

For now, I turn off the water, grab a croissant, and stand in the window looking out over the vineyard. The morning is the perfect temperature, and I have visions of the sparkling swimming pool. I go to the bedroom, take a robe out of the closet, and put it on. My head is a little tight from drinking more than I'm used to, and I take one long look at the bed. I really wanted to soak up its comfort last night. Perhaps I'll be able to make up for it tonight.

I scurry out of the cottage, itching to get into the pool. Anton is probably asleep—he didn't look as if he would stay awake for very long. Since he, Inés, and I are the only ones on the estate, I feel completely at ease taking off my robe and diving in. The water is lukewarm. I swim two laps, working off all the cheese and bread and wine I consumed in less than twenty-four hours. And oh goodness gracious, that chicken dish Inés made for dinner. She's the kind of cook I wouldn't mind having around three times a day, seven days a week. I take a break to catch my breath and swim another lap of backstrokes then butterfly strokes.

Once I'm breathing heavily, I float on the surface. Water plugs my ears, but I can still hear voices. I quickly let my body sink, look around, and am stunned by whom I see. This cannot be happening.

"I definitely like the view from here," says a man with Sean Connery's good looks. He's staring at my naked body that's now hidden underwater.

"What are you doing here?" My gaze flips between Dexter, Kristin, and the strange man with them.

"We're here to work," Dexter says, grinning as if I should be happy to see him.

My mouth is stuck open.

Kristin sets her piercing glare on Dexter. "She doesn't know? You said she knew."

I glance at my robe, which is too far away for me to reach without exposing myself. "Um…" I blink some more. "Are you really here?"

"Forget you ever saw us." Kristin starts to walk away.

Dexter catches her arm. "Don't forget you saw us. We're here to spotlight Bordeaux."

The good-looking older man hasn't stopped staring at me, as though he thinks if he stares hard enough, he'll get a really good view of my nakedness. Now I recognize him. He's Scott Whistler, the new host of their show.

"Let's talk, Daisy," Dexter says.

I sigh hard, and the water ripples in front of me. "Get my robe, put it near the edge, and you guys go wait on the front porch or something. I'll be there in a second."

Kristin points toward the house. "She let us in. The French woman."

"Oh well, I'll see you inside then."

Kristin shoots Dexter a harsh look. Dexter squats by my robe, gives me a naughty smirk, and sets the robe near the edge of the swimming pool. I watch them walk into the stain-glassed enclosed patio. Just to clear my head and make sure I'm not dreaming. I sink to the bottom of the swimming pool. I'm awake. I'm alive. I scream while underwater.

.   .   .

I WALK PAST THE KITCHEN. INÉS IS COOKING, AND the smell of shallots, garlic, and wine makes my mouth water. No matter what happens, I am not missing the next meal. Dexter is alone and waiting in the living room.

"Who lived here—Marie Antoinette?" he asks, grinning.

It's hard to be angry with a man who has the face of an angel, but I'm a little peeved. "I cannot believe you just showed up here! And you brought Kristin and Scott Whistler?"

Dexter thumbs over his shoulder. "Actually, the whole team's here."

"Then the whole team, including yourself, needs to leave."

"So this chateau has thirteen bedrooms, ten bathrooms, and a full staff?"

"There's no full staff, only Inés, and she's not going to cook and clean for a production crew."

"Then we'll hire our own staff. We have enough in the budget for that since you bailed on us." I'm on the verge of objecting, but Dexter lifts a finger and says, "*You* suggested we shoot in the South of France. We're good now, but without you, we'll murder our budget by making a bunch of mistakes." He lifts his hands to showcase the house. "You can at least give us room and board."

I sigh. Heck, I *am* the one who pushed for France. Was I ever really married to this whole project? No. I would've bailed on them sooner or later. I guess the fact that they're stuck between a rock and a hard place is my fault.

"How many?" I grumble.

"Four producers, one host, a cameraman, his assistant, an audio team of two, and our production assistant."

"Ten people. How many days?"

"As long as it takes."

"Wrong answer. I need a solid number," I say.

"How does three days sound?"

"I'll call my father. Wait here."

"Jacques? I'll call him." Dexter takes his phone off the clip on his hip. He slides his finger across the screen and taps it.

I shake my head. "You have my father's number?"

"Remember he invited me to Louisiana?" he says in a rush. "Jacques? She said yes… yes… right… staff." He widens his eyes at me as if to say, *I told you so*. "Thank you." He ends the call and clips his phone back to his hip. "So which of the thirteen rooms are you crashing in?"

"I'm not sleeping in the main house. But what are you doing here, Dexter? For real." My earnest expression demands to know the truth.

"I'm seizing an opportunity." His tone suggests a number of meanings.

"Well, I'm probably leaving tomorrow, so have a ball." I turn to walk away.

"Hey."

"What?" I ask.

"I missed you."

"I'm still married."

I wait to hear what he has to say about that. Crickets.

I was hoping he'd say his missing me has nothing to do with wanting me romantically, that he missed my friendship, my company, or my stellar work ethic. Since he's still speechless, I walk to the kitchen to get my cell phone. I can't believe I lost my appetite. I don't even pick at the small plate of cheese and bread that Inés has set on the table next to my cell phone.

"You take the cheese. I bring you more," Inés says.

I take the platter. "Thank you."

She presses her lips together. I catch the nonverbal "you're welcome" and head out of the kitchen to sulk in my cottage. However, the hallway that leads to the tower Anton showed me yesterday catches my eyes. Pretty soon, this house will be overrun by uninvited guests. Anton swept us past so many portraits last night, and I have a hankering to go take them all in while my moments are still private.

The cheese plate accompanies me to the tower. The sun shining through the frosted-glass roof illuminates the staircase. I study a close-up shot of my father with his brothers: Cyprus, Pey, and Dongo. I haven't seen my uncles since my parents divorced. They're handsome men with flawless dark skin, beautiful pouty lips, and strong bone structures. Uncle Dongo modeled in Paris in the eighties; then he went to dental school and became a dentist, which is why his teeth are so perfect.

There's Uncle Jean Luc and his wife, Adélie, Anton's parents. They're on the deck of a yacht, wearing Breton striped sweaters and waving at the camera. The wind blows Aunt Adélie's fine brown hair across her heart-shaped face. Anton and his brother, Leon, have her bedroom eyes and red mouth. I move to the next portrait. I'm sure it's

Anton's sister, Claire. She's in her early twenties in the picture and kissing Leon, who's making a sour face, on the cheek.

The more pictures I study, the more disheartened I feel. What have I been missing all these years? I've been going and going but getting nowhere. These portraits seem to hold the life I never claimed. Then I reach the fatal blow, a family photo with my sisters Daphne and Hannah, Heloise and her second husband Joseph's daughters. They are linking arms with Angelina and Randall and Joseph, my father's two other sons by his ex-wife, Shelly Price. By the trees in the background, it looks as if they're here at the chateau. The longer I study their faces, the more left out I feel. This one portrait is a dagger in my heart. Instead of walking back down the steps, I enter the tower. The single room is a lounge with an observation bench that rounds the walls. I think I want to cry, but I don't. I want to throw the cheese platter against the wall in anger, but instead, I sit on the floor and curl into a ball.

"I know the dead can't hear me, but, God, tell Daniel that I know he wouldn't be happy to know that I missed everything after he died." I can't stop my tears.

I picture how our portraits would look on the

wall. Daniel would have three children, all boys. He would've been a better father to boys than girls. His wife would resemble Kristin—he used to be attracted to blondes. But who knows? People change as they grow. Perhaps all the opposite would be true. But I still picture him with his wife and three boys, smiling at the camera with Belmont, Joella, who is ma fleur, and me in the frame. *If only.*

"Daisy?"

I sit up in a hurry and look at Anton. "Dang it, I fell asleep." I check my watch, but I'm not wearing it. I'm not wearing anything but a robe. My hair is all over the place, and there isn't as much daylight flowing in through the roof as there was when I entered the tower.

Anton sits next to me. "Were you crying?"

I look at the cheese platter on the floor. "Yes. I was just overwhelmed by all those portraits." I point toward the door that leads to the long staircase. "Don't you feel awful that you missed out?"

Anton shrugs. "Why regret what can't be changed?"

"I just want to be on that damn wall. There, I said it."

"Then you and I will take a picture, and I will put it on the wall."

I smile at him. He smiles back.

"How many years have we wasted not being in each other's lives?" I ask.

Anton pats my thigh. "What did I say? The past is the past. We'll work on the future. You still want a dress for tonight?"

I slump my shoulders. "I don't know anymore. Now that we have company, all I want to do is go home and…"

"And what?"

"I don't know."

"Then come with me," he says.

"Where are we going?"

"Out."

Getting as far away from here as possible sounds like the best idea right now. "Okay, but first I have to get a serving of whatever Inés was cooking."

"We don't have the time," he says. "I will get you food."

"Well…" I pick up the untouched cheese plate. "I'll take this."

Anton looks at me askew. "You eat a lot to be so thin."

"I'm not *so* thin."

Anton chuckles as if he knows he struck a nerve. "You are right. You are perfect in every way, Daisy."

I roll my eyes. "Now you're overcompensating."

"Perhaps but at least it is true."

I shake my head smiling. "Goodness your such an awesome bullshitter."

Anton laughs as he helps me to my feet. "That is a fantastic compliment."

The property is as quiet as a church mouse. The crew must've gone out to shoot for the day. One thing about Dexter is he's a professional. His goal in coming to Bordeaux wouldn't be only to pursue me but also to produce a superior show. So maybe he's actually here to make sure he can use me when needed. I can't knock him for that.

Anton waits for me to get dressed. I put on an old pair of jeans, a white ribbed tank top, and sandals and gather my wild hair into a hefty pony-tail. If only Belmont were here to see me. I would turn him on. The thought makes me grin.

I ride shotgun with the windows rolled down. My face catches the wind. French music streams out of the stereo speakers. The beat is as whispery as the songstress's voice. I want to snap pictures with my phone, but instead I lower my seat and pitch my feet on the window ledge.

"You are comfortable?" Anton asks.

I chuckle. "Yep."

"Your friend worried you had left."

"What friend?"

"Blue Eyes."

"Oh, Dexter," I say.

"Why is he in love with you?"

"Because he knows he can't have me."

"Ah, I see… That is the best kind of love."

I peek at him. "So why doesn't Angelina know that you're married?"

"Ah ha!" He shifts uncomfortably.

I hadn't expected that reaction. "You don't have to answer if you don't want. I'm not a prier."

The song ends, and an instrumental starts that I recognize. I bop my head to it. "'The Girl from Ipanema'?"

Anton sings along with Joao Gilberto in Portuguese. I shimmy my shoulders and take over singing when Astrud Gilberto sings in English. We sing the chorus together then bop our heads and sway to the instrumental sections. When the song ends, we smirk at each other.

"You are young at heart," Anton says.

"Well, I was never forced to grow up fast."

"I like what you are in a woman. Your husband is a lucky man."

"Oh no, I'm the lucky one." I look out the window as a new song plays, and I watch the landscape transform. The volume of the music is lowered, so I face Anton.

"We were married two weeks, then she died," he says.

My mouth is caught open. I'm speechless.

"It is not what you think. We were addicts, and we did not love each other, because we did not love ourselves. She overdosed."

I take my feet off the windowsill and sit up straight. I want to say something comforting, and I guess that shows on my face, because it appears as if Anton is waiting to hear it.

"What was her name?" I ask.

"Korina."

"Are you still in contact with her parents or any of your friends?"

He sneers. "It was not like that. No one knew. Only you."

"Oh shit, I told Angelina."

"Then I guess it is a secret no more."

I laugh because he took the words right out of my mouth. "Nope, it isn't. I'm so sorry."

"Is no problem. Nothing stays buried forever. But what about you? Are you ready to live beyond losing Daniel? I remember how hurt you were. My mother said you needed to be registered in an asylum."

I snort. That's what I remember about Tante Adélie—she was so extreme, and it drove Heloise mad. "I don't know about that, but I guess I never wanted to betray my grief or the life my brother could have had by enjoying all the things he would miss, including family. Recently, I've asked myself who I would have become if he were still alive. I don't think I would've ever met my husband. Before I met Belmont, I was with this guy for ten years." I roll my eyes at that extended mistake. "That relationship was definitely a product of my daddy issues, which became more severe after Daniel died."

"Daddy issues? What do you mean?"

"His name was Adrian, and I traveled a lot. We hardly saw each other. I didn't really like him as a person, and God knows I can't remember what drew me to him in the first place, but he was my boyfriend. I felt as if I needed to have a boyfriend just to be normal. It was stupid, I know. But all I had to say was, 'Oh, I have a boyfriend,' and people would leave me alone."

"But what does that have to say about Jacques?" Anton asked. "He is your father, and you say you have 'daddy issues.'"

"He wasn't father of the year to me, before or after the divorce. He was just there. I had one. At least I could say that."

"I see…"

"I don't blame him for anything," I say. "I used to, but I don't see the world or the people in it through the lens of a brokenhearted little girl anymore." A man's face fills my head and makes me smile. "Thanks to Belmont. I guess I can say I was saved by love and…" I glare out the window. We've just rolled onto the bridge over the Dordogne River.

"And what?" Anton asks.

"And I think I've been overly grateful for it," I whisper.

Anton grunts thoughtfully. He turns the volume back up, and I feast my eyes on the sluggish, murky river. A few unskilled kayakers row under the arches of the bridge. Bordeaux looms ahead. It's not a tall city, but blocky structures with straight lines and tall windows are abundant. Domed and steeple tops from as early as the seventeenth century are interspersed throughout. The structures have only been tweaked and refurbished here or there throughout the years.

Anton takes a roundabout off the freeway and speeds up a road into the city. The closer we get to the city center, the thicker traffic becomes until we're hardly moving at all. Anton turns off the main road. The back streets are extra narrow, but there's hardly any traffic. After a series of turns, Anton guides the car down an alley and into a parking structure. He presses a remote control on his key ring, and the gate opens.

"Are you going to tell me where you're taking me now?" I ask over the music.

He turns off the stereo. "My studio is in this building, and so is your dress. I have a sale to make, and you have a dress to buy. One stop shopping." He cheeses. "But I want you to first come with me."

"Ah, so you want me to watch you make money?"

Anton chuckles. "No, your father asked me to bring you."

"Why?"

"He wants you to approve the painting."

"Me? What the heck do I know about art?" I say.

"He said it is a gift for Angel. She is building a house, no?"

"Oh, right. She and Charlie are remodeling their home."

The tires screech as Anton swerves into a parking space. He opens his door as soon as he turns off the engine. I get out, and we look at each other across the roof of the car.

"You sure you want to sell the painting?" I ask, thinking he's bitter about what I said regarding Angelina and Charlie.

He taps the hood of the car as he contemplates.

"How much is the sell?" I ask.

"Twenty-five thousand euros."

My eyes expand. "Whoa. Your work commands that kind of price tag?"

He shrugs. "It's nothing. Not anymore."

My squint asks him to elaborate.

Anton walks, and I follow. "As an addict, I needed the money. I'm not an addict anymore, so I need something else."

"Like what?"

We walk down a short flight of stairs and enter

a corridor with two elevators. Anton smashes the down button.

"I do not know yet," he says.

"So what do you do with all the money until then?"

"I put it under my mattress."

"Really?"

The elevator doors open. Anton smirks as he waits for me to exit first.

"No, that was a joke," he says. "I put it in the bank."

I laugh as we walk onto the busy sidewalk. Tourists are abundant. They're sitting on patios, eating, drinking, and enjoying their moments. They're walking the cobblestone street, window-shopping. I love watching couples in Europe. They often get lost in each others eyes and touch each other ever so sensually. Europeans have learned to love love and passion no matter how old or young they are. After all the years of observing them, I feel as though I can finally relate. Anton and I are passing a cute little boutique, and the two women working the racks inside scowl at us.

"Is that the store you were talking about?" I ask.

"Yes." He doesn't even slow his pace so that I can do a little preview window-shopping.

We go through double glass doors in the same building then up another elevator to the fourth level. Anton's gallery encompasses the entire floor.

"Go browse. I must prepare for the buyer," he says and scampers in the opposite direction.

I walk over to study the nearest piece of artwork. I press my hand over my heart and gasp. I feel as if Anton snatched an emotion out of a human's body and heaved it onto the canvas. The hard part is figuring out which emotion or emotions are depicted. I tilt my head, trying to figure out if the obscure cityscape makes me feel angst or exhilaration.

"Do you like that one?"

I spin around. "What are you doing here?"

Belmont squints as if he doesn't recognize me. "Do I know you?" He smirks naughtily. "I would like to know you."

I also smirk. "You're my husband."

Two of Belmont's fingers journey down the side of my neck, slip down my chest, ride the slope of my breast and make an indulgent lap around my nipple. I skip a breath.

"I know who I am and who you are," he whispers as he lightly pinches my nipple. The sensation trickles down to my toes.

I bite my lower lip. Belmont tugs it from between my teeth and comes in for a sensual kiss.

We press our foreheads together.

"How are you?" he breathes.

"Fine," I barely say. "I've been trying to call you."

"Sorry, I've been waiting for a more worthwhile opportunity to connect with you." He kisses me again. "You look beautiful."

I taste his mouth on my lips and smile. "Thank you. So are you the twenty-five-thousand-euro customer?"

"Yes."

"So you set this all up?"

"Yes."

"Why?"

"Because I want us to start over."

I tilt my head. "Start over how?"

"I want to explore you."

"That still doesn't compute."

Belmont's large hand squeezes my ass and shoves me against his engorged cock. He licks his lips as if he's getting ready to kiss me. "I'll see you tonight. Let's have a drink, and see what happens next."

He'll see me tonight? "Oh, at the wine festival? So it *is* your party?"

"Hello? Daisy?" Anton calls.

I hear his rapid footsteps. Belmont releases me and steps backward.

"Oh," Anton says, looking between Belmont and me. I'm sure he notices the steaming hot tension between us.

Belmont extends his hand. "Hello, I'm Jack. You must be Anton Bisset."

Anton hesitates then shakes his hand. "I am Anton. Are you the buyer?"

"Yes, I am."

"You've met my cousin?"

Belmont gives me a smoldering look. I look at the painting I was studying earlier to keep myself from hyperventilating.

"I have. She's beautiful," he says.

Anton snorts. "Yes, she is beautiful, but Daisy is not for sale. Come this way. I'll take you both to the painting."

I plant my feet. "I'm fine. I approve." I need physical space from Belmont, because he has me all hot and bothered.

"Daisy, it is what Jacques wants."

I point my thumb at Belmont, still avoiding his

gaze. "Believe me, Jacques will approve whatever this guy buys."

Belmont chuckles.

Anton studies us. "Okay." He looks at Belmont. "This way."

Belmont flexes his eyebrows at me before rounding the corner. When he's out of sight, I can finally breathe. I walk over to the window and look out at the street. I hear Belmont and Anton, though I can't make out what they're saying. Anton laughs in a way that indicates he has been caught off guard. That's what Belmont does—he catches you off guard, and before you know it, you're putty in his hands.

A little while later, Anton says, "I will have it posted on Monday."

"Both of them?" Belmont asks.

"Only the one for Angelina. I will drive the other to the house on Tuesday."

I turn to face them when they're right behind me. Belmont's gaze peels me out of my jeans and tank top.

"There is a television crew on the property for three days, is that right?" Anton looks at me for corroboration.

Belmont's expression turns into a severe frown.

"Um, I think so," I say.

"What television crew?" Belmont snaps.

"They are with Daisy. I want to keep the painting safe. When they leave, I will take it."

My eyes bulge. I'm waiting for Belmont to blow his lid. He's not the kind of man who explodes into a rage, but this might be the sort of news that sends him over the edge. He clenches his jaw and stares at me as if he can see through my eyes and read my thoughts.

Belmont clears his throat. "I understand," he says in a carefully composed tone. "Daisy." He nods.

My heart is pounding. "Belmont."

Anton squints curiously. "I will show you out."

Anton walks Belmont to the elevator. I breathe a sigh of relief. I'm a little curious about what Belmont intends to do next. He's not a talker; he's an action taker, which means the plot may have gotten thicker.

18
MOMENTS LIKE THIS

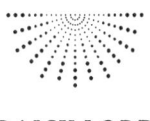

DAISY LORD

I order a sandwich with emmental, creamy chévre, and mozzarella cheese layered with prosciutto between a flaky baguette. We sit on stools at an oversized table set against the window.

"So you don't believe your theory on what you call 'daddy issues,' do you?" Anton asks.

I'm momentarily confused, but then I remember what I said in the car. "Yeah, why? You don't believe me?"

"Are there mother issues?"

I give that thought. "Humph, probably."

"So then maybe your issues are not 'daddy issues' but 'parent issues,' no?"

I grunt sarcastically. "I'm sure Heloise has worked on my psyche."

"Daddy issues imply that a woman needs a man to be her father, her dictator, her guide, and her father has failed to be that for her. The work I showed you—the man, the woman and the wheat —do you remember it?"

Ah, last night before I passed out at the table. "I remember that."

"A woman does not need influence by her father. That is patriarchal bullshit. A woman needs a partner. Your father cannot be your partner unless he is a pig. He is your mother's partner. Together, the parents show you what it means to be the Adam —the man and the woman as one. But if they are held accountable for their failure, then what shall all the societies do? We change everything, right?"

My confusion shows on my face.

"Your mother and father are equal in your issues, that is all I mean."

I stare at Anton's face. Memories, theories, and conclusions race through my mind. He's saying that both parents are culpable because they failed to pattern true partnership. "I never looked at it that way, but you're right."

"No, Daisy, no one is right and very few people

are." He tilts his head. "Possibly you and your husband will be the few. What is his name… Jack? My buyer?"

I laugh and pound the table gently. I feel so caught. "I so meant to tell you. Did he tell you?"

"He did not. Jack wears a gold band with your name engraved."

"That's right…"

"He wears a ring, but you do not?"

"That's because he had never taken it off, and I had. It's a long story. Do you want to hear it?"

"Do you need to tell it?"

I tilt my head to think. "Actually, I don't."

"Then I don't need to hear it."

I grin at Anton. He is such an enigma. He certainly teeters on the edge of pompous intellectual self-indulgence, but he's not puffing up his ego or trying to make me feel inferior. He was trying to get me to challenge Jung's Electra complex theory, and it worked!

"So… when are we going to get my dress?"

Anton stiffens his shoulders. "We can go now."

I notice the change in his demeanor as he pays for lunch. He's more sullen, and we walk silently up the narrow cobblestone street.

We're nearing the shop doors when Anton

shakes a cigarette out of the package. "I will finish this."

I nod. "Okay." I leave him to linger under a lantern while I go inside.

I'm a lucky shopper, because as soon as I walk in, one dress catches my eye. It's a red silk, spaghetti-strap jersey dress, and it will look nice with the sandals Angelina packed for me.

Other shoppers browse the racks, but the two ladies who watched Anton and me walk by earlier haven't taken their eyes off me. They're both pretty brunettes in their late twenties or early thirties. One of the women touches the other on the shoulder, consoling her.

"He wants to torture me," the consoled woman says in French.

They stare at me as if I'm the enemy they can't banish. Then the woman doing the consoling approaches me. I stare at her like a deer trapped in headlights.

"Can I help you?" she says in English.

I knew she wouldn't be friendly, but I didn't think she would be downright harsh. I hold out the dress I've selected. "Um, yes, I would like this."

"Is that all?"

"Um, sure, yes," I say. She reaches for the dress,

but I pull it back. "Is there a problem?" I ask her in French.

"No problem," she says in English.

"Just so you know, Anton is my cousin. So…"

Her eyes widen, and I watch the wheels turning behind them.

She reaches for the dress again. "May I take it?" she says in a nicer tone. I hand it to her, and she holds it up. "For you, this is a good choice." She smiles.

I accept the olive branch she's holding out and smile back.

"Come this way."

I follow her to the counter. As soon as she gets to the register, she tells the other woman that I am Anton's cousin. The information doesn't make the other woman's bitter expression ease.

"I am Anna," the woman who took the dress says. "This is Nina."

"I'm Daisy." There's an awkward moment of silence. "So you are friends of Anton's?"

Anna and Nina look at each other.

"Is something like that," Anna says.

"Oh?" My tone rings with intrigue.

"We were lovers," Nina says. "Then he dumped me for his cousin."

I'm a little caught off guard. I think she's referring to Anton's relationship with Angelina. "Well, Anton and I are not the sort of cousins who have sex," I say. We're blood related."

Anna chuckles cynically. "Blood or no blood, cousins fuck."

I wave my finger. "There will be no *fucking* between Anton and me."

Anna blurts a laugh. Nina smiles sheepishly. I think the iceberg has fully come crashing down.

Anna spreads the dress on the counter. "Well, you are lucky. This is our last like this."

I'm still a little rattled by Nina's insinuation, but I force myself to smile and move on. "I guess I am."

"Where will go you in this?"

"I'm wearing it to a party tonight."

In unison, their gazes shift toward the doorway. I turn to see what has captured their attention. Anton has come inside, and he's watching them. Anna looks at her shaking hands as they fold my dress and wrap it in white tissue paper. After she pulls herself together, she looks at Anton, who has come up to stand beside me, with a smile.

"Bonjour," Anna and Nina say to him.

"Bonjour," he replies.

Anna asks Anton how he has been, and he says

he's been as well as to be expected. Their interaction is very strange, as if they haven't seen each other in a long time. However, Anton's studio is upstairs. I'm sure they run into each other every now and then. Nina still hasn't said much to Anton. She's the one who thought my mere presence was her torture.

Anna hands me the bag. "Daisy, have fun at the party."

"Thank you. Do you live near Chateau Mes Fleurs?" I'm making a last-ditch effort to force this moment past the awkwardness and unspoken words.

Anna shakes her head. "I do not."

"Oh, it's my father's vineyard."

"That's right, your father is Jacques Blanchard," Nina says. She gives Anton a cross look.

Of course she's heard of him. I sometimes forget how popular my father is, especially in France.

"I see the resemblance," Anna says.

"Do you see the resemblance between Daisy and me?" Anton asks, grinning.

Anna sniffs cynically. "She is more beautiful than you. But then, you were always pretty like a girl," she says in French.

She and Anton share a lingering gaze. As soon as they realize they've stared at each other for too long, they cut their eyes away.

Two women stand beside me, ready to have their purchases rung.

"Do you have paper and pen?" Anton asks.

Anna retrieves both from beside the register and hands it to Anton. He writes the address of the party and the time it starts then slides the paper on the counter between Anna and Nina. "I hope to see you tonight."

"Is the invitation for one or two?" Anna asks.

"One or two." Anton takes the bag out of my hand. "Daisy, let's go. It is already late."

We say *au revoir*, and I follow Anton out the door. I have to trot to catch up with him. Once we're out of Anna and Nina's eyesight, he leans against the wall to catch his breath.

"What did I do?" he asks, fumbling through his pockets for his pack of cigarettes.

"You invited Nina and Anna to the party tonight," I say.

He shakes the package, but he's all out. "Fuck!"

"We can just stand here until you even out."

He nods. We lean against the wall and watch the people passing by watch us, although Anton doesn't really see them. One minute passes, then a few more.

Anton takes a deep breath then releases it. "Okay, that is enough."

We start down the sidewalk, heading back to the car.

On the way home, Anton tells me that he and Nina were lovers during the two years he spent as a university student in Paris. They broke up when he dropped out. Four years later, he had his first successful gallery showing in the 3rd Arrondissement. Nina happened to wander into the gallery with a group of friends. Before he knew Nina was present, Anna had walked into a circle where he was struggling to tell potential buyers that he wouldn't explain the piece they were interested in.

"If it only attracts your eye, then leave it. If it grabs your heart, then take it," he had said.

"You sound like a pompous egomaniac. Their relationship with the art does not need to satisfy you," Anna said, which intrigued him.

They had bantered back and forth. He was about to ask her to join him in the artist den, which was a small room at the back of the gallery that had a red velvet bed, but then Nina eased up beside her. That changed everything.

"Oh, so you're interested in Anna, not Nina?" I ask.

"Nina and I were together again for three years, but I was an addict. I made her leave me."

"So where does Angelina fit in?"

"Angelina was two weeks of making love and being in love. She was my one perfect lover a man has in his life. I knew she would never be mine."

"But how did you and Angelina get together?"

"After I cleaned myself, she visited Jacques in Paris. He was taking care of me. She was more satiating than the drugs."

I picture Anton and Angelina humping on the sofa in Anton's cottage. I realize that Angelina and Charlie screw often, but the longer we are sisters, the more I don't want to picture her engaged in the act. I throw up a hand. "Okay, got it. But back to Anna and Nina—I'm still confused. Which one are you interested in?"

I indulge in the mystical purple evening as Anton works on his answer. An apartment community off to the side of the road catches my attention.

"Anna. I like her a lot, but we can never be together because Nina will always love me," Anton says.

"Have you ever told Anna how you felt?"

"Never, no."

"Then how do you know she'll never be with you?" I ask.

"Because they are kiss, kiss like sisters. Also, Nina went into depression after I broke off from her."

"Oh… how long ago was that?"

"Two years ago."

"But you were seeing Angelina? Oh… you cheated on her with Angelina?"

"My heart did not cheat. I did not love Nina," he says.

"I'm sorry to hear that Nina was so hurt, but she's an adult. I kind of think that this one is in the Anton Bisset repertoire—you can choose who you love, but the best kind of love is the kind that chooses you."

Anton chews on that for a moment. He smiles. "That is very good."

"I think so…" I smile and put a hand on his shoulder.

He puts his hand on top of mine. The moment passes. I get comfortable in my seat and look out the window as Anton turns up the volume on the stereo. I inhale the wind blowing against my face. The Cyprus and oak trees along the sides of the road shuffle past like a deck of cards. This moment is perfect, and I didn't go looking for it. It just happened in real life. I've come to the conclusion that I want and need more moments like this.

THE TIRES CRUNCH THE DIRT ROAD. THE RIDE becomes smoother as we roll up the paved part of the driveway, which has a shaved lawn on both sides.

Anton drives slowly past the production van. "Over there."

Dexter and Kristin are standing on the side-walk. She's shaking her arms, visibly upset. Dexter's hands are on his waist, and he's looking at the ground, taking the tongue-lashing. She says something, and Dexter turns to glare curiously at Anton and me.

"Lovers' quarrel?" Anton says.

I've never pictured Dexter and Kristin as a couple. She has a fiancé, I think. I always got her situation confused with the other women on the production team. If they spoke less about their personal situations, then maybe I would be able to differentiate. It was always this boyfriend, that boyfriend, his mother, his job, our honeymoon, we this or we that… after a while, I stopped absorbing whatever they were discussing that wasn't work related. But Dexter and Kristin? No way. She's the barn house in Kansas, and Dexter has just stepped on the yellow brick road. I may not be his happily ever after, but Kristin isn't either.

"They just work together," I say.

"That is how it starts."

I squish my face. "She's not his type."

"Then you are Blue Eyes's type?" Anton asks.

"No," I say, sounding defensive. "Not *me* but someone like me would be his type."

"And what are you like, Daisy?" Anton asks as he approaches an old barn that has been converted into a garage.

So this is where Anton parks his car. The door is already open, and he drives in.

"I'm not like her."

"And how is she?" he asks.

"Kristin is the woman you get stuck with in the rut. Dexter is the kind of man who doesn't want to be stuck in the rut." I lift a finger. "My husband, however, is the kind of man who wants me to stay in the rut with him. Unfortunately, it's him I love and not Dexter."

"Ah, your husband…"

Something in his tone makes me look at him askew. "What did he do?"

Anton seems hesitant, but he gets out of the car and leans on the hood. I follow suit. Our faces are close, as if he's on the verge of spilling a juicy secret.

"He was curious about our night. I think he thought possibly we could have made love." He grins as if I should know what he's thinking.

Indeed I do. "It's not that he's jealous. He just hasn't figured me out yet."

Anton gives me a doubtful look.

"Well… he's a little jealous."

"He is more than a little jealous." Anton looks at Dexter, who peeks around the corner. "You are lost?"

Dexter steps into full view. "No, I'm not. I need to speak to Daisy."

Anton looks at me with raised eyebrows. "I see you later."

He walks off, although he keeps looking back as though he doesn't trust Dexter and I to be alone. But finally we are alone. All I can think about is what Anton said about Dexter and Kristin. Are they a couple?

Dexter holds up his cell phone. "I got a call from Gill Abbott today." He doesn't look as if it were a good call.

"Oh?" I say.

"Production has been canceled in France. We have to fly back tomorrow—bright and early. But here's where it gets odd, Daisy... we've been green-lit to shoot not only four but ten episodes in the U.S. anywhere we want. That's a full fucking season! You know Gil has been pinching us for every dollar. Suddenly we have a bottomless budget, but not for France. Why is that?"

I shrug. "I don't know."

"You know what I think?"

"What?"

"I think your husband had something to do with it. Because I'm here, and he's somewhere in the goddamn USA, probably chasing tail!"

"Chasing tail? The only tail he's chasing is mine. He's here in Bordeaux. I saw him today," I say.

"Then fuck! I was right!" He sounds as if he's whining about it.

"Not about the chasing tail part or about him being in the U.S. So what were you right about?"

I'm ticked off. I don't appreciate him describing Belmont as a womanizer.

"He's fucking with our production."

I sigh and slump my shoulders. "Dexter, I'm exhausted, and I still have a party to attend."

Dexter throws up his hands. "That's it? You're just going to let him do that to us?"

"What do you want from me?"

"You know I'd be happy as fuck if Gil had increased our budget on his own."

"Then pretend he did."

Dexter flinches and studies my nonchalance. "You're okay with him messing with our gig because he's jealous? I heard what your cousin said, and Jack's not a little jealous. He's a *lot* jealous."

"Look, if Belmont had anything to do with shutting down your production in Bordeaux, then I'm sorry. But you are at my father's chateau because I'm here. You know he doesn't think you're here simply because you appreciate my professional point of view, and neither do I."

Dexter looks me in the eyes. He releases a long sigh. "Damn, you're beautiful."

I frown.

"I wish I would've met you first," he says.

"Dexter—"

He raises a hand. "It's okay. No need to crush my ego any more than you already have."

"I didn't mean to," I say. "I thought we were really good friends. I don't know what else to say."

"Don't say anything." He turns around to look over the land. "We got some good stuff on video today."

I step up next to him. "Kristin must be pissed that you have to scrap the work you put in so far."

Dexter nods emphatically. "Oh yes, she is, but she's always pissed off about something."

I sigh long and hard. "I can't believe I'm going to say this…"

Dexter widens his eyes excitedly. "Are you coming back to work with us?"

"Ha… no."

"Okay, but one question?"

I look at him askew. "What?"

"If it wasn't for him, would you have joined us in Provence?"

"Truth?"

"Truth."

"Probably for a little while," I say.

"A little while is all I needed." Mr. Blue Eyes is flirting with me again.

"I'm sorry, but Kristin called it all along. She never thought I was serious about the job."

He shakes his head with a tiny eye roll. "That's not it. She doesn't like you because you're hot and your husband's rich. If she could switch places with you, she'd do it in a minute."

Wow, maybe Anton was right. "Sounds like trouble in paradise."

He's taken aback. "What do you mean?"

"Are you and Kristin…?" I lift my eyebrows.

"Hell no, and that's the truth. I wouldn't want someone like her influencing my daughters. You on the other hand…" He grunts. "Shit! They were supposed to fly out next week and spend the month here with me. I have to cancel their flights and the nannies.'" Dexter squeezes his head and shouts, "Fuck!"

I pat his shoulder, and he takes my hand.

"Don't touch me if you can't go further." There's passion in his eyes.

I remove my hand. "I was going to say that we can change Belmont's mind and you can keep whatever money he banked in your budget, but you have to promise to leave first thing in the morning, and we can't be friends. This has to be where we end."

Dexter studies me as he scratches the back of

his neck. We both know there's only one thing to say, but I give him the time he needs to come to grips with the truth—after all, I'm the one he can't have. That's never easy for a man to accept.

"All right." There's a hint of reluctance in his tone, but it's not enough to vanquish his reason.

"Then come to the party tonight," I say.

"What party?"

"Belmont's party."

"Ugh…" Dexter rolls his eyes and bobbles his shoulders. He recovers. "Okay, but since we're going to finish shooting in France with our bottom-less budget, can you come with me to the van and take a look at our footage? I want to know what you think about Whistler. I think he's a tool. Maybe I should get in front of the fucking camera and do it my fucking self."

I slap his back. "Now that's the best idea you've had yet."

Dexter and I spend an hour going through the footage. He was right—Scott Whistler is a tool and should be replaced by the blue-eyed sexpot beside me. Whistler performs as if a canoe ride down the La Dordogne is a raft ride down the Amazon River with piranhas plucking at the bottom. I laugh during all the shots in the Lascaux Caves. Whistler speaks as if they're trapped with no oxygen and he has to search for a way out or else.

"Scrap it all. Go to Provence and follow the shooting script," I say. "I mean, what happened to all the interviews we set up?"

"Half of them fell through without you."

"Then convince them to deal with you. Come on, Dexter, use your power of persuasion."

He snorts. "Yeah…"

"This is your career, for goodness sakes. Live up to your reputation."

He stares at the table, nodding thoughtfully. "You're right. I guess all that's left for you to do is work your wiles on your husband."

I chuckle. We lock gazes. Dexter holds out his hand, and I put my palm on top of his. He kisses the back of my hand. His lips are so soft, just as they were when we kissed. It's our way of saying good-bye.

I head back to my cottage to get dressed. I think I see Melissa, the receptionist, swimming in the pool. She's one of the last people in the world that I want to see. Inside, I'm dancing a happy jig that Dexter and his crew will be out of here before sunup.

I walk into my cottage and remember that I

left my dress in the car when I see it spread out on the sofa. Anton must've put it there. I smile. I love this little place. My eyes gravitate to the table and the fresh plate of cheese and bread Inés has placed on it. I don't mind putting on a few pounds if the culprit is chévre cheese. I pull off my tank top on the way to the table and unclip my bra.

"Just the way I want you," a familiar voice says.

I jump and spin around. Belmont has just walked through the door.

"What are you doing here?" My heart is beating fast. He walks toward me, and my legs turn to mush.

Belmont stops in front of me. "You like this little house?" His gaze rolls around the kitchen and living room.

"A lot," I whisper. I want him to just grab my tit and squeeze it. I want his hands all over me.

"You like that cheese and bread?"

I swallow what's in my mouth. "Um-hum."

He grins. "Have you been eating a lot?"

I roll my eyes. "I'm not pregnant."

He chuckles. My expression matches his flirtatious expression.

"So if I can't control myself and we end up

having a one-night stand, this is where you'll bring me?" he asks.

"I'm not the kind of girl who takes a man home on the first night."

"Been there, done that with a woman who looks, feels and..." He kisses me tenderly. "Tastes a lot like you—and cheese."

I chuckle and drop my face bashfully. His bulge is pressed against me already. I'm so ready for whatever he wants. We can skip the party. He can stretch me out on the couch, part my legs, and slam his dick inside me. He can eat my slit until I scream for reprieve.

I'm so very disappointed when he lets out a deflated sigh and takes one giant step back. I do something I've never done—I step close to him again and massage his rock-hard cock. Belmont sips air as he removes my hand.

"I'll see you later, baby." Belmont kisses my cheek and pinches my nipple before backing away.

I watch him longingly as he moves through the living room and out the door. I cross my legs, push out my hip, and wait. When Belmont returns, he'll find me in a sexy pose. The seconds tick by. I feel stupid standing here topless and alone. I rush to the window and look out. There's no sign of Belmont.

He's gone! I can hardly believe he left me wanting. I guess it's true—there *is* a first time for everything.

I swap the bath for a long hot shower. I wash my hair with some sweet jasmine shampoo. It's the same brand as the bubble bath. By the end of the shower, my skin and hair are soft. I dress my face with the makeup Angelina packed for me. The red dress fits like Marilyn Monroe's gloves, hugging my curves. I slide my hands down my hip, up my waist, then puff up my rack. Someone knocks on the door as I tie my black sandals.

"It's open," I call as I sashay into the living room.

Anton walks in and raises his eyebrows. "You look magnificent."

"*Également*. Likewise," I say.

He's wearing a lightweight black V-neck, sleeveless sweater with nicely fitting black Bermuda shorts. I like his shoes. They're the same kind of black leather tennis shoes Belmont often wears. Anton's hair is out of its ponytail, and it's long and wavy. I hadn't realized how supremely attractive he is until now.

"Your French is very bad," he says.

I look around the room to make sure I'm not leaving anything. "And still I try."

"There is no need. Your English is much better."

I snicker. "Does my hacking of your language offend you?"

"Not at all. But I like your English. I want to hear you at your best."

"All right then, English it is." I give the room a final once-over. I feel as if I'm leaving something behind. I don't need my purse or my cell phone or keys. I don't need to take anything but myself! "I'm ready."

Anton and I flow into the night. Dexter and his team, including Kristin, Damien, and Braden, are waiting for us under the pavilion. Red, green, blue, and yellow lights streak across them. Jacques must have installed special-effect lighting in the roof. Oh, and my eyes did not deceive me—Melissa is with them. She notices me and whispers something to Kristin, then she wrinkles her nose as she shakes her head. At least she had the wherewithal to not look at me while she did that. I swear, I've never met such a bunch of catty women. Leaving them in the past is definitely one of the best decisions I've ever made.

The night is warm and spicy. Creatures whistle, squawk, and hiss. Anton leads us up the driveway, and I'm slightly confused because I hadn't seen another chateau in walking distance. I'll get around to asking where Mer Rouge is after I finish marveling at how the sprinkles of multi-colored light coat the tall poplar trees. The tiny dots start thick at the bases and thin out the higher they go. I've never seen that effect before, which is rivaled by the pink-lighted water pouring out of the three-tiered stone fountain. All the effects could easily cross the line into tacky-Christmas-decorations-ville, but it's all tastefully done.

Braden shuffles up and stops at Anton's side to inquire about the sort of girls who live in these parts. Anton goes into a rant about how some girls are fat and some are skinny, some are tall and some are short. I chuckle when he goes into a silly story about a short man who has a tall wife with large breasts. Braden looks utterly confused. He has no idea that Anton is screwing with him.

Behind me, Melissa chirps in Dexter's ear about how Scott Whistler left in a huff. She lingers on the part where Whistler exploded when he learned he was being let go.

"'Your time is short-lived,'" Melissa says, mimicking Whistler. "'You're all going to be replaced. Every single *fucking* last one of you.'" She laughs.

"What a tool," Kristen says, going on about how she should've never hired him. Apparently she knew he could be difficult to direct.

Damien steps up beside me. "How's it going, Daisy?"

"Good, and you?" I reply.

"It's been…" He shrugs.

I read his gesture as him saying it hasn't been that good. "Sorry I didn't make it to Provence. Family issues."

He looks down and snorts. "I heard."

"Oh yeah, what did you hear?"

Damien checks over his shoulder to see who's listening. "Some crazy shit."

"Like what?"

He comes in closer. "Were you kidnapped?"

I toss my head back and belt out a good laugh. "Gosh, the juicy stuff always travels fast."

"You weren't?" he asks.

I think about it. "I guess I was kidnapped. That's what happens when you have a crazy family, I guess."

"But you're free now."

"Thanks to my husband."

"He's the one who kidnapped you?"

"No, my sister and my husband's brother and cousin did. They're very peculiar people."

"So are you coming back or what?" he asks, getting to the point.

I shake my head. "That would be a no."

"Why not? It's your shit they're fucking up."

"Are they really fucking it up?"

"Big time."

"I can hear you, Damien," Kristin says.

He gives me a look as if to say Kristin is the culprit.

I pat Damien's shoulder. "Well, the articles and the book are the only two forms of my work that matter to *me*. However, I think Dexter is ready to get you guys back on track. I also think you should speak up more. Hell, it's your career on the line too."

"Yeah," he says as if that's easier said than done.

"Fear is the root of all stagnancy," I say. "Believe me, I know."

Damien looks at me as if something just clicked inside him as we reach the dirt road. A cattle truck with white lights strung along the rails awaits us.

"Is that our ride?" I ask Anton.

"It is not your ride." Anton thumbs over his

shoulder. "This is for them. You and I, we go to the lake."

"What's at the lake?"

"We will take the canoe."

Dexter throws up his arms. "What about us? We can't take canoes?"

"I only have one, and it is only for two."

Dexter takes my arm. "Don't forget," he whispers.

"I won't," I say.

Kristin widens her eyes at me. Dexter must've filled her in on what we talked about. She could be a little more gracious about it. A kernel of defiance inside me wants to say to hell with convincing Belmont to undo whatever deal he made with Gil Abbot, but I'm not trying to set things right for Kristin's sake. This is about settling up with Dexter.

19

THE HOST AND I

DAISY LORD

*A*nton rows me across the opaque lake in a red canoe. He says that arriving this way to the Mer Rouge Wine Festival is customary.

"So this isn't a party thrown together at the last minute?"

"Why do you think that is true?" Anton asks.

"I thought it was one of my husband's elaborate schemes to impress me."

"You do not care for his elaborate schemes?"

I feel myself beaming. "Yeah, I care for them. I just wonder sometimes. When is he going to stop cold turkey, ignore me, and find a mistress to wine and dine?"

Anton narrows an eye. "What is cold turkey?"

I chuckle. "It's just an expression. It means he

stops cold, like I bore him. It's over. He moves on to the next Daisy."

"There is no other Daisy. If there were more Daisies, then more men would be happy."

I snort. "Ah, now you're a marvelous bull-shitter."

Anton winks. "But do you think your husband wants a mistress?"

"Don't they all?"

"No, they do not."

Of course I'm being overly cynical. The bright moon beaming down upon us has put me in some sort of mood. I'm not sullen or tranquil—I just feel like being candid. Anton paddles, and we glide across the water.

"What about you, Anton? What are you going to do about Anna and Nina?"

"What do you mean?"

I watch how smoothly he rows. "Hey, can I do that?"

"Do what?"

"Row the boat."

Anton shrugs. "Okay, but we will be careful when we make the exchange."

Anton and I keep the boat steady and balanced

as we slowly change positions. I sit at the helm and clutch the oars.

"Ready?" I ask him.

"Are *you* ready?"

"Why all the questions to my questions?"

He chuckles. "It is my way."

"Well, answer my questions, damn it." I pull the oars, and we're off.

"Okay, I will answer your questions directly." He's silent for a moment. "I have not made love to a woman in a long time. I would like to have the body but not the mind. Actually, it would be nice to have Angelina's body. Is she really in love?"

I nod. "Um-hum. Very much so."

"All right, well… I don't want the headache of Anna and Nina."

"Do you think they come as a package deal?" I ask.

"A package deal?"

"Think about it."

Anton smirks. "Yes, I do."

"And if they weren't?"

"Then I would want Anna's body."

"But not her mind?"

"Yes, that too. But first, her body."

I laugh and shake my head. My arms are getting sore. I glance behind me to see how far we are from our destination. The chateau is close. It sits high on a hill.

"What a sight," I say.

Two canoes pass, one on each side of us. We say bonjour.

"Daisy, I wanted to say this to you," Anton says.

"What is it?"

"Don't wait for the cold turkey. Live." He shakes his hands at the sky. "*Live!*"

His enthusiasm is infectious and I toss my head back. "I'm ready to *live!*" I shout.

Anton and I beam at each other.

"Good," he says. "I am ready to see you live."

"And you—are you ready to live?"

"Very much so."

I REACH THE EDGE OF THE LAKE. AS IF HE'S DONE this a million times, Anton hops out and pulls the canoe onto the muddy shore. He takes my hand and helps me off. "Fame" by David Bowie plays in the distance. Anton and I trot up the scarcely lit stairway.

"Do you like this song?" he asks when we reach the grass.

"I do!"

"Then let's dance!"

Anton lifts my arm, and the natural thing to do is spin. He breaks away and shakes his shoulders and moves his legs. He's a pretty good dancer.

"Dance, Daisy!" he says.

I realize that I'm just walking and watching him, so I move my hips, legs, and shoulders in response. I'm an okay dancer. I get by.

Anton curls an arm around my waist as we continue to bop up the grass. The lawn is large. Red, yellow, and blue disco lights light up the front of the chateau, which is set on a hill above. The closer we get, the more people we run into. This party is well attended. I'm having a good time dancing up the quad with Anton, but I wonder, *where is Belmont?*

BELMONT LORD

Daisy hadn't arrived yet, as far as Belmont knew. He watched his guests file out of trucks or walk up from the lake. He'd had a long phone call with Meg earlier, who updated him on how she and Audrey had made the event look and feel as if it had been planned months in advance, which wasn't a simple task to perform outside of the U.S. They'd booked popular groups like Simple Road, Hang-a-ran and Dirty Green, pop-rock artist Orange Tank, and pop-soul artist Michael Preston. A few more special guests were also booked just to appease him.

The hefty set-list and the promise of the steady flow of Mer Rouge and Mes Fleurs wines affected turnout more than his name, and oh, what a turnout! Meg and Audrey had put their heads together and issued seven hundred fifty invitations. They'd received three hundred eight yes replies, one hundred forty-six nos, and one hundred twenty maybes. There were already enough guests present as far as Belmont was concerned, but more just kept coming. Only one person mattered, and she hadn't shown up yet.

Belmont sneered when he saw Dexter hop out of the back of one of the trucks. Belmont didn't like to get into physical altercations, but Dexter had earned a good punch in the throat for all he'd done to get between Daisy and Belmont. As if showing up at Chateau Mes Fleurs would work. Dexter's love for Daisy was unrequited.

Belmont smirked. Daisy wanted *him,* and he sure as hell wanted her. Twice that day he'd had to force himself not to grab her by her wet pussy and overdose on just flat out fucking her. He wanted her hard knot against his tongue. He wanted to drink her nectar. Just thinking about kissing her and running his hands up and down her body made his pants tight. Then he saw her dancing across the grass with Anton. His heartbeat sped up as he studied Daisy's thighs, hips, waist, and breasts. Hell, he could tell she wasn't wearing panties or a bra.

"Fuck," Belmont muttered. He took a deep breath. He had to get a fucking grip.

Daisy and Anton were laughing, seemingly in high spirits. Belmont smiled. Daisy was radiant. He wanted to snatch her away from Anton, carry her to his suite, and rip that dress off her. *Not yet.*

Daisy said something to Anton, and he tossed his head back to laugh. Belmont wondered what she had said. Now Anton said something, and Daisy laughed. She glowed in a way he had never seen before. What was it about her? Anton spun Daisy around at the exact moment the answer came to him—Daisy was his Earth.

Karl Livre and his date, who looked like the kind of girl Belmont used to pick up in Divin, sauntered up to Belmont to shake hands. Belmont kept his eyes on Daisy as Karl said it was good to see him in France and asked if he planned on visiting Paris.

"What do you have in mind?" Belmont asked. It was always business between him and Karl.

"We want to refurbish some power plants in West Africa. The business is good. And you have the means to make it happen fast."

Daisy was engaged in conversation with Anton, but her eyes flitted toward the stage, to the tables and chairs along the dance floor, and to the bar.

"I'll have Meg call Rita. They can set something up for us. Next week?" Belmont said in a rush.

"Yes, that is perfect," Karl said with a deep French accent that was sprinkled with German.

"Excuse me, please." Belmont dipped behind a wall just as Daisy glanced in his direction. Watching Daisy from afar was becoming his favorite habit.

A knot formed in his throat when Dexter walked up to her. Anton dismissed himself, and Dexter put a hand on Daisy's back as if he owned her. She shook her head. Belmont could read her lips. She was saying, "I will, I will, I will." She nudged his shoulder and said something else.

Dexter reluctantly turned away and rejoined his group at a table.

Belmont watched Daisy walk into a tent where the caterers, who were also shipped in from America, were preparing the food. The next time Belmont caught sight of Daisy, she was picking a cheese hors d'oeuvre off a platter. She winked at the server when he caught her. The guy said something, and she blew him a kiss. Humph. He would've never guessed that his wife was a flirt, but he shouldn't be surprised. Whenever Daisy chose to seduce him, she could bring him to his knees and leave him begging for more. Like when she'd grabbed his cock earlier. Belmont had thought he would burst. When he made it out of the cottage, he'd had to stop and collect himself. He had no idea how he would make it through the night without pinning her up against a wall or spreading her across a table and fucking her brains out, but he would give it the old college try.

Belmont watched Daisy walk out the back of the tent and sashay along the flower garden. She stopped to incline her face toward the white gardenias. She took a deep sniff, held it, and let it go. He smiled when she smiled up at the moon. Daisy skipped up the steps of a stone pavilion. When she reached the marble floor, she noticed the darkness lingering between the ancient walls. He knew Daisy well enough to know that she was paying homage to the life and times of the structure. Daisy often revered sunsets, moon risings, architecture, and landscapes. He had never asked her to tell him what she was thinking when she looked at the world that way. All he wanted to do was make love to her. But from now on, he was going to start asking.

It was the perfect time to approach Daisy, but Belmont knew he couldn't. He could see how vital the moment was to her. Perhaps it made her feel just as he felt after his conversation with Karl. Belmont's work gave him purpose. Daisy loved her job as a travel writer, and from the very beginning of their time together, he had been fucking with her purpose.

He'd started with trying to get her to start a travel magazine with A&Rt Media. It hadn't even excited her. She'd gone through the motions for about a month, had all the meetings with potential editors and staff writers, and decided to put off the project indefinitely. Belmont had made himself believe it was because she was having a difficult pregnancy, but deep down he knew the reason. Daisy wasn't a publisher! She just didn't want to sit in an office and worry about numbers. She wanted to hit the road.

Belmont dug deep. Could he do it? Could he let her travel all over the world, mostly without him? There would be men like Dexter lying in wait. There would be many nights when he would ache to hold her, kiss her, and make love to her. He would want to see her roll her eyes and listen to her grunt while reading the *Times*. She had a love-hate relationship with the opinion section. Reading it was one of the few things in life that got her fired up. She would ask him, "Who gives these people a license to draw these conclusions?" Belmont would shrug. He knew she wasn't asking for his response.

Daisy squinted at the chateau. Belmont thought about his session with Dr. Calvet. He may not have treated her as his father did his mother, but he had had certain expectations of her, which didn't include racing all over the world to write articles. Why should she when he had enough money for the both of them? But damn it. Daisy wasn't one of those people. She didn't do anything for the money, not even love him.

She smiled as if she'd just figured out his secret and skipped down the short set of steps. She moved in his direction as if she knew exactly where she was going, and Belmont smirked. He was staying in the tower suite, and that was where she was headed.

Belmont scrambled to stay out of her eyesight. He rushed down the walkway, pretending not to see those who wanted to capture his attention. A lot of women were present, and they watched him like flesh-eating hawks. Belmont dipped around a group of guests, waiting for Daisy to pass. If she hadn't been so focused on her destination, she might have seen him. Belmont planned to follow her all the way up to the tower. Screw abstaining—he grew wood just thinking about all the things he would do to her in a matter of minutes.

"Daisy!" a woman called.

Daisy stopped dead in her tracks and looked toward the voice. "You made it!"

"Shit," Belmont muttered. His cock throbbed. "You're going to have to wait," he told *it*.

Belmont looked to the right. A woman was approaching him, smirking and batting her eyelashes. He recognized her face, and her name was on the tip of his tongue. Sadly the line between friendship and fuck-buddy had always been fuzzy for him before Daisy came along. The woman's hair was long and thick. Her eyes were brown and almond-shaped. She had long, shapely legs. Her dress was tight. Belmont turned to walk in the opposite direction just as he remembered that her name was Yvette. She was an American. A girl he met in L.A. The last thing he'd said to her was, "I'll call you." He wondered what the hell was she doing there.

After evading Yvette, Belmont had to find Daisy in the sea of bodies. It appeared as if all those who'd said they would attend had showed up, plus the nos and maybes. By the time Belmont caught a glimpse of Daisy, she was with Anton and two women. They were laughing. Anton put his hand on Daisy's back, and one of the women noticed. Then Daisy turned and spotted him. All Belmont could do was wave.

DAISY LORD

I wave at Belmont. All the talking around me ceases as I watch him walk toward me. He's wearing black slacks that fit his body like the perfect pair of designer gloves. His black button-front shirt shows off his sexy physique. He's so *GQ*, and he's mine, all mine.

"Who is he?" Anna asks.

"That is Daisy's husband," Anton says.

"Oh," Nina says. "I did not know you were married." Her eyes go right to my hand. She's looking for that damn ring.

Belmont embraces me. Our kiss is quick, but our gazes lock. Belmont rubs his cheek against mine, and my head feels light. The endorphins have kicked in. I'm high off love.

Belmont and Anton greet each other with a manly hug, patting each other hard on the shoulders. I smile. I feel as if the hug is their way of saying, "We're family from now until forever."

"Who are your friends?" Belmont asks.

"Um, this is Nina and Anna."

He shakes their hands. "I'm Jack Lord."

Both women look at him as if he has entrancing rays flowing from his face.

"He does not look like a frog," Anna says.

I chuckle. "Why would you think he would look like a frog?"

"Because men with his kind of wealth, they look like ugly animals."

"Like a parrot," Nina says.

"Or a turtle," Anna adds.

Belmont and I laugh. Anton looks at Anna with

stars in his eyes. I do understand his dilemma. Anna and Nina are very tuned-in to each other.

"Do you want to dance?" he asks, although it's not clear which woman he's offering the invitation.

Anna looks at Nina.

Nina shrugs. "Okay."

Anton and Anna look at each other as he takes Nina's hand. I shake my head. What in the world is he doing?

"Hey," Belmont whispers in my ear.

I look at him.

"What about you? Do you want to dance?"

I turn to Anna.

"Go." She waves. "I am fine."

I hear the disappointment in her voice, but I nod. Every molecule in my body is compelled to stick my nose where it probably doesn't belong. I take a deep breath and just go for it.

"Anton wants you," I whisper to Anna.

She looks at me as though I'm the headlights and she's the deer. I squeeze Belmont's hand and give him a look that says "get me far away from here." He's happy to oblige.

Belmont leads me to another patio where there are mostly high tables and a full-service bar. Many of the guests eye Belmont as if they want to say something to him and would if they could only get his attention. So many women are dressed as if they're out for a night at a disco. One woman sitting at the bar hits another on the arm when we pass them. They eye Belmont and sneer at me.

"Did you hire prostitutes or something?" I ask.

Belmont pulls me into his arms, and our bodies melt together. "That would sure get me into a world of trouble. They're just looking for a fun night out."

"A fun night out with you?"

"They must've heard I was giving a party. As you can see, it's a little over the top. Plus, they haven't gotten the memo."

"What memo is that?" I ask.

"You know what the memo would say, don't you?"

"'Jack Lord is no longer split from his wife. So back off, hussies.'"

Belmont interrupts my chuckling with a passionate kiss. We moan, frustrated that our mouths won't merge into one. He's hard, and I'm wet. We're both willing to ditch this shindig and go straight to bed.

I stare him with a heavy-lidded gaze. "Where do you really want to take me, Jack?"

Belmont presses his forehead against mine. "Don't tempt me. I need you to dance with me."

Our moment is interrupted when a girl bumps into us.

"Fuck you, Jack Lord," she snarls.

Belmont turns.

The woman scowls as if she wants to rip off Belmont's face. "You don't remember me?"

Before Belmont can find his words, I see her arm shift, then I catch the tail end of the wine she throws in his face. My mouth is caught open. I can hardly believe what just happened. A series of camera flashes go off. Belmont stands in front of me, his arms wrapped around me as if he has to protect me from her.

She goes crazy. "That's why your reputation is fucked! You can't keep your dick out of bitches like her!" She points at me.

I gasp. "What are you talking about, lady? He's my husband, you skank!" I don't know what's gotten into me, but I feel like roaring as I try to climb over Belmont's back.

"Skank?" the woman shouts as if I've just deeply offended her.

Belmont's too strong for me to break free, but

two men in security uniforms carry her out as she calls me different kinds of bitches.

"That's why you're getting what you deserve, Jack!" she yells before going back to insulting me.

I'm shaking. Everybody's looking at us.

Belmont faces me. "Are you okay?"

I nod, although I'm still shaken up. "Who in the world was that?"

He frowns as though he doesn't want to answer.

"It's fine, Belmont. I can take it."

"There's nothing for you to take. She's not stable, baby." Belmont rubs my arms. "You're shaking."

I remind myself that the confrontation is over. *I think.* I frown at another woman who's wearing a very short skirt. She's watching Belmont with that look in her eyes.

"How many of your ex-flings are here?" I ask.

"Daisy, come on."

"What?" I snap.

He draws back to get a better look at my face. "You don't have to be jealous of other women."

"I'm not jealous." That didn't sound convincing.

"She was a woman I used to see way before I

met you. If I had known she'd upset you, I would've her thrown out earlier."

My heart takes a dip. "You saw her earlier?"

Belmont lifts a hand. "Not in the way you're thinking. She walked past me. I was too focused on you to pay attention to her, though."

I sigh. I know a thing about the past rearing its ugly head. A few weeks ago, Adrian, my ex, tried to seduce me. I'd never told Belmont about it because he'd probably do something drastic, like confront Adrian.

"Oh well… it's over," I say.

Belmont raises an eyebrow. "'Skank'? You were really trying to claw your way to her."

I roll my eyes. "Well, she needed her eyes scratched out."

Belmont looks off playfully. "Damn, I would've loved to see that."

I nudge his chest and take him by the collar. "We should get you cleaned up."

Belmont shakes his head. "First you owe me a dance."

"But you're all covered in wine."

He curls his tongue out of his mouth and licks the wine. "At least it's the premium brand." He smirks.

That was sexy. "Oh?" I lick the same spot his tongue left wet.

Belmont's mouth seizes mine, and we engage in a luscious kiss. The guests nearest us clap.

Belmont presses his lips against my ear. "Let's pick up where we left off."

I nod, looking at him with stars in my eyes.

He takes my hand and leads me across the same grass Anton and I had danced up earlier. We're walking adjacent to the lake, toward the darkest part of the lawn. Belmont and I aren't the only ones seeking privacy. The darkness masks lovers enfolded in embraces. We reach a fence with vines growing through the wire. Belmont opens the gate.

"Where are you taking me?" I ask. It's just so dark. It looks as if there's nothing back here but buzzing night crawlers and wild trees.

"You'll see."

I take it he had this moment planned out. That's one reason why Belmont is so successful—he never disregards the smallest details. He glances at me as he guides me through the maze of trees. I smile at him then look up. The stars are brighter than they were last night. The birds of night, which hide in the bushes, do a little squawking. Applause erupts in the distance.

Belmont checks his watch. "Damn it."

"What?"

"It's nine o'clock."

"How are y'all doing tonight?" I hear my father say through the party speakers.

My eyes expand and I tug on Belmont's hand. "Is Jacques here?"

We step out of the trees into a small clearing. The grass looks trimmed, and pink roses surround the circle.

Belmont gathers me in his arms. "Yes, it's your father. You owe me a dance and not to just any song."

My father plays a string of his most popular notes on a trumpet. The crowd applauds and whistles.

"Oh, Betty," Jacques calls.

A beautiful voice fills the air with a few notes of "God Bless the Child." The guests are mad for Betty Moreland.

"Is she here, Jacques?" Betty asks.

I beam at Belmont, who's smirking.

"She's somewhere around here," Jacques replies.

"All right, then. Ma fleur, wherever you are, this one's for you and him…"

Jacques starts playing "God Bless the Child."

"You should've danced this with *me*," Belmont says.

I roll my eyes playfully. "Oh Belmont, what am I going to do with you?"

Betty Moreland starts singing. Our lips press against each other's, and the tips of our tongues touch. We're merely making contact. Belmont's hands massage my back, working down to my ass. His breaths are heavy.

"You're so soft," he whispers.

I lick his lower lip, and the next thing I know, Belmont spins me around and stuffs his fingers between my legs. I gasp when he smashes my clit and grinds against my butt. Our dancing has ceased. There's neediness in the way he's stimulating me. I reach back to hold his neck, and he goes completely still. All I can feel is his package twitching.

"Daisy?" he says breathlessly.

"Yes?" I'm in a daze.

"What do you want from me?"

"I want you to make love to me."

"No… we'll get to that." He chuckles. "I had a long session with Luc Calvet yesterday. I want you to tell me what you want, and I'll do it. Whatever it is you want, baby."

I understand that he's not talking about wishes that are fleeting. Belmont is referring to changes in the way we make our lives together. It's time for me to speak up. It's time for me to *live.* "I want you to know that you don't have to raise the dead to make me happy." The fact that he said that still bothers me.

Belmont stuffs his tongue in my ear. His breath is warm, and so is his tongue. "What else?"

"My family. Thank you for making things better between Heloise and Jacques and me."

"You're welcome…" He sighs. "What else?"

It's hard for me to think with him stimulating me like this. "Huh?"

"What are you going to write your next article about?"

I close my eyes, and my hips gravitate toward his finger. "Yes, I want that…" I sigh.

"I want you to travel and write. I won't stand in your way. Is our house too big?"

"Belmont…"

"Is it, baby? Don't hold back. I need to hear it."

I moan. "Yes."

"I hear you. We'll sell it."

"But it was your first."

"You're my first. Where do you want to live?"

"I don't know," I whimper. I raise my hips higher to catch the sensation.

"Not Santa Monica, baby?"

"Okay."

"And nowhere west of the 405."

"Ah…" My legs shiver as an orgasm pulses through my pussy.

Belmont shoves his tongue in my ear and jerks his finger quicker and harder against my swollen knot until the sensation subsides.

"Malibu is west of the 405," I say, breathing heavily.

"Do you think I like that fucking town?"

"I thought so."

"I don't. You ever considered Montecito?" he asks.

"Never, but I like that town."

"I always wanted to build something for us there. It doesn't have to be a mansion. It can be a country house. Six bedrooms?"

"Four," I say.

"Five?"

"Okay, five."

"Five baths?" he says breathlessly.

"Okay."

Belmont spins me around. "See how easy that was?"

That look in his eyes says he's about to devour me. "Uh-hum."

"Now get on the grass and open your legs."

I step away from him, sit on the grass, part my legs, and lay back.

"Pull your dress up. I want to see your pussy."

I do as he asks, exposing my lower half. Belmont skips a breath. He bites his lip as he unzips his pants and pulls them and his underwear off one leg at a time. He's so hard that his dick is pointing at his head. It's tantalizing, and I feel powerful that I've made a man of his caliber that excited.

I sit up. "Wait."

His eyes are glazed over. I take him by his erection.

"No, baby. I want your pussy."

"And I want your cock. Let me have it. Please…"

Belmont concedes by dropping his arms to his sides. I smirk. He's giving me anything I want. Finally. I stroke his dick. It's already moistened and rigid as steel. Belmont gasps as I lap my tongue around the tip. I don't want to fool around—I get right down to business and put it all the way in my mouth. I squeeze my lips around his shaft and press my tongue against the middle. I swallow as much of his ten inches of rock-hard cock as I can. I bob up and down, sucking him as though I want to milk him dry. Belmont mutters a string of curses. I grab his ass with one hand and massage where it meets the crease of his thigh, and I use the thumb of my other hand to give his taint a deep massage.

"Fuck! Daisy!" Belmont shouts, grabbing my hair. His breaths are loud and quick. His knees try to buckle under, but he recovers. "Shit!" Belmont pulls his dick out of my mouth.

The next thing I know, my thighs are pinned to the grass and Belmont's dick is so far inside me that I scream. He pounds me. One. Two. Three thrusts. His body quakes, and he grunts and whimpers. Belmont collapses on top of me, and I hold him. Our breaths slow as Belmont's body relaxes.

"What bag did you pull those tricks out of?" he asks.

I chuckle. "I tried some new things."

"You sure as hell did."

"Did they work?"

Belmont nods. "Every single one of them."

I chuckle. "Angelina and Maggie were talking

about how to give the best blowjobs on the New Year's Eve we spent on Martha's Vineyard."

"And it took you this long to try their suggestions?"

"I don't know…" I squeeze Belmont tight. "I feel uninhibited tonight."

"Are you rewarding me for finally wising up?"

"Did blowing you feel like a reward?"

Belmont shrugs. "I'm fonder of your pussy."

I roll my eyes. "I know."

Betty and Jacques have finished their set. Now the music is louder and faster.

"This grass is hard," Belmont says. "Are you uncomfortable?"

Now that he mentioned it… "A little."

He stands and pulls me up. We kiss some more.

"Now what?" I ask when our lips separate.

He flexes his eyebrows. "Let's go to your bed."

I narrow one eye. "Babe, my cottage is way too small for you."

"This trip is about you, not me. Maybe we should do that more often."

My eyes dance. "Take trips that are all about me?"

He chuckles. "Change them up. Take one that's about you, then one that's about me."

"Hmm, I like it. But where will we go on a trip that's all about you?" I ask.

"Can't you guess?"

My lips twist into a flirtatious grin. "A luxury villa, full service, on a bluff that overlooks the sea in Monaco, or a luxury yacht in the port. And me naked twenty-four-seven."

"How does Monday sound?" he jokes.

"Oh no, we'll still be on my trip on Monday." I kiss him tenderly. "But my trip does include me naked twenty-four-seven."

Belmont makes his penis jump. I chuckle.

"He'll be ready for round two by the time we make it to your pint-sized bed," Belmont says as he puts his pants back on.

I straighten my dress, and we're on our way.

20
I CHOOSE YOU

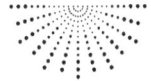

ANTON BISSET

*A*nton kept his eyes on Nina as they danced. She was definitely prettier than Anna, and Anna knew it, which was why she couldn't believe that he actually preferred her. Nina turned heads without much effort. Even as they danced, men watched her body move. They were the kind of men who collected women like Nina to lounge on their yachts or play the hostess of their mansions. But she wasn't sexy or interesting. She wasn't quick-witted or cynical. She didn't possess a come-hither look. Anton believed all women should possess a coquettish gaze. Nina had never had to develop one. She was just too beautiful.

He felt as if the song went on forever. Nina didn't look as though she were enjoying herself. He smiled at her to perk her up. She returned a weak smile then clenched her lips. He had seen that look before. She was still hurt by their past. Anton couldn't apologize for hurting her more than he already had. The tension-filled dance was like torture.

He looked around to see who he could connect with, and he locked eyes with a girl. She had platinum blond hair, red lipstick, and wore a very tight cat suit. His lust chose her for the night since Anna wasn't an option. Anton smiled at the girl, and she smiled back. The guy she was dancing with was older. Anton snickered when he remembered what Anna and Nina had said about rich men like that one. Out of the turtle, frog, and parrot, that man looked most like a ferret. The women at the party were definitely more attractive than the men.

The song finally reached its last note.

"Thank you for the dance," he said, intending to ditch her for the rest of the night.

"Anton, are you leaving so soon?" Anna said when her dance partner swept her up against him.

He wasn't a turtle, parrot, frog, or ferret. Her partner was more like Anton: a good-looking guy out to have a good time and score a woman with a sexy body for the night. Anna had the kind of round ass and plump tits that made a man's mouth water. When the guy's hand settled on her ass, Anton thought he would lose it.

"Do you want to continue to dance?" he asked Nina.

Nina shrugged indifferently. "Yes, okay."

The deejay spun a new song, and Anton and Nina danced right next to Anna and her partner. The woman in the cat suit kept making eye contact with him, and Anna acted as if he didn't exist. Nina was boring as usual, but Anton wouldn't show Anna that he was miserable. He grabbed Nina's hips to help her loosen up a bit. For a little while, Nina followed his lead, and they danced much better. He caught a glimpse of Anna watching them. If only he could get to the blonde in the cat suit. She would really make Anna jealous. Then he saw Jacques and his band preparing to take the stage.

"No way!" He put his mouth near Nina's ear. "I must go." He motioned toward Jacques.

Nina gestured that it was okay. Like a gentleman, he walked her off the dance floor before he went to talk to Jacques. He and the blonde locked eyes as he passed her. He would claim her when the time was right. Anton leaped on the stage.

"Anton, how's it going?" Jacques said, and they hugged.

"I am good. Much better now that Daisy has been here."

"Where the hell is she?" Jacques's eyes swept over the audience. He looked disappointed by her absence.

"She is with, um, Belmont."

Jacques nodded. "Ah, then I hope I see her sooner or later."

"Yes, yes… are you lodging at Mes Fleurs?"

"We're flying back to Paris after this set."

Anton glanced at Anna. She was still dancing with the guy. The music had changed, and the beat was draggy and sensual—so were her moves.

"You want to play something tonight?" Jacques asked him.

Anton realized Jacques was curious about why he was up on stage with nothing to say. He shook his head. "I did not bring my sticks."

"Larry will share."

Anna rubbed her ass against the man's cock.

"I know but not tonight. I will see you later?" Anton jumped off the stage.

He was incensed. A travesty was unfolding right before his eyes, and he couldn't stop it. He wanted to avoid Nina, who was still standing where he left her. Anton searched for the woman in the cat suit, but she was no longer dancing. Someone tapped his shoulder. He spun around.

"You are looking for me?" It was the woman in the cat suit.

Anton nodded. "I am."

"Well, here I am."

Anton pondered taking the woman to a quiet place to convince her to go home with him so he could fuck her brains out. That would satisfy his biological need to connect with a woman on a sexual and emotional level. But first, he wanted to see Anna again. He could see her when he returned to the studio to pick up Belmont's painting, but he couldn't wait that long, especially since she was still rubbing her ass against the guy's cock. He wondered how far that guy would get with Anna tonight.

"Let's dance," Anton said.

Her eyes were smoldering. "You are sure?"

"Dance first, and we'll see what happens next," he said.

Anton took her hand before she could respond. Anna saw him as soon as he showed up beside her. The blonde twirled around twice, and her ass ended up right up against Anton's cock. He grew a boner instantly. He hadn't felt a nice, soft woman's ass against him in ages. Anna couldn't take her eyes off them, and neither could Nina, who was glaring from the edge of the dance floor.

Anton couldn't move because he was so hard. He didn't know what the hell was happening to him. He took the woman by the hips. Who did that to a poor, defenseless, sex-deprived man? If he had been sexed-up, he could have handled the stimulation much better. If he was going to come, then he wanted to do it while fantasizing about what he really wanted. He focused on Anna. She wore a white dress that contrasted with her peach skin. When they'd first met, her hair was cropped, and he'd thought that was sexy. It was now neck length, and the way the strands slid across her face turned him on. Anton had put his nose on her neck once when they were engaged in horseplay. She had been very soft and smelled sweet. He almost took her then.

Anton's dance partner had turned around, and she was smashing her pussy against his erection. There was no doubt about what she wanted to do.

"What is your name?" the blonde asked.

He snorted. He didn't think she cared to know. "I'm Anton."

"I am Mirabelle."

The music died down.

"Are we finished dancing?" she asked.

"How are y'all doing tonight?" Jacques said.

People clapped.

"Don't you want to stay for Jacques Blanchard?" Anton asked.

"Who is that?" Mirabelle asked.

"He's a famous musician. Believe me, if you miss this performance, then you will miss heaven."

She batted her eyelashes. "You are already missing heaven."

Jacques and his band started to play.

Anna tugged on Anton's shoulder. "Dance with me."

Mirabelle tugged on his arm. "He is with me."

Anna widened her eyes. "Anton…"

"I will dance with her," Anton said to Mirabelle.

Mirabelle gasped as if she had been slapped in the face. "Then you lose!" She stomped off.

Anna wrapped her arms around him. She looked down. "You actually became excited by her?"

Anton embraced her. "It was a little bit of her and a little bit of someone else."

"Nina?"

Anton stared into Anna's face. He wondered why her face had always captivated him. Her eyes, nose, lips, cheeks, and the way each was situated on her face made her naturally sexy. Some women had it, but most did not—Anna had *it*.

Jacques introduced Betty Moreland.

"Is she here, Jacques?" Betty asked.

"She's somewhere around here," Jacques replied.

"Ma Fleur, this is for you!"

As Betty sang, Anton and Anna stared into each other's eyes.

"Your cousin said something interesting to me," Anna said.

"Daisy speaks more interesting words than uninteresting ones," he replied.

Anna snorted. "I love your bullshit."

He tossed his head back to chuckle, remembering that Daisy had also referred to him as a bullshitter. "And I love your mouth."

"She said that you wanted me. Do you?"

Anton felt as if he had just slammed into a wall of relief. "Yes." His heartbeat sped up.

"Always?" Anna asked.

"From the moment we met."

"Then I was not imagining things?"

Anton shook his head. They hugged each other tighter. Anna rested her face on his chest, and Anton pressed his nose against her forehead. She had the same sweet scent that had turned him on so many years ago.

"You were not going to fuck that prostitute, were you?" she asked.

"Prostitute? She wasn't a prostitute."

Anna rolled her eyes. "Look at her. She was a very costly prostitute."

Anton chuckled. "It doesn't matter because I was thinking about you the whole time."

"No?"

"Yes."

Anton glanced toward where he'd last seen Nina. She was no longer there. "I want to show you something. Will you let me?"

He looked deep into Anna's eyes. Her expression indicated that she knew that this was the point of no return. It could actually happen between them, and it had been a long time coming.

"Are we leaving?" she asked.

"Can you leave?"

"Maybe. Yes."

He asked, "Will you come with me now?"

She raised a finger. "Give me a moment."

"Can I kiss you first?"

Anna gulped. "Yes."

His lips melted against hers. Anton could not believe what he was doing. Her mouth was warm and tasted like wine. He gripped her back and brought her closer. If he could not make love to her, then he would die.

"What are you doing?" Nina asked.

Anton and Anna forced their lips apart. Nina's face was red and her eyes watery.

Anna looked flabbergasted. "Nina…"

"Fuck you, Anna! You too, Anton."

Anna reached for Nina's shoulder, but Nina whacked her across the face. "No!"

Anna grabbed her cheek, and they watched in horror as Nina ran away.

"Why are the women so feisty tonight?" a guest said.

Anton sneered at the man for making light of their situation.

Anna hugged him. "Take me away from here."

"Gladly." He wrapped an arm around her waist and led her off the dance floor.

They headed to the canoe. He was positive Daisy wouldn't need a ride back to the chateau. She was in her husband's hands now, and Jack Lord wasn't going to release her.

"I am sorry," Anton said as they marched across the grass.

"It is not your fault. I wanted to kiss you too."

Anton tugged her into his arms and kissed her deeply. He wondered how far Anna would let him go. There was no one around so he squeezed her scrumptious ass, and she let him. He hiked up her dress, and she let him slide his fingers under her panties. Anna whimpered against him when he slid as much of his finger as he could up her slit while reaching for her clit. She was so wet, but Anton didn't want his first time with Anna to happen on a bed of scratchy grass.

Anton sighed as he retracted his hand. "We go to my house."

Endorphins made Anton and Anna's legs wobbly as they walked to the canoe. Anna was very quiet, which worried Anton.

"You don't have to go through with this," he said.

"Do not doubt my feelings, Anton." She sounded as if she was chastising him.

"I don't, but you and Nina are like sisters. That is why you never acknowledged my feelings for you."

Anna pulled up to a stop. "You say you wanted me since we met, but you had a relationship with Nina. Why?"

Anton searched her glassy eyes. "I did not think you would have me without her."

"I would have and I will, although I prefer the both of you."

Anton searched Anna's sad expression. He could not believe what he was about to ask, but he was willing to delay his gratification to make her happier. "Do you want to wait until you make it better with her?"

Anna petted his chin. "Do you remember when you did not shave your face?"

Anton smiled. "I remember. Nina did not like hair on my face."

"But you asked me what I liked."

"You said whatever Nina wanted."

"I liked the hair," she said. "It made you look so manly. Without it, you are like a pretty, pretty girl."

Anton grabbed her hips and shoved her pelvis against his erection. "Does this feel like a pretty, pretty girl?"

"No," she said breathlessly.

Anna tilted her head as glided his tongue down the front of her neck and sucked her skin between his teeth.

"I knew you could make me feel good," Anna whispered.

"I can make you feel a lot better."

They stared into each other's eyes. After realizing they would have to wait to make love, they held hands and finished their walk to the canoe. Once they boarded, Anna snuggled against his chest as he rowed toward the moon. Never in a million years did he believe Anna would be nuzzled against his heart. Perhaps he loved her.

"Anton, get your horny ass back up here!" someone shouted from the hill.

Anna turned her curious expression toward him.

Anton snorted. "It is Claire."

"Your sister?"

"Yes."

21

CAN WE START ALL OVER AGAIN

DAISY LORD

*B*elmont and I walk to the Mer Rouge chateau with our arms around each other, still charged by our desire for one another. We have to make up for all the nights and mornings we've spent apart. But I insist that he change his shirt first. We're taking the long way around since Belmont doesn't want to be stopped by the guests who only showed up to get some face-time with him. He's not the kind of man who shuns a casual ear-bend, but he wants me on my back, and the sooner, the better.

We've just come out of a hidden path through the woods. Hidden bugs have gnawed my bare skin. The grass has made me itchy as well.

Belmont moves my hand and takes over scratching. "I should've never taken you to that flea patch. I didn't think I would lose control like that."

"You didn't?" I ask sarcastically.

Belmont laughs.

I catch sight of Jacques and three men loading instruments into a van. "Look, it's my father."

"Jacques!" Belmont calls.

My father glares in our direction. His preoccupied expression turns into a welcoming smile as we approach. "Ma fleur, Jack Lord!"

The hug between Jacques and me is tighter than the one he gives Belmont.

"Leaving so soon?" I ask.

"We're just packing up. We're going to grab a couple of drinks with Leon and Claire before we head to the airport. You should join us."

I look at Belmont. "Leon and Claire are Anton's brother and sister."

Belmont dips his head toward the party. "Go. I'll change my shirt and come join you."

I give him a longing look before we give each other a chaste kiss. Belmont shuffles to the chateau, and the three men finish packing the van. Jacques and I head to where the action is. Most of the guests are around the stage dancing and listening to the band. I recognize the five skinny, dark-haired boys on stage as the pop group Hang-a-ran. The people who aren't into the music hang under the tent, socializing. Most of them are three sheets to the wind. French wine hits fast.

Jacques updates me on what's been happening in Leon and Claire's lives. Leon is married with three kids, only he's here tonight with a friend Jacques calls Boy. Both of them are architects, and they came to the party because they were already in Bordeaux, working on refurbishing a government building. Claire drove up from Paris. She's recently back from MIT, where she is studying for a degree in biological engineering. Claire has lived in the United States since her freshman year in high school. Personality-wise, she's more like Heloise than Adélie, her mother. He says that with one eye narrowed, which is his look of warning.

"I don't know if that's a bad thing," I say.

Jacques laughs. He knows exactly what I mean. Heloise still complains about how badly Tante Adélie overreacts. She's very spastic for a European. It's strange.

I recognize Leon at first sight. He and Daniel are the same age, which makes him two years older than me. His friend, Boy, walks up to us with Leon.

"Leon, here is my daughter Daisy," Jacques says in French.

Leon opens his arms. "Ah, Daisy!"

I accept the hug. "Bonjour, Leon."

"It has been a lifetime, no?"

"A few lifetimes."

I shake Boy's hand. Funny, Boy looks nothing like a boy. He gazes at me with stars in his eyes.

"Daisy, like the beautiful flower?" Boy smiles. His teeth are yellow. He smokes too much.

"Yes, like a flower," I say, smiling.

"What would you like to drink, Daisy?" He sings my name. Then his eyes veer over my head.

Belmont wraps me up from behind.

I turn and look up. "That was fast."

"I wanted to hurry up and get back to you." He glances at Boy. "Seems I'm just in time."

We get lost in each other's eyes for a moment.

"Leon, this is my husband," I say.

"Jack Lord," Leon says as he and Belmont shake hands, "is an honor to meet you."

"Likewise," Belmont says.

Leon's smile expands. "So, Daisy, I heard you write travelogues."

"I do! I'm a travel writer," I say.

"You know our paths almost crossed. You were in Tenerife in 2011?"

"Yes, I was!"

"You left a day before I arrived. I read your article. It was very engaging. I was impressed."

"Thank you," I say.

Jacques motions for a roaming waiter to serve us all a glass of red wine.

"So you're not staying at Mes Fleurs?" I ask Jacques.

"No, baby, I have a group in the studio tomorrow morning."

"Oh." I know I sound disappointed because Belmont squeezes me tighter.

"Why don't you come up? We have a concert tomorrow night," Jacques says.

Belmont and I look at each other.

"I think we can make it," he says to my father.

"Get there early and meet me backstage. Dongo and Pey will be there too. I want them to see you, Daisy."

I nod excitedly. Jacques kisses my forehead and shakes all the men's hands before waving good-bye. My father will never change. He can't stay in one place long unless he's playing music.

Jacques is close to making an escape when

Anton walks up, holding Anna's hand. A young woman is with them, and I recognize her from the pictures in the tower hallway. She's Claire, Anton and Leon's sister. Anton and Claire hug and kiss my father good-bye before Jacques continues leaving. I search for Nina, but she's nowhere to be found. I'm so curious about what happened between the three of them, but I can't take my eyes off Claire. She has Anton's eyes, Leon's lips, and a split chin, which is a dominant Bisset family trait.

Claire points at me. "You're Daisy, right?"

"I am."

She quickly gives me a hug. After letting go, she notices Belmont and bashfully looks away.

"This is my husband, Belmont," I say.

She shyly looks at him.

"Hello," he says.

Although Belmont moves in for a hug, she extends her hand for a handshake. I think she's intimidated by his presence. It's no matter to Belmont. He's used to that.

"You're prettier in person," she says to me.

"Thank you. You're pretty too."

She shrugs dismissively. "I've heard a lot about you from Anton. He says that you are addicting."

Anton and I smile at each other. As

Belmont, Leon, and Boy, whose real name is Augusto, discuss refurbishing historical buildings, we finally get into what happened with Nina.

"I know Nina is obsessed with you, Anton," Claire says.

Anna gives Claire a cross look.

"Sorry, Anna, but it's true."

"Nina is not used to not getting what she wants, that is all," Anna says.

"But she slapped you?" Claire says emphatically.

Anna has a sad look in her eyes. "Yes, she did. But we will talk. She will understand."

Claire rolls her eyes. "I doubt it. Anton, remember when she smashed all the pieces you were going to display in that urban contemporary museum? She said you were flirting with the curator."

"I remember," Anton says.

"I know she's your friend, Anna, but she has a *Fatal Attraction* side."

"*Fatal Attraction*? What is that?" Anna asks.

"It's a movie where the woman has an affair with a married man, and when he tries to break it off, she goes bat-shit crazy," I say.

Anna shakes her head. "Oh no, Nina is beautiful. Many men want to love her."

"Let's end this depressing conversation," Anton says. "Daisy, when will I see you again after you leave the chateau?"

I take a moment to think. "Why don't you come out to Martha's Vineyard for the 4th of July, all of you? The house is big enough." I nudge Belmont in the ribs.

"Yes, come for a visit." He kisses my ear, massages my ribcage, and whispers, "I've run out of patience."

"That is an American holiday?" Anna asks.

"It's like Bastille Day," I say.

"With fireworks?"

"Yes, and Belmont will make a bonfire. It's one of his many talents." I snuggle against him.

"I'm ready to show you another talent right now," Belmont whispers in my ear.

I look at him. He smirks. We tear our gazes off each other only to see that they're all watching us. We probably look like the start of an R-rated movie.

"Then it's settled, you'll come," I say to take the awkwardness out of the moment.

"I will see," Anna says.

"Don't worry about a flight or anything. I'll arrange Belmont's jet for you."

"Oh," Anna says, gazing at Belmont.

"Handsome and rich. I am lucky that I don't have to compete," Anton says.

I can't see Belmont's face, but I imagine that he's smiling while his hands get friskier.

"Hey, let's take a picture," Claire says.

She asks one of the guests to snap a picture of the eight of us with her smartphone. Anton tells Claire to send the picture to him and winks at me. A waiter brings us another round of drinks. Orange Tank takes the stage, and Anna and Claire scurry off to watch. It's evident that they've known each other long before tonight.

"Well, we're leaving," Belmont announces.

"But this is your party," Anton says.

"My mission is accomplished." Belmont grinds my butt. He's up and ready to go.

"I'll see you tomorrow then," I say to Anton.

"We'll see each other in the morning. I want to show you something."

I narrow one eye curiously. "Show me what?"

"You must wait and see."

I groan playfully. "Okay but it better be good."

Anton and I hug. Did we really only reconnect

yesterday? I feel as though we've been close cousins ever since the afternoon Daniel tried to teach him and Leon how to jump over the swimming pool on a skateboard. Daniel landed the jump every time, and I landed it only once. I remember Anton clapping when I finally succeeded, and I remember thinking, "thank you," and feeling proud of myself. I hug Leon then Augusto, who pats my hip as we let go. Belmont narrows his eyes at Augusto.

As soon as Belmont and I make it to the sports car he's renting, he pins me against the door and tongues me. His kiss is greedy. He pulls me against him by my dress.

"That was hard," he says breathlessly. "How long did that take? Five hours?"

I chuckle as he nibbles my neck. "Not that long."

"Hey, Daisy!"

Belmont turns to look behind him. "What the fuck does he want?" he mumbles.

I lean over to see around Belmont. It's Dexter. Shoot, I forgot he and the team were even here. Dexter throws up his arms as if to say, "remember me?"

I sigh. "Okay!"

"Okay what?" Belmont snaps.

"He knows you called Gil."

"And what does he want you to do for him?"

"Let Gil know that it's okay for them to stay in France. They'll keep the money you put in their budget, and my friendship with Dexter is over. He loses my number, and I lose his. The whole crew will pack up first thing in the morning and drive to Provence."

Belmont's grimace intensifies. "Who said I called Gil?"

I look at him askew.

"Okay, I called him. But Frampton is fucking stalking you, and you're a happily married woman." He smirks.

"He was making a grand gesture that didn't work. He gets it—you and I are never leaving each other. You would've done the same thing if the tables were turned."

"I don't want to have to think about that."

I flutter my eyebrows. "Oh, if the tables were turned, I would leave his ass in a hot second."

Belmont grins as if he likes the sound of that. "Is he still using the material from your books?"

"Yes."

"What if he has questions? I'm sure he's planning on calling you every second of the day in the name of work."

"Kristin will call me. I'll only deal with her."

Belmont lets out a hard sigh. "You know I'm not going to say no to you."

I lick his bottom lip. Belmont skips a breath then looks over his shoulder. "You got it, Frampton! I'll contact Gil."

Dexter shows Belmont a thumbs-up. Dexter's eyes gloss over me before he turns and trots away. I imagine he's going to tell the team that they're back in business and with a better budget. They'll all probably celebrate, drink like fish, and dance the rest of the night away.

Belmont pulls out his phone and types a message to Gil. Gil responds right away, and Belmont replies.

"Done," he says.

"Thank you." I grin.

Belmont forces his eyes off my face long enough to get us in the car, but once we get on the road, he tries to control the gear shift and finger-bang me at the same time. We almost run off the road twice before he's able to get two fingers inside me the way he wants and smash my clit with his thumb. I put my seat back and let him play inside my pussy. He moans and whimpers and mutters about how good it feels. We roll up the driveway to Chateau Mes Fleurs very slowly because Belmont refuses to switch gears. He stops near the front door, puts on the brake, and shoves his face in my pussy.

"Shit," he says as he pushes his tongue against my swollen knot. The car is too small, and he's unable to stimulate me the way he wants to.

I can't help but laugh. "Calm down, Jack, I'm not going anywhere."

The next thing I know, Belmont is out of his seat and opening my door. He picks me up, and I wrap my legs around him. He pulls up my dress and unsnaps and unzips his pants. I feel the head of his penis break through me. I gasp as he smashes deep inside me.

"I can't wait," he says. "I've been thinking about you all night and day."

I tighten my pussy around his erection.

Belmont grunts. "Not yet, baby."

We stand very still. Once his lust has settled, he carries me toward the cottage. We can't kiss. I can't move my hips or else. Belmont takes a path I didn't know existed, and we're at my cottage in no time flat. He opens the door and carries me inside. I chuckle.

"What?" he asks.

"You're like a giant trapped in a shoebox."

He smashes his mouth on mine. He tastes so good.

"The sofa," I mutter.

Belmont sits on the sofa with me on his dick. I shift my hips back and forth, and he tosses his head back.

"You like that?" I whisper.

Belmont moans and speeds up my hip action. His dick feels so good that I whimper like a puppy.

"Not yet," Belmont whispers as he holds me against him.

We calm our breathing. He lifts my dress off and gobbles up my tits.

"You have the most beautiful breasts," he says, squeezing them.

He bites, sucks, and licks one nipple then the other. I kiss his forehead as he devours me. He slides his hands up and down my waist then pulls back to get a good look at my nakedness.

Belmont dips his head toward the bedroom. "The bed is that way?"

"Um-hum."

He stands up really fast and takes me to the bedroom. My back comes down on the mattress.

Belmont holds my hips and rams his penis inside me. My pussy pulsates with every thrust. He goes faster and faster. His entire face is strained.

"So… fucking… tight…" He yells and quakes as he pops. He pitches his dick deeper to make sure I absorb all of his cream. "I love you, baby."

"I love you, too," I say with a sigh.

Belmont slowly takes himself out of me and clamps my legs closed before he trots to the bathroom for a towel. He wipes me dry. "I'm not the only one who likes to bite you." He chuckles.

"Oh…" I look at the red marks on my leg— they're insect bites.

Belmont throws the towel on the floor, and his eyes are hooded as he gazes at my pussy. "I've been hungry for this since I first saw you at that party."

He licks the length of my slit. It's a slow journey for his tongue, and he applies pressure so that I can really feel it. Our eyes lock as he does it again and again. Then his tongue sinks into my hole, and it goes in and out as he blows against my wetness. My thighs quiver in response. Now that he's got me good and excited, he latches on to my clit. I think he's sucking it because the sensation is so intense, it flows to my belly. I try to squirm, but he holds me still. I grunt and whimper as I clench my teeth, trying to bear the sensation. When my orgasm ignites, I claw the mattress and scream.

Belmont doesn't stop. He just keeps going. It happens again, and again, and again until his dick is hard and ready to enter my juicy pussy. He thrusts in me until he gets to the edge, then stops, waits to settle down, and guides me into a new position. I'm on my knees. My legs are over my head. I have one leg up and one leg down. He lies on my back as I lie on my stomach with my legs together to make my walls extra tight for him. This is the position that usually gets him, and Belmont blows after three thrusts.

He knows I love it when he lies on top of me like this. His dick is corked in my pussy, waiting to rise again. We fall asleep, and later he wakes me up with a few hard thrusts. He shifts my hair off my neck and kisses my skin. He's going nice and slow, shifting his hips indulgently.

"I'm going to make you come, baby," he says and slips his finger under me to stimulate my clit.

Belmont has every single live spot inside my vagina memorized, and he's probing the most sensitive area, using the clit stimulation as a guide. I whimper and sigh as I get closer to orgasm.

"Yes, baby," he says, encouraging me to go before he does.

I grab the pillow, grit my teeth, and hold on as the pleasurable sensations explode. I cry and whimper. Belmont holds there until I release the tension in my body. I tighten my pussy to make the finish line feel good for him. He jerks and sucks my neck when he comes. Just like before, we fall asleep until the next round.

SUNLIGHT ENGULFS US, AND BELMONT IS EATING MY pussy. I scream as I climax. My clit is so sensitive, and Belmont knows it. He's made me come so many times through the night that I can't count them all. We'll probably sleep through most of the day. He falls back on the pillow beside me. His dick is hard but tender. He's overdone it again.

"Are you sore?" he asks me.

"No. You've kept me too wet."

"Oh shit, don't say that, baby. You're going to make me flip you over onto your stomach, sore dick and all."

I give him a look that dares him to do it. Just as he's about to take my dare, his cell phone rings.

"I'll be back," he says.

I giggle as he reaches for the phone on the nightstand.

"It's Maggie," he says.

I lie on my side to watch him.

"What's going on Mags?"

She says something.

"I'm in France with Daisy." He listens. "You don't need to apologize. It worked." He pinches my nipple. "Not the way you thought it would work, but you got the job done, so I should be thanking you. Oh, except for the ankle monitor. Daisy didn't like it, and I didn't like to see her suffer." Belmont pauses then puts the call on speakerphone. "Maggie wants to talk to you."

"Hi, Daisy," Maggie says nervously.

"Hello, Daisy!" Javar Les says in the background.

She covers the mouthpiece of her phone and says something to him. When she takes her hand off the phone, she says, "Hey, Daisy, sorry about the ankle bracelets. It was the wrong call. But I'm calling to tell you that I'm sending you guys a video."

"It's okay," I say.

"I don't have my computer," Belmont says.

"I'll send it to your phone. We got extra lucky last night when Yvette threw wine in your face."

I gasp and crawl over to nuzzle against Belmont, who takes me in his arms.

"I wondered who the hell invited her," Belmont says.

"We can thank Javar for getting her there. We learned that she's the one who was feeding Reece Development those lies about you. She fabricated all of this 'proof' so that her lies could stick. They paid her a lot of money, but she didn't do it for the money. A woman scorned makes the best adversary —she doesn't think with her head."

"Tell Daisy about my part already, won't you?" Javar says in the background.

Maggie sighs hard. "He seduced her, manipulated her, and made her even angrier with you, Jack. Then Harold Doe told us about the party. We already had her on tape confessing to 'fixing' you, but we knew getting her to confront you at your party would be the nail in her coffin. By the way, the team of people who work for you are fucking brilliant. I'm going to send you the video now. This is what's out there. She looks like a bitter hag who set you up."

"Whoa," Belmont says. "Thanks, Mags, I'll

have payment for your services wired to your account."

"You don't have to pay me, Jack. You know I'd do anything for you, even fucking bury a body."

"I'd do the same for Daisy," Javar says.

"Could you please shut the fuck up," Maggie grumbles. "Don't worry, Jack, he's harmless. He's hit on every chick we've come in contact with."

"Oh, Javar is such a cheat," I say.

"Major," Maggie says. "Even Monroe won't sleep with him, and she fucks everything."

"Yet," Javar interjects, "Monroe's walls will tumble like the walls of Jericho."

"Anyway… Jack, Daisy, I'll see you when you get back. Love you both."

"Love you, Daisy," Javar says.

Maggie hangs up before Belmont blows his lid.

"Who's that guy?" he asks, grimacing.

"I thought I told you about him. He's the English guy who taught me how to swim. He doesn't love me. He hasn't fallen in love yet."

"So he just wants to fuck you?"

"Pretty much, but that's your job."

Belmont raises one eyebrow as though he likes the sound of that.

I tap the screen of his phone. "Let's see it."

He glances at his penis, which is sticking up under the sheet. It's as if he has to deliberate between screwing me and watching the video.

"Seriously? Babe, we've been doing it all night. Play the video."

Belmont chuckles, and I rest my chin on his shoulder as he pulls up the video and presses play. It's a clip from a Chicago news station.

"Yvette Maynard was allegedly paid by Holden Reece and Matt Silver of the Reece Development to defame billionaire Belmont Lord of Lord & Lord Development in order to foil his bid to acquire prime riverfront property in downtown Chicago. The two corporations have been locked in a bitter battle since early May. We have acquired recordings of Maynard claiming that she will ruin the billionaire who has been named six times as *Luster Magazine's* sexiest and richest man in the world."

Words are displayed over a black screen as we hear Yvette say, "Jack Lord can just go (bleep) where his (bleep) (bleep) (bleep). I don't give a (bleep) he's married."

"But you said he hired you to have sex with his competitors and make them pull out of the sale. Is this true?" a man asks.

I recognize the voice. "That's Javar, but he's speaking in an American accent."

Belmont furrows his eyebrows.

"It is if I say so," Yvette says.

"Now that's a hefty allegation."

"Jack Lord lies so much, who cares if someone lies about him? He deserves it."

The anchor says, "Last night, Maynard assaulted Lord at a private party in France. Mr. Lord was accompanied by his wife, daughter of famed composer Jacques Blanchard and Hollywood producer Heloise Krantz."

They show a photo of Yvette throwing wine in Belmont's face and my shocked reaction.

Belmont and I laugh at how insane this is. The video ends. Belmont writes a text message.

"What are you doing?" I ask.

"Making sure Maggie is paid."

Once he's done he slams his phone on the nightstand and pulls me under him, parts my legs, and winces as he holds his sore rod.

"You're overdoing it," I say.

There's a loud knock on the front door. "Daisy! Daisy! Get up! I want to show you something!"

"What the fuck," Belmont mutters.

I peck him on the lips and scoot out from under

him. "Take a soak in the bath. It may help soothe your man pole."

"My man pole?"

I tug a plain white tank dress out of the cabinet. "Mm-hmm."

Belmont watches me slip on the dress, and he lets out a frustrated sigh. His glistening eyes focus on my horns. I look down at my nipples, and they're stiff.

I tug a robe off the hanger and put it on. "I'll be back. Take a bath. It'll help."

Belmont groans and shoves a pillow over his face as I head out of the bedroom. I slip into my sandals and open the door. Anton is standing there in pajamas and a T-shirt.

"Come, come... I am excited to show you." Anton takes my hand and guides me around the hedges and through the backyard.

"Where's Anna?" I ask.

Grinning, he glances at me. "She is in my bed."

I grin too. "You had sex?"

"Yes."

"Was it everything you thought it would be?"

"It was more than I could imagine."

He holds the door to the main house open for me, and I knock on his chest.

"You smell like sex," he says.

"Belmont is insatiable."

He gives me a lopsided smile. "So am I. That is why I show this, and that is that."

"What do you want to show me?"

"I cannot tell you, only show."

Anton leads me down the hallway. Inés is baking bread, and it smells like heaven. I must stop by the kitchen on the way back. He opens the door to the tower, and I follow him up the steps.

He stops abruptly. "Is here."

Anton faces the wall. My heart skips a beat. It's a black-and-white selfie of Anton. I'm behind him, curled up and sleeping in the passenger seat of his car.

"What the..." I smile so hard. "Did you take that while driving?"

"I did," he says with a laugh. "Don't you think this sort of photo is fitting for you and I?"

I inspect it. I look peaceful. "It is. It looks so professional."

"That's because I am an artist."

We smile at each other.

"I also have this one," he says.

We walk up three more steps, and there's the picture we all took last night.

"You did this already?" I exclaim.

"I have the tools. It did not take long. You are now with the rest of the family, so you do not have to cry anymore."

I give Anton a big hug. "Thank you. Really, thank you."

"It is I who thank you. You told Anna my secret, and now my dreams have come true."

We do the double cheek kiss.

"And now… good-bye." Anton rushes back down the stairs.

I chuckle until he's out of sight. As soon as he's gone, I really take it all in. Belmont and I fit in perfectly with my family. Our smiles are real. He's so sexy, and I must admit that I look really good standing next to him. Then there's one of Anton and me. That's the picture that makes me feel as if I've been on this wall all along. Life can't get any better. I take in a deep breath… actually, it can get better.

I trot down the stairs and skip into the kitchen. Inés smiles at me as she squeezes jelly into the croissants.

"This is for you and baby," she says.

I'm taken aback. "I'm sorry. What baby?" I say in French.

471

"No more wine for you."

I shake my head. "I'm not pregnant."

"You have this." She hands me a platter loaded with warm bread, jellies, meats, and cheese.

I'm still processing her claim. I don't know, maybe something got lost in translation. It happens. I take the food. "*Merci.*"

She smiles and turns toward the sink. I'm half in a daze as I return to the cottage. I see that Dexter and his crew stayed true to their word to leave before sunrise. When I get back to the cottage, I scarf down a croissant with cheese.

"Daisy, are you back?" Belmont calls.

"Yes!"

"I need you."

I grin. "Here I come!"

"I agree!"

I snicker and shake my head—that was too easy. I finish eating the croissant, walk into the bathroom, take off the robe, and toss it on top of the bed.

I stand in the bathroom doorway, wearing my dress. "Hey, you."

Belmont's hooded gaze falls over my body. "Get in here."

I peel my dress over my head. His man pole is sticking straight up. "How does he feel?"

"He'll feel better after you get in here and sit on him."

I chuckle and walk seductively to the tub, get in, and sit on it. "Ah…" I gasp.

THE NEXT BOOK TO READ IN THIS SERIES IS STILL IN LOVE WITH HER (MAGGIE & VINCE, #1) LOVE IN THE USA, BOOK 5

ABOUT THE AUTHOR

Z.L. Arkadie has been an author since July 2011, debuting with her Parched series. She has been a best-selling author in the iBooks store, holding the top spot for two weeks with her LOVE in the USA, series, which is still her most popular series to date. Currently she has written 40 novels and counting, which span over 7 series. She enjoys merging erotic romance with a solid mystery. Her favorite characters to write are sexy, strong and brooding men who find love with beautiful, independent and smart women.

When she's not writing, she loves to cook and read good books, which have the power to take her somewhere she's never been.

For more information:
zlarkadiebooks.com
contact@zlarkadiebooks.com